WRECKED

Also by Charlotte Roche

Wetlands

WRECKED

CHARLOTTE ROCHE

Translated from the German
by Tim Mohr

FOURTH ESTATE • *London*

First published in Great Britain in 2013 by
Fourth Estate
a division of HarperCollins*Publishers*
77–85 Fulham Palace Road
London W6 8JB
www.4thestate.co.uk

Originally published in Germany as *Schossgebete*
in 2011 by Piper Verlag GmbH

2

A catalogue record for this book is
available from the British Library

ISBN 978-0-00-747876-7

Printed and bound in Great Britain by
Clays Ltd, St Ives plc

MIX
Paper from
responsible sources
FSC® C007454

FSC™ is a non-profit international organisation established to promote
the responsible management of the world's forests. Products carrying the
FSC label are independently certified to assure consumers that they come
from forests that are managed to meet the social, economic and
ecological needs of present and future generations,
and other controlled sources.

Find out more about HarperCollins and the environment at
www.harpercollins.co.uk/green

For Martin

WRECKED

Tuesday

Every time we have sex, we turn on both of the electric blankets half an hour in advance. We have extremely high-quality electric blankets, and they stretch from the head of the bed to the foot. It's something you just have to spend a bit more on—at least, my husband had to spend a bit extra on them. Because I've always been terribly scared of those types of things, scared that they'll heat up after I fall asleep and I'll be roasted alive or die of smoke inhalation. But our electric blankets automatically switch themselves off after an hour. We lie down next to each other in the bed—heated to 105 degrees—and stare up at the ceiling. The warmth relaxes our bodies. I begin to breathe deeply, smiling on the inside with the excitement of what's to come. Then I roll over and kiss him as I put my hand into his XL yoga pants. No zipper or anything else that could catch on hairs or foreskin. I don't grab his cock at first. I reach down farther—to his balls. I cradle them in my hand like a pouch full of gold. At this point I'm already betraying my man-hating mother. She tried to teach me that sex was something bad. It didn't work.

Breathe in, breathe out. This is the only moment in the day when I really breathe deeply. The rest of the time I tend to just take shallow gasps. Always wary, always on the lookout, always bracing for the worst. But my personality completely changes during sex. My therapist, Frau Drescher, says I have subconsciously split myself in two—since my feminist mother tried to raise me as an asexual being, I have to become someone else in bed to avoid feeling as if I'm betraying her. It works very effectively. I am completely free. Nothing can embarrass me. I'm lust incarnate. I feel more like an animal than a person. I forget all my responsibilities and problems. I become just my body and leave my anxious mind behind. I slowly slide down in bed until my face is in his crotch. I can smell his masculine scent. I find the male scent isn't very different from that of the female. If he hasn't showered right before sex—and who does when you've been together as long as we've been—a drop or two of urine has started to ferment between his foreskin and the head of his cock. It smells the way my grandmother's kitchen used to after she'd sautéed fish on her gas stove. Eyes closed. Just get through it. The smell disgusts me a little, but that feeling of disgust also excites me.

Once I've given everything a good suck, it doesn't smell anymore. Like a cow licking its calf clean. I bury my face in his balls, then rub my cheek along his outstretched shaft. He always gets stiff as soon as we first kiss. My husband, Georg, is a lot older than I am, and I'm curious how much longer his erection will function this well. I kiss the crease where his legs are attached to his body—whatever you call that spot. By now he's moaning and asking for more. For the time being it's all about making him happy. I carefully consider the rhythm I do everything in—I want to drive him absolutely wild. First, let's tease him a little. I stay on the seam where his legs and body meet, holding his balls firmly in my hand. I slowly switch from kissing to licking. I make loud smacking noises so he can hear what I'm doing as well as feel it. Beneath his balls I feel the erectile tissue—the extension of his cock inside his body—that stretches to the perineum. Do you call it a perineum on a man? There's a line there that looks like a set of labia fused together. It's all the same, isn't it? The way I like to approach it is to imagine he has a vagina. Just a very elongated vagina that sticks out! Way out. I hold his balls more tightly and massage the erectile tissue below.

To get myself going, I rub my vagina against his knee. If I arch my back a little, it hits just the right spot. My tongue slowly wanders from the line between his legs up his shaft. I lick it until it's totally wet, and then I breathe on it so he can feel the chill of the moisture. From the shaft I run my tongue down to his balls. I take both of them into my mouth and play with them. I've learned to make sure not to twist the cords attached to the testicles. I've done that a few times with Georg, and it really hurt him. Farther down I massage his perineum with my tongue and let some spit dribble down for my finger on his asshole. I make my tongue stiff and pointed and run it upward from the bottom of the perineum, between his balls, and then all the way up to the acorn-shaped tip of his shaft, all while rubbing my pointer finger slowly around his asshole. I wet my lips and the tip of his cock with spit. When I start to suck on the acorn-shaped head of his cock I barely open my mouth so it feels tight to him. And I let just the very tip in and out again. In and out. In and out. In and out. I let more and more spit run out. I learned that from another man—that it hurts if it gets too dry. I start to take his cock a little more deeply into my mouth. As I go down, I wrap my lips tightly around his whole cock. When I come back up I suck. Because of the vacuum that creates, it makes a popping noise when I get to the top.

I always pull the foreskin up with my mouth, up and over the acorn tip. And then I always swirl my tongue around the end. The tip bulges out of my cheeks from inside my mouth. In porn films, women always jerk the foreskin back and forth with their hands. But that—particularly the downward jerk—doesn't do it for my husband. In fact, it hurts him. No idea why they do that in porn films. I read once in a sex book that if a woman is going to do that, it's better if you're right-handed to do it with your left hand. Supposedly you don't grip it as hard and you have a nicer touch as a result.

Unfortunately I can't do the trick the women in porn films do where they take a cock all the way into their throat without gagging. I tried a few times in the past but nearly threw up, so I quickly gave up. You don't have to do everything the way they do it in porn films. I've also tried to swallow many times. But I just can't do it. I find the taste and the consistency in the back of my throat so disgusting that I just can't choke it down. I have a strong gag reflex, and the sound of me nearly throwing up isn't much of a turn-on for the man, either. It takes a huge acting job to be able to manage it, and it's just too much trouble. I could probably pull it off for a one-night stand, but I can't fool my husband. He knows I hate it, so he doesn't want me to do it anyway. So, instead, our deal is that he can come in my mouth but I push the shooting sperm back out with my tongue.

Sometimes my mouth and neck need a break, so I take the spit-moistened cock in my hand and carefully pull upward, always pulling the foreskin only upward over the tip. I wouldn't have hit upon that myself. But one time when we were just getting together, I asked him to get himself off in front of me. When you're new with someone, you do funny things like that.

And I now copy a lot of things I saw him do to himself that time. I figured out that the closer I come with my hands and feet to the way he masturbates, the better it feels for him. Your own ideas are never going to counter decades of sexual habit. So my challenge is to get as close as possible to the way he satisfies himself, but with other means, of course. He can only use his hand. I have my tongue, my mouth, etc., etc., etc. If I do continue with my hands, I lift his balls toward his cock with one hand while I run my other hand upward toward the tip of his shaft. That gives him the sensation that I've got everything tightly gripped together.

At this point he's lying there like a beetle on its back, surrendering himself to me completely. Legs spread, arms stretched out, eyes rolled up like he's in a trance. I get a serious feeling of power when he's lying there like that. I could cut his throat and he wouldn't even notice. Now and then I step back from the role of sexual servant and observe the scene like an outsider. And when I do, I have to smirk, because from that vantage point what we're doing is rather comical. But I quickly wipe the smirk away and continue with the requisite level of seriousness.

Most of the time we start out with one of us devoting him- or herself to the other. When we try something in a 69 position, we always find that, while it's nice to see all the parts up close, you're too distracted doing things to enjoy what's being done to you. One or the other! Not that we ever actually talked about it. It was one of those tacit understandings. Our sexual accord. While I'm tending to him, I always make sure that I can rub my vagina on something—otherwise he's miles ahead of me in terms of being turned on. As I treat my jaw muscles to a rest and put all my effort into the whole two-hands-lifting-and-tugging thing, I sit with my legs splayed and my vagina on his thigh, getting messy from all the wetness. It's such a rush—we work ourselves into something like to a drug-induced trance. It makes me proud, all the things I can do with my husband.

Beyond the electric blankets, there are a lot of other steps that I have to take before I can have sex. I'm petrified by the thought that our neighbors might hear us. So part of our fore-play is making sure all the doors and windows are shut. It's the only way I can be relaxed. It's happened only rarely that I left it to my husband and he forgot to close a window. But if I do discover an open window after all our noisy sex, I turn bright red from shame. It must be terribly annoying for the neighbors, though my husband constantly makes fun of me for thinking so. Of course, if I look at it like a therapist, it's dead easy for him to play the easygoing role, because he can always be sure that I'll be the uptight one in our relationship—and you take on the role in the partnership that's available. I play the parts that are panicky, obsessive, ashamed. That leaves him to be the cool one, the exhibitionist. But I make sure that nobody hears him anyway. I close the windows, doors, and curtains. Sometimes at night I'll go outside in my bathrobe, tell him to lie in bed with the light on, and double-check that nobody can see in from outside. Because sometimes I worry that our curtains are too thin. They're made out of the same kind of silk as a tie, with a brown paisley pattern on them.

Sometimes during the winter, the electric blankets aren't enough, so we get the infrared lamp Georg occasionally uses for his back pain out of our basement storage space and use that as an additional source of heat. It's a big, broad, expensive model, and we're lit up all red by it. It's like being in one of those window displays in Amsterdam—which makes me worry even more that the silk curtains might reveal two sweating interlocked bodies to passersby. Georg knows I'm crazy. I always have to go outside and double-check that we won't be visible, however the lighting is set up. How many times in life have I seen that people apparently pay no attention at all to the shadows a 100-watt bulb can cast through a window. A normal person might find it pleasing to be able to watch a woman undressing that way. But all I can think is, *Oh God, I hope that never happens to me—I have to make sure it never happens to me.*

I continue to cater to my husband. Sometimes he'll lie there for ages and just let it all happen. Most of the time he lies on his back because for years he's had back pain—and because I know him so well, I feel pain in my back, too, anytime he does. He hates to appear weak in front of me. The only reason we're together is because I invented this idea of him being ridiculously strong. If I were to ask him how his back was every day, it would be emasculating. But even so, I want to be polite. I want to show that I commiserate. It's the kind of problem that can come up when you are together with someone who's older. But in the end it's not about what I do, it's about the fact that he thinks it's terrible to show he's in pain when I'm around.

I think it's new for him, too, just to lie back and enjoy. He used to be with women he had to put incredible effort into pleasing, and there was not much left for himself afterward. For that, thank the women's movement. But that's not the way it was supposed to be. That only women get their way and men just have to see what happens. He loves it when I play his sexual servant. I repeat everything I've just described, first quickly and then at a slower pace. I don't even have to think. Everything seems to happen on its own, like when you're high.

When we're in the middle of having sex, I lose track of time and space. It's the only time during the day when I can just shut everything off. I really think it has more to do with the breathing than with the sex itself, but maybe it's a combination of both. Contrary to what my mother wanted, I've learned through years of therapy that I am indeed a sexual being. I'm slowly learning to be conscious of my own desires.

Earlier, for years and years, it was just like the old cliché of marriage with us: the wife never felt like doing it and the husband did—constantly. But once the right buttons were pushed, I would always think, *Why don't I ever decide to make the first move? Why don't I seduce him sometime instead of him always seducing me?* It was humiliating for him to have to constantly ask, to get rejected—always to be the one who had to initiate things. It often led to fights. I would have been lying, though, if I said I felt like having sex. I didn't feel like it one single time. I just went along as a favor to him—and because I knew our relationship would go down the tubes otherwise. Everyone knows that: if things aren't working in bed anymore, it's just a question of time before the whole relationship stops working, too. Of that much I am sure. But as soon as we'd get past the initial paralysis, I'd really get into it—every time. And every time I'd say to him, "Why don't you just remind me how much fun I have, and then you won't even have to ask!"

Thanks to my therapist, I initiate things myself more and more often. About twice a week I say, "Again today?" I can only be so selfless during foreplay because I know I'll get the same treatment back afterward. No matter how much effort I put into pleasing him, I'll never be as good as he is at oral. I ask him all the time whether he thinks what I do to him is as fundamentally good as what he does to me. It's a dilemma. We'll never know.

When I feel I've done enough as far as servicing him, I gradually stop. He always understands and then very grate-fully starts to do the same for me. He spreads my legs apart and positions himself with his head between them so he can see everything. He examines me millimeter by millimeter, like a gynecologist. Do you say "playing doctor" when adults do it? That's what it's like. It's best if you've showered that day. Because anyone who looks and smells so closely will pick up any impurity. He takes my hand and puts it on my vagina. I know exactly what to do. He wants me to get myself off for him. I never play with myself when I'm alone. My mother brought me up as a feminist. I think something went wrong during that upbringing, though, and I became some sort of sexual Catholic. I've never gotten myself off. The only thing I ever do that comes even remotely close to masturbating is a shame-ful scratch or two in my pubic hair. And in those instances, I think I'm tricking myself. First I think, *Hey, something itches in my crotch*, then I scratch a bit in my shortly cropped pubic hair, then I realize it turns me on, and I stop immediately. For whatever idiotic, archaic reason, I don't continue. I mistake my own lust for some sort of uncomfortable condition because I just don't want to admit it.

If it's been a few days since we've had sex and I've done this secret scratching beneath the bedsheets, sometimes I get so horny it hurts. But I don't want to admit that I'm horny, and think instead that I have a yeast infection or a bladder infection, or that I've contracted herpes, despite the fact that I'm totally immune to it—otherwise I'd have gotten it long ago. They say that about herpes—either you get it or you don't. And I appear to be immune. At least I'm immune to something. These thoughts about being ill stay in my head until I have sex—when my husband initiates it, of course. Then all my ailments are pleasantly fucked away.

But when my husband wants me to, I put on the best masturbation act of all time. When he's watching and encouraging me, I really go for it. I rub and flick and finger. He doesn't look at my face at all. I exist only as a vagina. I am my vagina. He keeps his head between my legs and watches closely as I go through all the masturbatory techniques I've seen online and on DVDs. His eyes, his nose, and his mouth are just a few centimeters from the inner lips of my vagina. I rub crossways on my clitoris, push the lips open and rub between them, and once in a while I shove a finger inside and fuck myself with it. Even if I find it more amusing than stimulating, when I see how it affects him, how much it turns him on, I get turned on, too.

He can't take it anymore, and he wants to do with his cock what I'm doing with my finger. I lie in front of him, completely naked, and spread my legs as wide as I can. He shifts forward and smacks his hard cock a few times against my vagina. I think he must have seen that move in a porn film. But I like it when he does that. Even though I can't explain why I like it. He smacks his cock against me a few times and then in he goes. I usually come very quickly. A few thrusts will do it. And then that's it for me. My mother—and leading feminists—brought me up to think there was no such thing as a vaginal orgasm. They sit between me and Georg and whisper in my ear: "There's no such thing as a vaginal orgasm!" Now, at thirty-three years old, I've had to find out all on my own that that's not true. I've always felt it during sex, but when I came I always dismissed it as a psychological effect. I figured tht it was just because I liked the idea of being fucked, that the thought—*fuck, fuck, oh fuck yes, he's inside me, filling me*—was enough to make me come without touching my clit. Because I was convinced—for political reasons—that there was no other way to really come except through clitoral stimulation. No surprise that eventually I started to think I was crazy or, at the very least, had a powerful imagination. In bed, I realized that my feminist upbringing was miles away from reality. Secretly, behind my mother's back, and behind prominent feminist activist Alice Schwarzer's back, I began to think, *They're wrong! I come that way almost every time—there is such a thing as a vaginal orgasm. Fuck it and fuck them.* And now, finally, I've gotten scientific confirmation, too. In *Geo Kompakt* magazine, number 20. It's a science magazine—and it's my favorite. The theme of issue number 20 was "Love and Sex." I learned a lot from it, a lot more than from Alice Schwarzer's journal *Emma*. And yet, Alice Schwarzer still sits between me and my husband during sex, whispering, whispering: "Yes, Elizabeth, you only think you're having vaginal orgasms, you imagine that in order to subjugate yourself to your husband and his penis." From that issue of *Geo Kompakt* I learned that women have two ways to have an orgasm—and can even come both ways at the same time. A vaginal orgasm is—speaking in layman's terms—transmitted to the brain via the vagus nerve, whereas a clitoral orgasm is transmitted through nerves that run through the spine. Sometimes I come really hard, and that probably means it's being sent to my brain both ways at the same time. I also feel I come quickest if I do it the way I need it. What I mean is that I actually do the thrusting—I grind against his cock more than he actually shoves it into me. That way I can create the perfect rhythm for me. And then it's just a matter of seconds before I come. I'm really loud. I flip out every time. And then I'm done. He has to be careful that he doesn't come right away, too, because it turns him on when I just take what I want. He loves the way his cock gets me off. But that's probably just something he's convinced himself of—in reality, I'm pretty sure I get myself off. Anyway, he has to really concentrate—or think of his Catholic mother or whatever—until I finish. So that he doesn't come before me, in which case it's all over. I'm really thankful that he takes it so seriously—that he makes sure I come first. I'd guess that in the seven years of our relationship, he's come first only three times, meaning there were only three times I didn't come with his cock. But in all of those cases, he still made good with his fingers, his tongue, and his toes. In those instances I really benefited from his bad conscience.

With the exception of those three incidents, it's always his turn after I come. At that point, I'm his servant, like at the start. This is the only moment during sex that I say anything. I'm no good at talking dirty. Probably for the same reason I don't masturbate. It's all my mother's fault. As always. I ask Georg: "How do you want to come?" There aren't *that* many ways. He gets to choose from the following menu: in my hand, my mouth, my vagina—I get on top and fuck him, because of his back—or, on rare occasions, because it is always pretty painful for me, in my ass. When I get on top of him, to fuck him so he can come in my vagina, he usually wants me to sit backward. That way he can grab my ass and see everything. He pulls my cheeks apart so he can watch his cock going in and out of my vagina.

He tells me exactly what he sees. Unlike me, he can talk dirty very well. He feels bad that I can't see the way the skin of my vagina wraps around his cock as I lift my body. He says it looks as if the skin of my vagina forms a hat for his cock—the skin clings to it and is pulled slightly downward, getting dragged along the entire length of his shaft. A few times in our seven years together he's pulled my cheeks apart so far that it's slightly torn the tissue around my asshole, leaving me feeling slightly wounded. I tell him the next day, after I go to the bathroom: "Please don't pull my ass cheeks so far apart next time, you broke something, thanks." He immediately feels bad and promises to do better next time. I guess it just happens in the heat of the moment.

I often feel as if intense sex makes you overlook injuries. It's the same with the way he pulls apart my vagina so he can really examine it. Sometimes the sensitive skin tears a little. Up to a point, a little pain turns me on even more because I think to myself that he is so horny that he can't control himself anymore, that he no longer knows his own strength. It sounds as if I'm talking about a man with Down syndrome. But that's what goes through my head during sex. If I can bear it, I wait until we're finished before complaining—in a friendly tone. Often he squeezes my hard, stimulated nipples, and that can really hurt. Very carefully, I try to let him know that he hurt me—I don't want him to feel too bad and then be tentative the next time we have sex. I don't want that. And I also don't want him to feel as though he's some kind of brute.

But now it's time for him to come. Over the years I've developed a trick. I first saw it in the documentary *Chicken Ranch,* by Nick Broomfield. In the movie, prostitutes use the trick on drunk clients so the fuck is over more quickly and they are able to raise their hourly earnings. As soon as a client has blown his load and his hard-on is deflated, the prostitute is done. So she earns the same money in a shorter time and can move on to another client. I use the same trick on my husband at the end of our sessions. Once I've come, I don't really see any reason things should go on for an eternity. Over the years I've developed extremely good control over my Kegel muscles. I can make myself much tighter inside than I normally am. I have no idea whether having a baby slightly widens you—my gynecologist says that it doesn't, that everything goes back to the way it was beforehand. Anyway, it's also perhaps less than ideal for the feeling of tightness that my body produces so much fluid during sex. During foreplay it's great, but later, when I want to make him come by rubbing his cock with my vagina, it's more of a hindrance. If he puts his cock in before I'm really wet, I can tell from his reaction that it turns him on—because the friction is more intense. But anyway, after I've already come, I don't have any great desire to prolong things. Unless it's Christmas or our anniversary or something—in that case I let myself get carried away and will take a long time to get him off even after I come. So now I squeeze my Kegel muscles with everything I've got and he comes immediately. I mean *immediately*. There's just nothing he can do. It always makes me feel good—the fact that I have his cock in a vise grip inside me and can pull the trigger whenever I'm ready. Cool. He moans and groans a lot when he comes, and usually I then ask him, as a joke, "Did you come yet?"

I think that being loud increases the intensity of sexual sensations. It highlights the rush, the animalism. Earlier, at the beginning of our relationship, I was the only one who always screamed. I would scream until his ears rang. But these days he screams right back at me. It's great fun.

I'm totally against any kind of postplay. I get really jittery from sex and always want to get up and do something afterward—like take a shower. Not because I feel dirty or anything. It's just that I am prone to the number one female ailment: urinary tract infections. And I can never get rid of the impression that I usually get UTIs after sex. So in my mind—with no scientific basis—I can't help thinking male bacteria are responsible. So I wash them away and leave my husband lying there at the scene of the crime. He always falls into a state of complete relaxation after sex and then falls fast asleep—sometimes for hours. How does a cliché become a cliché? I've read that it's totally normal for men and women to behave completely differently after sex. Having that scientifically confirmed makes me feel much better—for years before that I had to hear how unromantic I was for hopping right up afterward and starting to clean up or whatever. In the article it said that the clichés that form the basis of the jokes everyone makes—about the hyperactivity of women after sex and the "little death" of men—are the result of different hormones. I love science because it absolves you of your bad conscience about things like that. Now that we know, I can get out of bed immediately and do something without being given the evil eye. He's already deep asleep, and I switch off the electric blankets so he doesn't get broiled in his sleep. I grab one of my daughter's stuffed animals that's lying on the floor of our room. It's an orangutan. I hold it against my vagina so none of the sperm drips out on my way to the bathroom. You never see that in the movies after a sex scene—the soupy fluid running back out of the woman at some point. Probably wouldn't go over so well. I smile. My head is never clouded with problems after sex. It always seems to me that I can't possibly get more relaxed or free. And then I feel even more relaxed and free the next time. He outdoes himself. We outdo ourselves.

Right in front of the bathroom is our rattan laundry basket. We like old, dark brown things—prepares us for our eventual death. I toss the orangutan into the basket and head into the bathroom. If my daughter finds the stuffed animal in there, the sperm will have dried. And anyway, a child would probably just think it was snot. Definitely. I sit backward on the bidet and wash myself—the way I saw it done in *The Tin Drum* as a kid. My mother often showed us movies with adult-only ratings. She was of the opinion that art films couldn't be rated that way. But ever since, that image has stuck in my head: the working girl from *The Tin Drum*, played by Katharina Thalbach, trying to perform retroactive contraception by washing out the sperm of her client. I don't think that image will ever leave my head. After washing myself first with soap, I rinse again with clear water.

I grab a towel—which, for the sake of the environment, is air dried, and as a result is brittle and scratchy—and dry myself off a little too roughly. I want to finish quickly. My daughter will be home from school any minute, and then we'll want to have dinner. I haven't prepared anything.

I look at myself in the mirror, nude. I always look best after sex because my facial features are so relaxed. My breasts are slightly larger because they're engrossed with blood, the nipples are hard, the pupils of my eyes are dilated as if I'm high, my clitoris and the inner lips of my vagina are thick and swollen from the stimulation and friction and hang out of my outer lips. On my throat and chest I have the telltale red flecks I always get when I come. You can't fake those. My husband is always happy when he sees those red flecks on my white skin. He's always worried that I might be faking it. But I don't—and I don't have to. I brush my hair so I don't look too deranged when Liza gets home. With makeup remover and Q-tips I clean up the smearing beneath my eyes that could be a giveaway. And I fold two squares of toilet paper into my underwear before I pull them on. But no more than two. I teach my daughter not to waste paper when she goes to the bathroom, too—for the sake of the environment.

As quietly as possible, I slip into the walk-in closet off our bedroom and rummage around for some comfortable clothes to wear for the rest of the evening. Before dinner, I have to briefly stop by to see my therapist, Frau Drescher. I can wear anything to her office. That's the beauty of it. I can go there regardless of how I look, how I smell. I can go there in any state. Isn't that what religious nuts say about their gods? Maybe so, but they aren't so confident that they don't wash up for him—just in case he's not quite as magnanimous as they pretend.

Frau Drescher even wants me to go to the bathroom at her place—number two, no less. But so far I haven't been able to get up the nerve. We're working on it.

Once I'm dressed, I go upstairs to the kitchen. I close all the doors along the way so I can make as much noise as I want with my daughter without waking up Georg. I know he'll sleep for at least an hour. I like to tell myself that I've worn him out. That makes it easier for me to let him sleep—because I'm proud of myself. During the hour I have while he's asleep, I'll cook something healthy and, by breathing deeply, get rid of the red flecks on my throat. Don't want my daughter to see those. Kids don't want to know that adults have sex. From our stack of cutting boards I pull out the one with the words *garlic and onions* branded onto it. And from the magnetic strip that holds our knives I grab the knife I've written *garlic* on with a Sharpie. Ever since I quit smoking, my senses of taste and smell are so sensitive that when I eat a piece of fruit I can taste whatever was cut with the same knife beforehand—and if it's onions or garlic it nearly makes me puke. When things that are supposed to be sweet taste somehow savory, it drives me crazy. It's something that has started to bother me only as I've gotten older. When I was younger, I was more easygoing. A lot more easygoing!

Onions live in a wooden box under the sink. That's what my grandmother used to always say: "Now, where do the onions live?" The mother of my ex-husband taught me a good trick for chopping onions. When I sauté them in a pan, as the beginning of almost every dish I make, I like them so finely chopped that they nearly disintegrate. I skin them, cut off the ends, and then stick out my tongue—just the tip. The acidity that emanates from the onion seeks out the closest moisture. If your mouth is closed, that ends up being your eyes, and the onions make you cry. I hate crying. For me it's best not to start, because I can never stop. But with this trick, your tongue attracts all the acidity before it gets to your eyes. Your eyes don't burn, and you never cry. I turn the onion so the top is facing me, and cut it horizontally and then vertically, and then cut it into tiny pieces. I throw the onion slices into a pan with organic olive oil and sauté them until they turn transparent. I get a head of savoy cabbage out of the fridge—it's just the most beautiful vegetable.

With a big sharp knife I cut it in half and pause to look at the coloration inside. It goes from dark green to light green, with each layer toward the middle slightly lighter. I make two cuts and remove the hard part around the stem and throw it into the compost container under the sink. Then I cut the head of cabbage into small strips. I always think it's going to be way too much, but as soon as it's in the pan it cooks down dramatically. Next I throw in a handful of my special ingredient: organic vegetable broth with no yeast extract. It's very hard to find. Even in most organic markets they have only vegetable broth with yeast extract—which is just a new "green" euphemism for monosodium glutamate. As a good mother, I can't allow *that* in our kitchen.

When we still had meat at our place—that is, before the Jonathan Safran Foer era began—I conducted an experiment several times: I made chicken broth from scratch, using an entire chicken carcass. It went over okay. The next day I would serve chicken soup made with a prepared broth I bought at the organic market. Everybody loved it. The only difference was the flavor enhancer, either glutamate or yeast extract—which sounds so harmless. But if my family were to get used to that stuff, they'd only like the enhanced flavors and they'd lose their taste for the real thing. So I avoid the stuff.

To the organic vegetable broth powder with no MSG I add some water to steam the cabbage a bit. Then I add an entire container of cream, some butter, and plenty of salt and pepper. Dinner is ready.

The doorbell rings and I let Liza in. On the way to the door I think to myself, *Cooking helps you stay sane, and vegetables help keep you from going crazy.*

"How was school?"

"Good."

When she comes in wearing her teenager-style jacket, skinny jeans, and heels, I can hardly believe how big she's gotten. This is my child? Great. I guess I've succeeded—she's out of the woods, as they say. She's still alive. That's not something we can take for granted in our family. One of my brothers died at six, another at nine, and the third at twenty-four—though there's still a while before my daughter reaches that age. But I've already achieved more than my mother. My child is still alive. One hundred percent of my children have lived beyond age six. My mother had five, and three are dead. One of them was younger than my daughter is now—that is, my mother lost 20 percent of her offspring before they were eight, which is how old Liza is.

I quickly wash up the things I dirtied making dinner. I don't have to wash away the onion smell completely because this cutting board is used exclusively for onions and garlic. What bourgeois trick will we dream up next?

"Could you please not throw your jacket on the floor every time you come in?"

"Why not?"

"Do you have a servant who cleans up after you?"

She points at me.

Then we both laugh. She picks up her jacket and hangs it up in our children's wardrobe, which is only half my height.

"Can you please set the table?"

"I don't want to."

"Otherwise you'll get no dinner."

"Okay."

She stomps over to the kitchen counter, hops up like a gymnast, wedges her toes in the handle of the cabinet, and gets up on the countertop.

"What's for dinner?"

"Savoy cabbage."

I lift the lid of the pan.

"That's it?"

She rolls her eyes and sticks out her tongue like she's throwing up.

"Yep, that's it."

I smile at her. It's one of my old tricks—just to make a big dish of a single vegetable. She comes home from school hungry, and even if she complains about the vegetable I've chosen, she eats a lot of it—because there's nothing else. It makes me very happy as a mother. Kids need proper nutrition. They need lots of vitamins in their tummies. Which is why I do it all. Because I love her.

Over the years you think of all sorts of things you can do in order to act like a good mother. And when I write "act" I mean it. What's the best way for me to act so that I am the best I can be *for my child*? I want to provide an anchor for her at home as much as possible. Really, I want her everyday life to be boring and predictable—something I never had as a child. I want her to have the luxury of wanting to go out into the world because life at home is so boring.

Everything was too exciting during my own childhood—constantly moving, fathers constantly changing. There was nothing else I could do but become a homebody and shun travel and excitement. Always cook proper meals. Hardly ever go out to eat, maybe four times a year. And never, ever eat at McDonald's. Over my dead body.

We always sit together at the table, everyone who is around. Nobody is allowed to answer the phone during a meal, nobody reads or sings. I have no idea why it is, but singing seems to be a major problem—both my daughter and my stepson seem to want to sing at the table all the time. But it's strictly forbidden—otherwise no food goes into their mouths. These are the less important things that I do to act like a good mother for my child. Above them on the list are things like signaling through my behavior every second of every day that she is wanted and loved. I let her know that I am happy she was born. That I'm proud of her, just the way she is. That I'm proud of the things she does. And I tell her all the time that I love her, that she's smart, pretty, and funny. That she can learn anything if she puts her mind to it. I try to make her understand that it's okay with me if she does things differently than I do, that I'll still love her regardless of whatever craziness she ends up going through in her life. My mother never did that. In fact, she impressed the opposite upon me: either you are like me or I don't love you. That will not be passed down through the generations. I will make sure of that. Ha.

Liza gets three plates out of the cabinet, squats down, puts them on the counter, and then hops down nimbly, like a monkey. In order to set the side of the dinner table where Georg and I sit, she has to remove the picked-over remains of the two newspapers we read every day. The table sits seven. We only use one end of it, though, so we can be close together. I have her set the table because I read in a book that it's good to have kids do things like that. My impulse would be to do everything

for her—to show that I love her. But then she'd never learn
anything and she'd grow up unable to do laundry or unload a
dishwasher. So I have to get past that impulse and ask her to
do things that she really doesn't *need* to do. In the book I read
about bringing up kids, by Jesper Juul, it says you have to have
taught a child everything they will need to live on their own by
the time they are twelve. Otherwise it's too late to teach them.
I've got five years left. I'll do it quickly. Setting the table, folding
clothes, tidying your room, cleaning the toilet.

Georg comes upstairs. It's obvious that he's just gotten
out of bed. I smile at him in a way that's meant to telegraph a
message: I can't talk right now because a child is in the room,
but that was fucking hot. He smiles back. He's wearing his
loose-fitting, long white underwear with a button fly. I always
tell him how good he looks in them—he looks like a cowboy
on his day off, and I like it. And when I run my hand across his
ass, which I often do when Liza's not looking, the cloth feels
unbelievably soft. The undies have been washed hundreds of
times and are practically see-through in some spots.

I read a theory in *Geo Kompakt* (which has become my
new sex bible) that seemed to perfectly capture the relationship
between me and my husband. It was called "the hanging bridge
theory." An attractive woman—the bait in the experiment—
stopped random men in everyday situations and everyday
places—like at the mall or on the sidewalk—and asked them
a few questions, supposedly for a scientific study. The men
answered gallantly, and she gave each respondent her number
in case he was interested to learn the results of the study. Then
she did the same thing, except she approached her subjects on
a hanging bridge in a park. The bridge swayed back and forth in

the wind as she again asked the questions and handed out her number. The result of the experiment: many more men from the hanging bridge called her afterward than did men from the normal situations. Meaning that people create connections more quickly when they are in more extreme conditions. On the swaying bridge, men thought, *Oh, we both survived that together and, man, she was rather attractive*. People seek connections to those with whom they go through a tough situation. The hanging bridge that brought me and my then new husband, Georg, together was pregnancy and birth.

We got to know each other in a totally boring way, like so many other couples—at work. He ran a gallery and I wanted to exhibit my photography. His wife was about to have a baby, and I had just given birth. We had both just started families with other partners. There was the hanging bridge. Then things went crazy. We careered toward each other like two comets. It was love at first sight—though neither of us noticed. Love took root and grew on its own somewhere in the back of our heads, undetected, like a Trojan-horse virus on a computer. All we thought was, *Cool, we understand each other, we should become friends*. We felt like kindred spirits, strictly platonic, of course.

So birth was our hanging bridge. He wanted to know everything about my birth process. We hardly talked about anything else. Along the way we started to work together. Much too soon—before the end of my maternity leave—I had to, or rather was permitted to, exhibit my photos in Georg's gallery. As a result of the stress, good stress, mind you, my milk stopped flowing after just three months of nursing. At that point I could work full-time again, and my then boyfriend could finally help me feed the baby bird. When my future husband had his baby, with his wife obviously, I was more excited than for my own birth. It felt as if I was having a second child because I felt so close to the father. Our children are so close in age that I've never been able to shed the feeling that they're twins. Everything seemed predestined. Yeah, yeah, I know, there's no such thing as pre-destination, God, fate, fuck you—there's only coincidence and hanging bridges. We thought we were friends. We didn't lie about our relationship because we didn't know any better ourselves. The moment his son was born, who did he call? Standing in front of the hospital, as men do, after the birth, he didn't call his own mother or relatives. Nope. He called me. I was so happy for him. Everything had gone well.

I watched my then husband during our birth and thought, *Hmmm, he could really do a bit better than that*. And my future husband watched his wife give birth and thought, *Hmmm, she could really do a bit better than that*. And we both knew who could do it a bit better. Us. By the time he had his own child, there was no stopping our love. I thought he was stronger than my then husband. He thought I was stronger than his then wife. Naturally, later on those impressions turned out to be mistaken, just as almost everything you initially think about someone when you fall in love turns out to be wrong. He's the man; naturally he had a son. I'm a woman; so obviously I had a daughter. Everything fit perfectly—if only there weren't the previous partners. We needed to get rid of them. But how? Leaving my partner wasn't difficult for me to imagine. I had my mother as a role model, a consummate pro at leaving people. Georg, on the other hand, had his religious and uncompromis-ingly loyal parents, married for more than fifty years. In his entire family, zero percent of the marriages had ever ended in divorce. How could he get out of his marriage? What's more, his wife had picked up on the whole thing. "You're not going to fall for her, are you?"

As far as I'm concerned, women notice that kind of thing more quickly than men. Or at least they are crazy enough to bring it up, and when that happens everything goes downhill. "Do you still love me?" "Uhhhh." It takes a second too long to answer. Busted. What a terrible actor Georg is. Just say this, for God's sake: "Of course I love you! What kind of a question is that?" Then we'd have had a little more time to figure things out. The way it happened, it was already over between them before there was any chance to save it.

That's what he was going to do at first. He had pangs of Christian guilt, felt it in his genes, I guess. He wanted to save his family. "We can't see each other anymore. I just had a child with her, and I have to give her—and our relationship—another chance. For the child."

I had to wait. All through the painful waiting period, I was sure they would work it out. That's the way you are when you are in love. You're not sure of yourself and you just keep telling yourself, *Sure, no problem, he'll be back*. I didn't even tell my then husband. Either he didn't want to notice or he actually didn't notice anything. There wasn't much to notice anyway.

We hadn't even had sex one time before we left our partners. That's why it's always amazed me how well that aspect of our relationship functions. In fact, it's always getting better. I've never experienced what it's like to have sex with the same person for such a long time. Thanks, Mother!

*   *   *

I'm convinced that people come together only because of sex—even if it's just because they *think* you will be a good fit in bed. Because of genetics—you can smell it. And then it does turn out to be a fit as good as a couple of trapeze artists. If you have a good sense of smell and don't ruin it by smoking, you'll find the best genetic match—someone with whom you can perform sexual acrobatics. I'm totally convinced of that. I must have smelled it. Everything. His sexuality. His ability as a provider. We never talked about money or sex. Our love was just there, and everything made sense in retrospect. Though nothing did at the start. I read a quote somewhere—I think it was from Goethe, though it could just as easily have been from Yoda—that went something like this: Love is just a romantic philosophical superstructure that permits us to avoid admitting to ourselves that we just want to get into someone's pants. He put it somewhat more eloquently, but I can't find the exact quote. Maybe I just dreamed that I read it. But I believe the sentiment nonetheless. It's the key to all the craziness that happens between fully grown adults.

My husband isn't physically attractive at all. Obviously love has nothing to do with looks. Fuck all of you with your my-dream-man-should-look-like-this-or-that bullshit, your star signs and height and hair color requirements. That's not the way love works. The first thing I noticed about him—and that stood out in a negative, though interesting, way—was his fucked-up elbow. The first time I met him he was wearing short sleeves. Strong white arms with hair on them, and then a strange crippled elbow—there was some sort of cyst or tumor sticking out, covered with scars. The Phantom of the Opera, except only at the elbow!

I asked very directly what it was. I always do that in the heat of the moment because I'm worried the person has already noticed I'm staring. It turned out to be an affliction from childhood. He broke his arm once, and all winter long he had to take the bus alone to the clinic where he was doing his physical therapy. And one time after an ice storm he got off the bus and slipped and fell on the newly healed elbow. It had to be operated on several times after that because he'd shattered all the bones. They never managed to reconstruct it properly, and that's why there's a piece of bone that sticks out like a shark fin. That made an impression on me straightaway.

After the arm business, I noticed a big scar across his cheekbone. The second thing I asked him was where he got *that* scar. And that one was from cancer. Shortly before we met he'd had skin cancer. Nothing serious. It was discovered early enough that they were able to remove the entire melanoma before it spread, and that was that. Well, except for the fact that in the back of his head he would always remember how death had come knocking. After my very first conversation with him I knew that we belonged together and also that I would end up burying him. I'm going to be a grieving cancer widow. He told me that he comes from a family with a history of cancer. Members of his family either died of cancer or managed to beat various forms of it to earn a brief reprieve. I knew what the story was and what this great love of mine was bringing with him—even if perhaps I understood only subconsciously.

At the front of my consciousness I thought to myself that we would end up working together. What a great gallery owner! What a great guy! But what an odd set of icebreakers. First, childhood injuries. Second, cancer in the family. It pretty much says everything about our relationship. He also asked me about the car accident in which my three brothers died. Death was intertwined with our love right from the start. One of the first things we did as a couple was to fill out organ donor cards and write and sign living wills and actual wills. For us, that was the height of romance.

Georg sits down at his laptop in the kitchen and scans *Spiegel Online* to see if anything has changed in the world in the last few minutes. Liza wanders around grumbling. She's bored.

"What should I do now, Mama? I'm bored."

"See if anything is missing. Drinks, perhaps?"

"Oh yeah, what do you want to drink?"

The same answer we give every day comes from Georg and me in perfect harmony: "Tap water."

We never drink alcohol in front of the kids—for the sake of setting a good example. And sugary drinks are strictly forbidden at our place—both for the usual anti-American reasons and because of the fact that they are totally unhealthy. Why would you drink something that amounts to candy when you're thirsty? Sweets exacerbate your thirst. It's like a form of torture. How can anyone pay good money for drinks that actually make you more thirsty? It's like giving Jesus vinegar and gall to drink when he was thirsty on the cross. Torture upon torture.

She climbs up onto the counter again to get glasses out of the cabinet. She jumps back down, fills the glasses too full, and carries them to the table while trying to keep them from spilling. I have to stop myself from saying something. Bad, bad to be a mother and want to comment on everything a kid does. You feel it coming on and then the impulse hits you. Terrible, terrible, terrible.

"Can you please put a trivet on the table, too, my child?"

Now that my husband is fully awake, I leave my daughter in his care. I say good-bye. They know the drill. They're free to do what they wish until I'm back. I'll be there and back quickly; it's not far. I turn off the burner under the pan as I walk out—don't want the two of them to go up in flames in the apartment while I'm unable to keep an eye on them. Gas stoves are dangerous. I won't let fire take any more of my relatives.

"See you soon, you nut jobs."

Neither of them answers. That's the way it is when the routine is so well rehearsed.

I drive to my therapist's office in another section of town. I go three times a week for an hour-long session—though an hour to a therapist is fifty minutes in normal human time, no more, no less. I go there to work out my everyday life, and I think I'd have died many times over without my therapist. She has often saved my life—psychologically speaking. In my daughter Liza's mind, it's just Mama going to see her weird doctor. She's not interested in what I do there. I hope she waits a long time to ask, too, because the older she is the better I'll be able to explain to her what it is. "Mama goes there so she doesn't get on your nerves, my child, and so she doesn't weigh you down with her own issues. That way you can live more freely."

The drive is usually a pain. But my therapist, Frau Drescher, says that's part of the therapy, too. I complain to myself about a therapy that includes such an array of annoyances even before you get there. Because I know the car accident plays a big role in her mind, I feel as if I don't even have to go to her office: hey, I'm doing great—what's the point? I think up all sorts of reasons why I shouldn't drive, and once I'm in the car I convince myself that Frau Drescher is a bad therapist—that she overestimates the value of her couch and psychoanalysis. What the hell is analysis anyway? I do it, but I still have no idea what it's about. Will I get some kind of certificate at the end? Like the report you get after a blood test? A psychological report? That would be useful—I could give it to my husband as a sort of instruction manual, and later my daughter could read it, too. It would make all of our lives easier. I'll ask Frau Drescher. She thinks that my assessments and criticisms of her as I drive to her office are also part of the therapy. Great, that really puts me at ease. I feel better already.

I try to follow every rule of the road—I have to avoid an accident at any cost. Not necessarily because I don't want to die—in fact sometimes I feel like an old woman who thinks it would be nice to have peace and quiet, the ultimate peace and quiet—but because I have a child. That gives me added worth. I can't do that to my daughter. Cannot get killed or injured. Which is why I'm such a careful driver. I let everyone in, but especially women. It's a chance to contradict any accusations of cattiness, even in traffic. I drive very defensively and leave plenty of space between me and the car in front of me. I avoid all mistakes and keep all the things I learned in driving school at age eighteen in the front of my mind—all in order to survive and to avoid killing anyone else. Because of my past, even just driving across town to my therapy session is a life-and-death scenario.

I get out of the car in the parking lot. I take all my valuables with me because, oddly enough, my therapist has her office in a bad part of town. And her office is on the eleventh floor. Which for me is a catastrophe. I've told her a million times that I don't like it. She needs to get a new ground-floor office somewhere else. That would be much nicer. She laughs at me and says, "You'll have to get over it, Frau Kiehl, because the practice is staying put."

And then she wants to sit peacefully and discuss my fear of heights and of elevators, my fear of fire and smoke. I'm also afraid that such a tall building might collapse while I'm in it. When I walk into the high-rise I talk to myself. "I can't believe I have to get on this elevator because of Frau Drescher. I just can't believe it." I usually smell smoke or gas in the lobby. That's a funny old habit of mine—it's because my mother found her own mother in front of the oven with the gas on. She had taken sleeping tablets and also drugged her young son, whom she wanted to take with her. But not my mother, who was also just a kid at the time. Who knows why? That was the big drama in our family—at least until the car accident overwhelmed every-thing else. So I sniff my way around the lobby like an animal, searching for the source of the dangerous odor. For most other people, hearing is the sense that most frequently sets off their alarm bells. In my case, it's my sense of smell. Because I just know that my family will be snuffed out by fire, smoke, or gas. That's probably also the reason I avoid smokers like the plague. They trigger a flight instinct in me. Whenever I smell a lit ciga-rette I think something is on fire and cringe with fear. Just for a second, of course, but it's still enough to make my heart jump and cause a jolt of adrenaline. Very unpleasant.

When I step into the elevator to go up to my therapist's office, it really does smell like smoke. Some nicotine-addicted asshole must have lit up on the way down for a cigarette break. Most smokers just can't wait. I stand there and think something's on fire. And before I realize it's just the remains of cigarette smoke I get so scared that I feel like I've aged several years. That's why I hate all smokers—they spread the smell of death. It clings to their hair and their clothes and hangs in the air wherever they go.

When I look at the digital number panel in the elevator, I can see what floor it's come down from. It sends another shiver of fear down my spine. The building is *that* high? The eleventh floor is not even the top floor. Often the elevator has come from much higher up than that. And I wonder, *Do I really want to do this to myself?* All the things that can happen on the way up. It could get stuck and catch on fire, and I'd be trapped, burning up in this tin can. The floor would get too hot to stand on, so I'd sit down; but the skin and flesh of my ass would burn, so I'd stand up again and that's when I'd see the smoke snaking into the elevator carriage. I scream for as long as I can still get air, the smoke stings my throat, burns my vocal chords. I'm coughing and my voice gets thinner. I push the emergency button over and over. Nothing happens. In a mortal panic, I climb onto the top of the elevator carriage to try to get some air—but everything is shrouded in dark smoke. I'm in a smokehouse, unable to escape. Nobody is going to save me, and I can't even scream any longer. I cry, and then lay myself down to die atop the glowing elevator. I think of my daughter and don't want to die. Then I black out.

That's the way it plays out in my head every time I have to ride up those eleven floors to see my fucking therapist, who insists on having her practice all the way up there. And I stare the whole time at the sign in the elevator that represents all my fears: IN CASE OF FIRE, DO NOT USE ELEVATOR. I can definitely agree to that. But what happens if a fire breaks out when I'm already using the elevator? Didn't anybody think of that? Of course not. When I reach the eleventh floor and, miracle of miracles, the doors open normally, I march out like a survivor. A passerby might think from my demeanor that I'm relaxed and happy. But then comes the next problem. Someone on her floor smokes in his apartment. We're eleven floors above the earth and he's playing with our lives! The building seems to sway. I tell my therapist all the time that the foundations aren't solid. You can tell when it's windy. When it's windy I can feel the way we're all swaying inside the building.

Once in a while I encounter someone in the hallway on the eleventh floor. When that happens I'm immediately diverted from the frightening images swirling in my head. Because I suddenly think, *So that's what my therapist's patients look like?* Though of course there's no guarantee that the person has come from her office. I get upset that she even has other patients. I read in a biography of Brian Wilson that he had his therapist live with him. What a good idea! That would be my dream—to have Frau Drescher at home, all to myself!

I'm totally convinced that I simply couldn't live without her. But I want to be her only patient. I know only monotheism—from my mother, of course. She never taught me anything else. It's always mother's fault. I'm sure someday my child will think I'm to blame for everything, too. That's just the way it works.

I try to glean as much information as possible in the few seconds during which I can actually see my therapist. She shrouds herself in a mysterious cloud of noninformation. She says I should know as little as possible about her. All I know about her is what I can see. And what little she divulges. Which is next to fucking nothing. Particularly in comparison to what I divulge about myself. It's not fair. But I guess that's the way it's supposed to be with therapy. I'm not meant to understand—I don't have a degree in it, after all.

My soon-to-be-former best friend also briefly went to a therapist—though naturally she didn't do it very intensively or for very long because otherwise she would actually have had to do some soul-searching. But she went to a therapist that every one of her friends—except me—also went to. What a sick idea. My therapist thinks so, too. You can't talk openly in a situation like that. What if you had a problem with one of your friends? The whole idea behind therapy is that the therapist doesn't know the people you are talking about. That way the therapist can't have an opinion about them independent of yours—her information is limited to what the patient says. If you're insanely jealous about all your therapist's other patients, just imagine what it would be like if you constantly ran into your friends coming out of her office. "Oh, hi, I was just talking to your therapist about your abortion! Oh, sorry, you hadn't told her yet? That explains a lot!"

Aha, I think to myself in the hallway, looking at a person who must be another patient, *she takes on boring-looking patients, too, eh? She does it with any old person! Hopefully that person's psychological issues are more interesting than his clothes!* The patient doesn't make eye contact with me. How uncool. Hey, we're all fucked in the head, don't worry about it. But you've got to be able to meet my gaze when I say a friendly hello.

Perhaps he's more ashamed than I am that he has to go to therapy? That's annoying, too. Once he's walked away, I can ring the doorbell. There's a sort of agreement among all the patients that there should never be more than one in the office at a time. Not like at a normal doctor's office, where all the patients sit in a waiting room together. When I'm in her office, I can be sure that the only other person there is Frau Drescher.

She's furnished the place oddly. I hope it doesn't reflect her true taste. I hope she's furnished the place this way just to meet patients' expectations and make them comfortable opening up. If not—if this is how she actually wants it to look—it would be really tragic.

I ring the bell now that the other lunatic is gone. A buzzer lets me in. As usual, she is hiding in her office, a room I've never seen. Through the frosted glass I can see only that she's sitting at a desk in there. It's very fuzzy, but there's a large desk, and I can make out the shape of a person dressed in pastel clothing. She likes to wear pastel-colored sweaters, often cable-knit. I can also vaguely make out her blonde head of hair. She looks very feminine and friendly. She's got a 1970s kind of sexiness to her. Sometimes I worry that she's a lesbian, but I'll never find out. I wouldn't like it if she were a lesbian. I want her to have all the same difficulties in life that I have: husband, child, the whole shebang.

I have to wait until she's ready. She always needs ten minutes between patients to clear her head and cleanse her soul—which, of course, does not exist. I have no idea what she does for those ten minutes. I suspect she looks over her notes, because it doesn't seem possible that she could remember all the mothers-in-law and ex-husbands and children's and pets' names that people jabber on about all day. In eight years with her, she's never made a single mistake about things like that with me. I keep waiting for her to refer to my husband as Oliver or whatever. Or to say "your son" instead of "your daughter." That's why I think she hoards notes about all of us loons behind that frosted glass—notes she quickly updates after each hour with the various new names that have come up. I imagine her partner—hopefully a man—quizzing her about all the names of her patients' family members.

I have my choice of sitting on a chair in the hall or going into the room where she hosts group sessions. There are probably a dozen chairs in that room. It's where the group marriage counseling takes place. Back when we went to marriage counseling to save our relationship, my husband and I chose to do it privately, just us two, rather than with a group. My husband is very much opposed to groups—whether it's tai chi, therapy, or whatever. Only when it comes to sex is he not opposed to groups.

There are pictures on the walls that I think Frau Drescher painted herself. They depict naked people in the Garden of Eden. Snakes are wrapped around the bodies. There are brightly colored flowers all over the place. The people aren't fully visible—they're more like silhouettes. In the group room is a well-stocked bookcase, which I find reassuring. It's proof that she did study the stuff she uses to fiddle around with my head. It shows she's clever, and if she doesn't manage to make progress on something she can consult her books. When I arrive much too early, I grab a random book off the shelf, open it to a random page, and try to understand what's written. But it never works. It's insanely complicated stuff.

At the top of the hour she quietly emerges from her office and comes to look for me. I hear her footsteps, always following the same route: first she looks in the hall, then she comes down to the group room. She stands in the doorway and says, "Right." She smiles encouragingly.

I stand up, go confidently toward her, look her in the eyes—as my parents taught me to do—shake her hand, and say, "*Guten Tag.*"

I find it uncomfortable making physical contact with her. But it's part of being a member of society. Still, I'd rather not touch her. Not because I find her disgusting, but because I feel as if we should have a strictly mental connection, and physical contact of any kind disturbs that. Disturbs me, anyway. I've never talked about it with her. Maybe I should sometime. Then perhaps we could forgo the handshake. A lot of what I think I want to talk about vanishes from my mind once I've had to use the elevator or see Frau Drescher. Things usually go in a completely different direction than I anticipated.

"*Guten Tag,*" she replies, and we release each other's hands from the handshake. It's all rather embarrassing.

She's usually wearing a pantsuit. Or a masculine blouse with a V-neck sweater over it. She likes pastel colors. Pink, lilac, salmon, light blue, mint green. She has long blonde hair. And breasts. Big ones. A nice body—not too thin, not too chunky. She looks very healthy. Thank goodness—I want her to live a long time. Did I mention her breasts? She has breasts. And breasts are a major theme of my therapy. My breast complex runs my life. I complain to her regularly about women with big breasts and blonde hair. And she has big breasts—at least from my perspective, as a tadpole in the breast department—and platinum blonde hair. Sometimes I feel funny saying what I want to about it. I ask her if I'm not going too far for her. But she's totally supportive. It's not about her feelings or sensitivities. She's a doctor. She stays above the fray. I have to be able to say anything in therapy without thinking about how she will feel about my breast comments.

She's also a lot bigger than I am, which I like. She wears a lot of mascara, jet-black, and light blue eye shadow. It works perfectly with her dark blue eyes. Her whole face reminds me of Agnetha from ABBA. She always smiles at me so knowingly and kindly. She's on my side. It's nice. That's the way it works with therapy—the therapist is on the patient's side. She puts a lot of effort into understanding me.

She lets me enter the sacred space of the consultation room ahead of her. There's the couch where I've already spent so many hours. The room has been nicely aired out so it doesn't smell like another patient. We wouldn't want that. The idea is to pretend that other patients do not exist. But I don't let myself be fooled. Not even by Frau Drescher. She closes the window, and I wrap myself in the fleece blanket with the strange pattern on it—to protect myself from all the forces of nature about to be released upon me. Then I lie down. She always puts a freshly washed light blue cloth on the pillow where I put my head. Sometimes, when I show up with freshly washed hair, I get it all wet. She says it's no big deal—that each patient gets a new one anyway. A thin piece of cotton prevents any direct contact between the oils of the various patients' hair. Where Frau Drescher stores these cloths is still a riddle to me. At the foot end of the black leather couch is the type of mat you would usually place just outside the door of your apartment.

It has hard bristles. Frau Drescher knows that it scratches me and she's said I can remove it from the couch. But I never do. I want to get right down to business. So for the entire hour I just hide the fact that the mat bugs me. Especially in summer, when my legs are bare.

Once I'm lying there, I wait for her to close the door and sit down behind me. The door is soundproofed, which, being paranoid, I like. I lie there in my usual funereal position, with my arms outside the fleece blanket—don't want anyone to think I'm secretly playing with myself. I put my hands together and interlock my fingers the way people do when they're praying. Despite the fact that I'm totally against prayer. I look up at the ceiling: white wood chip. And at the wall to my left: white wood chip.

When I look past my feet, there is a huge painting leaning against the wall. No idea why it's propped against the wall instead of hanging from it. What is Agnetha—as I like to think of her— trying to signal to me with that? I always think she's trying to tell me something. But in the case of the painting, I have no idea what. Maybe it's something like, *Hey, check it out, dear patient, I'm human, too, and don't always follow through on everything.*

The poorly painted image is of a colossal devil figure. He's a naked man, and he's squatting on the ground. I keep looking at his crotch, but his balls aren't hanging down. A bunch of kitschy little birds are flying around his head. As I'm talking about my latest problems, I keep racking my brain for a reason she might have for putting this image right at the feet of her patients. She's probably crazy herself. Anyway, I've stared at that painting for hours upon hours. I've seen it blurry, at times when I've been crying. And I've seen it shaking, when I've had a panic attack.

I've had to look at that image of the devil with little birds flying around his head in every imaginable emotional state. What is she trying to tell me?

If I were to look to the right—which I never do—I'd see a room stuffed full of tasteless objects. Two fake trees, a black vase out of the 1980s that must be three feet tall, on top of which she's put a huge polished purple stone. The entire windowsill is crammed with useless stuff. A steel turtle sculpture with evil eyes, some sort of ashtray filled with black sand, a beanbag gecko. I guess Agnetha came of age style-wise in the 1980s. In fact I'm sure of it. But what do I know? Funny thing. I've never thought about how old she is. She's definitely older than I am. Definitely. I read somewhere that psychologists and psychiatrists—what's the difference between them again?—try to trick their patients by decorating their offices completely differently from their homes. The patient should have something to get annoyed with. The decor in Frau Drescher's office functions extremely effectively that way for me. When she moves or takes down a painting, I'm thrown into crisis. I walk in, immediately notice the change, and ask her, completely dumbfounded, what the story is. Why do people always have to change things around? Where's the painting gone? When is it coming back? The way she looks at me, I can tell that five other patients have already reacted exactly the same way. So much for my wonderful individuality.

Then we begin.

"First I need to apologize to you, Frau Drescher, just in case you can smell anything. It's best if I just tell you directly, rather than spend the entire hour wondering whether you've noticed anything."

"That's right, Frau Kiehl, it's better just to say it. You don't want anything to distract you or weigh you down here. Let's just get everything out in the open right from the start. What is it that I might have noticed?"

"I just had—shortly before I came here—sex. So there you go, now it's out. And I only washed up quickly afterward. You always say I don't need to be perfect when I come to see you."

"Nice. With whom?"

"Haha. Are you making fun of me? With whom? With Georg, of course."

"Yes, of course. I was just asking because of the sexual fantasies you've talked about recently."

"I know, I know."

"Do you feel good as a result?"

"Ha, of course! What do you think? I always feel good after having sex with Georg. I'm kind of amazed that we still have sex, since we've been together for so long. In previous relationships, I lost any interest in sex after about three years. This time it's still going after seven years. Pretty amazing. But I worry that it will end soon. You know how it is: once the sex is gone it's just a question of time before the love withers and dies, too."

"Really? You think that's how it works?"

"Yes, I do. That's what happened in every single one of my relationships since I was thirteen. That's exactly how it works. I keep trying to figure out why it's stayed so good with Georg for this long. And I'll tell you this, Frau Drescher: I think I'm letting myself be fucked by his money. That's what I think. The reason it's worked for so long is because he's the first guy I've been with who's had more money than me—as a result I still find him sexy. I don't mean sexy in the sense that he looks so good, but in the sense that I want to fuck him. I'm pretty sure that's the reason."

"You've told me this theory of yours before. Aren't you underestimating the love you feel for your husband? You reduce it all to money and sex. I would posit that you're doing this as a defense mechanism—to shield yourself from your deeper feelings in case things do eventually go bad, or he dies."

"And I've heard that theory from you before, too. We're not going to get anywhere talking about this topic. Today in town, I thought for a second that I saw my father."

"What did you do?"

"I just kept walking. I wouldn't say hello to him. You know that I hope I never see him again. So I couldn't just say hi to him on the street. The same shit would just start right back up again with his fucking wife—my evil stepmother. You put it so well last time. What was it you said again? That I'd let myself remain passively at the mercy of my parents for long enough and that now I had decided to be proactive, to actively break away from them, even if it was difficult to do so. But that way they could no longer hurt me. That's it. Exactly. And you said, 'You can only put physical distance between you and your parents; inside they will always remain with you, because they are your parents.' Horrible."

"But you understand that now, don't you, Frau Kiehl? That you can only get away from them physically, right?"

"Of course. But I still think it's best to try to cut them off once and for all, forever. I know you don't like the word 'forever,' but I'm allowed to use it because I mean it—even if you don't like my saying it, and even if you think I can never get rid of them on the inside, like a fucking virus. One that doesn't just go away. AIDS in parent form. And even if I do still suffer inside, I think cutting them out of my life is the right thing to do. Because I'm doing something, taking action. I'm sick of being a fucking adult and still wondering every year on my birthday whether or not my father has remembered it. He still manages to mess up my birthdays, and I still think about how he always forgot me when I was a child. Okay, sure, he didn't forget *me*—like you always say, he *only* forgot my birthday. Sure, sure, but when you're a child that feels as if he has completely forgotten about you."

"Don't you associate anything good with him?"

"I'd rather not."

"I'm sure something good will occur to you."

"Yeah, well, if it's mandatory. He taught me and my dead brother to make pancakes. The whole process. One egg per person, a little seltzer in the batter to make them fluffy, how to flip them up in the air—though a lot of the time they never landed back in the frying pan. We would sit at the counter and watch him in amazement. They were our favorite thing to eat, his pancakes. Typical kids of divorce. The parent who isn't there is a wonder, while the parent you end up living with you take for granted. Our favorite foods were the few things our father made—pancakes and curries—instead of any of the thousands of dishes our mother made. She was a much, much better cook. And the curries were really something he showed us for later in life. We wouldn't eat just pancakes for our entire lives, he said. So he taught us how to make curry from scratch, using whole spices—not just some mix out of a jar. No, we measured out turmeric and coriander, made garam masala mixtures, everything. It was way too spicy for kids. He wanted to show us what a hard-ass he was. Although it occurs to me now how crazy that was. Showing kids he was tough—by eating spicy food! Ridiculous!"

"Still, I'm pleased you were able to say something positive. When people decide to shut someone out of their lives, they tend to limit themselves to seeing the negative aspects of that person. Like you and your best friend. It's as if you feel bad for thinking you should quit the friendship, so you convince yourself, in retrospect, that there wasn't a good side to it. But it couldn't have been all bad, or else you wouldn't have been friends in the first place."

"I still only see the negatives."

"That's the way you rationalize ending the friendship. You are afraid of the vengeance of the person who is being abandoned. Because you're actually afraid to leave anyone, no matter who."

"Right. That's why I have you. You help me get away from the people in my life who are bad for me."

"If you say so. But it's interesting nonetheless that you need help to leave people."

"That's the way it is. Without you I wouldn't have left my parents, and I wouldn't be about ready to finally get rid of my best friend."

"I would like to point out that I did not encourage you to take such steps."

"I know. You say that every time. I know. I know. I'm here with you but I come up with the ideas myself. Obviously you never say, 'Do this or that.' Tomorrow is another push-Elizabeth-to-the-limits day, by the way."

"You're going to a brothel with your husband again? You already know what I think of that."

"Yes, I know. But it helps me get further away from my mother and closer to my husband. It's proven, Frau Drescher, an empirical fact, and you can't change my mind about it. Maybe most of your patients don't pursue a healthy marriage that way, but I remain convinced these brothel visits are good for us. The same way that every time I make pancakes for the kids, I can feel my father sitting on my shoulder and watching. Everything has to be perfect, for Papa, so he'll love his daughter. Everything takes effort. And just like when my mother sits on my other shoulder when I'm giving my husband a blowjob. She hates men. She hates cocks. When I was a child, she constantly told me that men were only good for procreation and that sex was never the slightest bit enjoyable for her. Unfortunately that lesson didn't take. From that perspective, I'm definitely cheating if I go to the brothel with Georg tomorrow. And just thinking about it gives me diarrhea."

"Would you like to go here? I'm happy to wait."

"No, thanks. You know the story. I can't go number two anywhere but at home."

"We need to work on that some more, Frau Kiehl. You must obviously know there's nothing wrong with using the toilet here. It's human to leave odors behind."

"Yeah, well, then I guess I don't want to be human. Let's not talk about it anymore—it'll just make the situation worse. And no matter how bad it gets, I'm not going to use the toilet here. Except to pee. Anything else is out of the question."

"How long have you been with me? Eight years. And still so little trust in the surroundings. The other patients go here."

"That's great, but the last thing I want to hear about is the toilet habits of your other patients. Yuck. It's disgusting of you to even bring it up. Seriously, I'm going to be sick just thinking about it."

"All I can do is invite you to use the facilities here and reiterate that you are very welcome to do so."

My intestines make a horrible noise.

"That's your fault, for talking about this. Let's change the topic. You and your strange invitations. So, where were we? The important things!"

My intestines make more ugly noises. I attempt the impossible—to ignore them.

"Ah, yes, right, we were talking about the fact that I think it's good to do a favor for my husband and in the process to betray my mother. I always feel free, relaxed, and happy when I do the opposite of what I was brought up to do. She was completely off the mark with her hatred for men. And as a result, I had to come see you for eight years before I realized that men weren't the enemy. Or at least definitely not the only enemy. In my case, unfortunately, Mother is the enemy. My husband is a much bigger feminist than my mother."

"Yes, I think you're right."

She laughs. I sometimes think that's my job—to get my therapist to laugh. Even the most awful things I try to express in a funny way—that way she has fun working with me. I want so badly to be unique and to stand out from the other patients. The smartest, the funniest, the bravest, the favorite. I want to be the patient who lets my therapist in the fastest and furthest so she can have the most success with me. With me! I push myself hard, too. I reveal to her all the most disgusting parts of my personality—the bad, the evil, everything has to be aired so she has plenty to work with. In therapy, protecting yourself is completely wrongheaded. She's on my side and only wants to help. So, everything out. I don't bother hemming and hawing and vacillating. I don't think, *Should I tell her this or that?* Get it out, speed up the healing process. And learn as much as possible from her about the process, so I can take over and always be a good wife for my husband and a good mother for Liza.

During this hour we talk for the hundredth time about the connection between sex and parents. How you have to do everything well so your parents love you and how upset I still am about all the crap my parents planted in my head. I tell her about the outing planned for tomorrow and how proud I am that I can suck cock better than any hooker. I explain to Frau Drescher how we choose our prostitutes. Georg and I are actually too polite for the red-light district. We've often slept with unattractive women because we can't bring ourselves to say, *No, she's not for us.* We're too gentle for that. We'd rather sleep with an ugly woman and pay her a ton of money—about three hundred and fifty an hour, because she has to service two clients at the same time—than to tell her she doesn't appeal to us. I'm tougher than my husband. He gets disgusted afterward and spends ages in the shower trying to wash the images of the fat woman from his mind. I always have to laugh, thinking what a couple of idiots we are for being too shy to just say what we want, like every other customer.

Over time we've developed a signal to use if one of us finds the woman or her body repulsive. We say, "Wow, it's warm in here." Because I don't think we are particularly attractive, it doesn't really bother me if someone isn't good-looking. In the book of life—where I mentally record all the extraordinary experiences I have—it's good to have slept with a fat woman or, accidentally, with one with huge fake silicone breasts. But Georg can't roll with the punches as well as I can.

We also never pick young prostitutes. They are too insecure. And so twitchy with their hands. The women we choose for threesomes need to be at least twenty-eight or so. But we're happy if they are a lot older than that. Up to fifty works for us. A lot of customers seek out extra-young women to fuck. They think the youth will rub off on their cocks. It doesn't.

Does it make me a lesbian if I'm always messing around with women? Even if it's my husband's wish rather than mine? It's not always easy to unravel the difference when people are in love and together. Drawing a line between what he wants and what I want is difficult. But in any event, my husband doesn't want to touch another man, which is a shame, because then we could change our sexual adventures around. A woman here, a man there, and always me and my husband in bed with them. But if I ever do something in bed with a male prostitute—if we could ever find one who didn't look too gay—Georg would never participate. He might watch, but I find that idea strange.

I also talk to Frau Drescher for the hundredth time about how proud I am to send my husband to the brothel alone sometimes, and how it absolutely sparks my desire for him. It's crazy the effect it can have. Sending your husband off to another woman. I'm always trying to be less of a control freak, trying to get beyond my normal urge to be like that, which is strong. And when I loosen up enough to send him off to a brothel alone, it makes me feel so good. My husband is still afraid of the fits of jealousy I used to have—or, let's be honest, had until recently—because of my fear of losing him. Million-dollar question: I wonder how long Frau Drescher thinks it will take—how long must I behave well before he's no longer afraid of me? How long—how many years do I have to spend proving to him that, with her help, I've cut out many of the evil, aggressive, ugly parts of my personality—before the good outweighs the bad in his eyes?

Every once in a while I ask whether we still have time. She answers, "Yes, we have a few more minutes."

Then I start on another topic. I ask her how long it will be before I stop thinking about my mother while giving blowjobs, how long it will be before I stop hearing her whisper that I'm debasing myself. Which isn't true. He goes down on me just as often as I go down on him.

And then at some point Frau Drescher answers my question about the remaining time with "Now the time is up."

I lift myself and sit upright, take a deep breath, then start to fold up the blanket. Frau Drescher always says, "You can leave that, I'll take care of it."

That's part of the ritual she has for preparing for her next patient. Folding the blanket and putting it over the chair as if I had never been there. Hopefully she likes me the way I like her.

I say good-bye, survive the elevator ride down, as always, and then listen to loud music in the car on the way back home to Liza and Georg. I'm a good mother and wife. I try to clean up my messy psyche for the sake of a healthy future together, as a family and as a couple.

I drive along the ugly street toward home. There's a patch of grass and a few trees at one point along the way, and I always look for a rabbit or squirrel. Sometimes there are a few there.

At night I've even spotted a fox. The happiest moments of my life are when I catch a glimpse of a wild animal. In my case, it's usually normal woodland creatures because I never go very far away. I'm against traveling to distant places. When I see a squirrel I'm even happier than after I have sex with Georg. I don't know why we don't live out in the country somewhere, near some woods where I'd have the chance to see more wildlife. The feeling I get when I see a deer or squirrel is overwhelming. I'm no longer myself, and that feels great to me. Time stands still. I hold my breath and smile. Like a hunter, I've developed a good eye. I notice every movement in the bushes. On the highway I keep one eye on the road, to preserve my family's life, but the other one is on the fields and woods along the side of the road. I always see the most deer. Then, for an instant, my life has purpose. I try to convey my enthusiasm to our kids, but it just doesn't work. "Yeah, yeah, Mama, a deer, great." I can't explain why I don't try to create more of these moments of happiness by going for walks in the woods or even training to become a forester. I'm a big believer in happiness through scarcity. It's precisely because you see wild animals so rarely that it makes you so happy. I've noticed that it seems to be the same way with other adults. I know a lot of adults who are happy to report that they've seen a squirrel in their backyard. And if it comes back often, they convince themselves it wants to be near them.

Unfortunately, there's nothing to see today in the strip of green grass. Too bad. Maybe next time. Happy moments really are rare in my life. But before I can let my mind wander too far down this depressing path, I'm home.

I turn the stove back on. As soon as it begins to sizzle, I take the pan off the burner and put it on the trivet on the table.

"Dinner is ready."

I always have to say it three times before my husband gets up from his computer and comes to the table. My daughter and I are already sitting at the table. Nobody can start before all of us are seated. Everything is strictly regimented at our place. Manners, manners, manners. Perhaps they'll come in handy one day.

"*Guten Appetit.*"

Liza goes first. Lately she also wants to serve us. That means that a lot of food gets dropped on the table. But it also means she learns a new skill, which is one of my goals as a good mother.

My husband and I discuss the plans for tomorrow, and my daughter complains that nobody is talking to her. That's her latest thing, complaining that nobody is talking to her. I've learned over the last few years that everything comes and goes in phases. Whenever children start to do something incredibly annoying or terribly worrisome, they grow out of it—and it's replaced with the next annoying or worrisome thing. Nothing lasts. Something new always comes along and displaces the old.

"Okay, how was your day at school?" my husband asks his stepdaughter.

"Great. Today we voted to decide what new clubs will be funded at school."

"Oh yeah? What did you vote for—nose-picking and farting clubs?"

My daughter cracks up.

Anytime he makes her laugh, I feel happier than I was at my own wedding. I think it's because he's not even her father. I don't laugh with them, though. It's childish humor, and only children get it. I telegraph my feelings with a put-on frown. It makes it even funnier for the child when the mother distances herself from that type of humor.

All three of us eat very quickly. Too quickly. I've read that you should chew your food thirty times before swallowing. But when I've tried it, I find it disgusting. The food turns into a thin mush that no longer bears any relationship to whatever it was I originally shoveled into my mouth. So far nobody in our family has had any stomach trouble, despite us all wolfing our food down. I've tried a few times to teach the kids to chew their food thoroughly, but when I don't do it myself there's really no point. So I don't bother anymore. I can't do everything perfectly. Just nearly everything.

We hop up immediately after dinner and put everything in the dishwasher. I think it's bad for the environment that we use it daily. But my husband and others have told me that even though the dishwasher uses electricity and water and pumps out soap, it's actually better for the environment than washing dishes by hand. I just can't get that through my head. But I go along with it anyway, even though I don't believe it for a second.

Protecting the environment drives me insane. A lot of the things you're supposed to do seem illogical. I'd really like to have everything explained in detail sometime, so I'd know how I—and how we—should act at home going forward. I definitely don't want to be one of those people who does nothing just because nobody else is doing anything. And I don't want to fool myself, either. There's a tendency to convince yourself of all the things you're doing for the environment when in reality—with the things that count—you're making things worse. This thought is unbearable. For the most part, ways to help the environment are about limiting yourself, sacrificing—you just stop doing things that other people don't think for a minute about doing. The point is not to take yourself or your luxurious lifestyle so seriously; instead you live more simply in some areas. But making these sacrifices takes an iron will, because nobody checks up on you. Unfortunately there's no such thing as an environmental inspector who can come into your apartment and take the dryer away because it's both pointless and terrible for the environment. Nope. Our dryer is sitting right there. We just can't use it. Laundry has to be hung to dry or else we are wasting energy.

The dishwasher is loaded. After each item was placed in the dishwasher, Liza said, "Okay, finished."

And we said, "No, you're not finished. There's this still, and that . . ."

With kids, there's somehow never one big task that needs to be taken care of. Any big task is divided into lots of small tasks, and after each small task is accomplished they're ready to call it quits. Parents have to keep pushing children so that later in life, when they have their own place, they won't live like pigs.

My parents didn't manage to make it stick with me. My own parents fucked up royally when it came to the most important things parents need to instill in their kids—understanding money and maintaining a clean home. I wonder how they would justify that now. I doubt they'd ever accept the blame for it. Of course, I can't ask them at this point because I've cut them out of my life. I've decided my parents don't deserve to have children. I'm thirty-three now, and I said good-bye to them at twenty-nine. I don't mean literally. I never said, "Good-bye, I'm cutting you out of my life now." I just broke off contact. Forever. That means I don't go to see them on their birthdays,

I don't send cards. I won't be at their funerals and I won't visit if one of them gets testicular cancer. (I think my mother has balls, too.) I won't visit their graves. I simply no longer have parents.

Even to me it seems like something of a taboo. I'm constantly plagued by feelings of guilt. We're all brought up in a society where even hard-core atheists are taught that you should honor your parents and so on and so forth. But why should you honor your parents when everything they did to you was bad? I constantly try to convince myself that life without my parents is better and that they don't deserve me as a daughter. At Christmas it's just unbearable. Even as anti-Christian as I am, I get painfully sentimental and feel in my bones how bad it is to celebrate Christmas as though I have no larger family unit—that is, without the older generation. It seems so wrong that I often break into tears, but it's still no reason to change anything. My decision is final: I will live without my parents. It's my right. Anyone is allowed to leave anyone else if they find out that person is bad for them. I have to keep telling myself that to calm myself down. I learned it from my therapist. Otherwise I sit around thinking what I'm doing is monstrous. Especially when I think further and imagine the same thing happening between my daughter and me. Awful.

Frau Drescher has convinced me, however, that I can't take my daughter's grandparents away. Despite the fact that I've decided they were bad parents to me, they could still be good grandparents to her. I doubt it, but fine, if she says so. Family! I have only one, so I'm by no means an expert. So I listen to her. Against my will, I arrange meetings between my daughter and her grandparents, my ex-parents. Other people have to help with the exchange, because in my pigheadedness I've decided I never want to see them again until they die. And not even then.

They pick my daughter up at her father's place. I won't take her to her grandparents. Yeah, yeah, Frau Drescher. I get it. Life is tough.

At Christmastime I have to hide from my little family the fact that I really miss my parents. Not necessarily those parents, but parents in general. The parents of one of my friends always say to her, "Whoa, you got fat!" when she comes home for Christmas. I told her just to stop going, but she still heads home for her annual dose of humiliation. I can't understand it. But it's possible that in her case it has something to do with an inheritance. If my husband hadn't popped into my life and made any inheritance unnecessary, I'd probably still see my parents regularly, too. I definitely think money keeps a lot of screwed-up families together, forcing children to humiliate themselves.

I was heavily indebted to my previous husband. The first thing my new husband did was pay off all my debts, and I've never been able to completely cast off the feeling that he bought me from my ex-husband like an old camel. I think it's true, I let myself be bought—because I badly needed security. I was such a mess mentally from my trauma that I couldn't have dealt with a life weighed down by debt. Georg was able not only to fill the financial role of the father but to fill the mental role of both parents. Naturally Frau Drescher thinks this is too much pressure to put on my new husband, and she's probably right again. But I'm still working through that with her.

*   *   *

I get my daughter ready for bed. For seven years it's been the same routine, like in prison: bathe, brush your teeth, go to the bathroom. For me, brushing your teeth is a matter of life and death. I think that only low-class scumbags ever have kids with bad teeth. Especially bad baby teeth. That's just not acceptable. You have to drastically reduce their intake of sweets. And you have to make sure they brush their teeth at least once a day. For a good long time. I've developed some nasty tricks to ensure proper oral hygiene despite the natural opposition of my daughter. I use the same trick that people typically use to impose moral behavior—they invent a god and say that he sees everything, so you'd better be good.

When she was still little, I talked to my daughter constantly about the tooth trolls named Cavity and Bacteria. They are children's book characters invented by the German government or something in order to get kids to stick to a good oral hygiene regimen. It's pure scare tactics. The book explains that the tooth trolls feed on bits of food left in your mouth and that their excretions burn holes in your teeth. I told Liza over and over, "If you don't brush, Cavity and Bacteria will come with their hammer and sickle and bludgeon holes in your teeth—and those holes will hurt, which will mean you'll have to go to the dentist, who will have to drill into your teeth before he can fill in the holes."

The comparison to God is not so apt, though, since Cavity and Bacteria are real, basically, and there are real consequences if you don't brush. With God there are never any consequences. God doesn't see everything or punish anything—because there is no such thing as God. Liza has so thoroughly internalized the importance of brushing her teeth that sometimes, when it's really late and I am inclined to lay her sleeping body in bed fully clothed, she wakes with a start and goes to brush her teeth because in her paranoia she thinks she'll wake up with loads of holes in her teeth. All the better. She'll thank me one day—or probably not. When friends of ours with kids the same age tell us that their children have cavities, I act as if it's totally normal. But in reality I'm thinking, *Oh, God, what a terrible mother she is!* I get off on the fact that my child has no cavities. All because of me and me alone! Ha!

Then we go into her room and I lie down next to her and read. Right now we're reading *Gulliver's Travels*.

She asks, "Mama, why are you whispering?"

No idea. I have to think about it myself. Why indeed? "Um, to make it more suspenseful?"

"Stop it."

I continue reading, without whispering. Then I stop at an awkward point and allow myself to be persuaded to read a little further. I learned that from Jan-Uwe Rogge. You should be hard and follow through on things, but once in a while you should also show children that they can convince their parents to change their minds, using charm and a good argument. They should learn to convince people, to change their minds. Liza learns that from me.

After reading, I sing the two songs that I've sung to her since she was nursing. Just so she has constants in her life—something I never had. The first song is "Sleep, Children, Sleep," and the second is an English children's song called "Baa, Baa, Black Sheep," which is about a sheep that takes its own wool to various customers' homes. No idea what lesson it's supposed to be teaching.

Finally I lie next to her in bed until she falls asleep. Our apartment is like a dungeon. There are only a few windows onto the street. The previous owners did all kinds of renovations in the building, almost certainly illegally. There's just no way they would have gotten permits for all the things they did. Long, narrow hallways, miniature rooms without windows. Because some rooms are in the basement, it's like a cold rabbit hole. People always get lost, even Liza sometimes. It's a very intestinal apartment—as if the rooms and hallways are part of a giant, subterranean colon.

I'm also slowly beginning to worry whether the apartment makes us happy or not. When we moved in, newly in love, we didn't care about the apartment's backstory. Now that the honeymoon phase of our relationship is over, the story of the previous owners bothers me more and more. When you're first in love, you think you are immune to anything bad in the world. Once daily life has begun to encroach on that feeling, you notice you're not so unique, as you so arrogantly thought at the beginning. And then the things that happen to others suddenly make you think, too. In the case of the previous owners, she had money—she was in banking—and he was an ordinary worker. She started to waste away. He did, too, for a while. Then he got a liver transplant and was suddenly healthy and lively again. Then he left because he couldn't stand her anymore.

And we moved into their apartment without even thinking about it for a second. If it were a movie you'd think, *Oh, boy, there's definitely trouble in store if you move in there.* Or maybe you'd move into a place like that if you didn't know about the history. But never with all the information at hand.

Liza lies down and acts as if she is ready to go to sleep. As a good example, I've closed my eyes and am breathing deeply, in and out. I learned to breathe that way from a masseuse—it's a way to stave off panic attacks. You fall asleep better that way, too. It makes you feel as if you have your life under control. Crazy. It also shows how poorly you breathe otherwise, during the rest of the day. I listen closely to her breathing, to see whether it's changed from the way it is when you are falling asleep to the way it is when you are deep asleep. But suddenly she speaks in the darkness.

"Mama, is Hitler still around?"

"What would make you think of that?"

Oh, man, please fall asleep. This is bad.

"At school, one of the kids said to another when they were fighting, 'You're as bad as Hitler.'"

"No, don't worry. He killed himself a long, long time ago."

"Oh, good. In that case I can fall asleep. If he hadn't have killed himself, would he have gone to prison?"

"Of course he would have been put in prison. He killed so many people."

"Mama, do we know anyone who has been in prison?"

"Why?"

"I'd like to visit someone in prison sometime. I want to see what it looks like in there."

"No, unfortunately not. Maybe someday."

I would love to take revenge on the newspaper publisher who capitalized on my family's car accident to earn dirty money selling our blood and agony to voyeuristic readers. If I didn't have a husband and child, I would have founded a terrorist organization immediately. I've sworn that as soon as my child is out of the woods, I will kill myself—which I want to do anyway—and take those responsible with me. If I get up the nerve. If the plan works and I don't die, I'll be put away for the murder of at least three people—as well as whoever else happens to be in the wrong place at the wrong time—and you'll have someone to visit in prison, my child. Maybe I won't accompany them to the grave, because I couldn't do that to my daughter or, to a lesser extent, my husband. But in any event I've already written in my will that Georg should seek out another woman immediately, that I want him to. He always seems to need absolution from me. He can even get together with a blonde woman with big breasts. It's not like I'll be around to see it happen. And it'll happen sooner or later anyway.

Liza is breathing more deeply. I can make out her long eyelashes in the dark. It's really funny the way every mother thinks her child is the most beautiful. Despite the fact that this can't be true. Holding my breath, I pry my finger out of the vise grip of my daughter's hand. Getting my finger out of her grasp while holding my breath is like giving birth. The child doesn't want to come out. She stirs. Of course. That's why fingers are constructed in such a complicated way. As an alarm system for when I try to escape.

She opens her eyes. Always the same sentence: "Mama, a little bit longer."

"Yes, but let go of my finger, or else I will wake you up again when I leave."

Always the same. Stuck in a loop, everything repeating itself. Not like the chaos I grew up in. I take my finger out of her hand. Then I lie down next to her again, but a little farther away, with no bodily contact. I know that she will now take four normal breaths and then begin to breathe deeply in and out, at which point she'll sound like an old drunk man. That's the sign that she's asleep. Finally. Suddenly she shudders, but I'm familiar with this. Behind her eyelids she's either falling or running into something. Free fall or, worse still, a collision. The same thing happens to me. And my husband. Right before you enter a deep sleep, boom, you shudder because you're having a scary dream. I need to ask Agnetha about it—what it means and why our brains do that to us. I absolutely have to ask her that before I die.

Liza is finally asleep. I can go. I'm free, free from childcare. My shoulders start to relax. I feel like a weight has been lifted from my shoulders. Kids look their cutest when they're asleep, so innocent and smooth, like newborns. Why is it that people always hope to have kids and then, when you have them, you're happy when they're asleep or somewhere else? And this thought makes you feel guilty every time it pops into your head. Sometimes I use the opportunity to work on my stomach muscles— lying silently with my legs stretched out, I raise myself without using my upper body. I use nothing but my stomach muscles and I raise myself slowly, without lurching. If I'm sitting down, I cross my legs Indian-style and stand up directly from that position. Then creep out. Extra careful on the wood floor by her door—it creaks if you step on one of the planks. I let out a deep breath outside and then dash up the stairs.

Georg notices the tension in my face. "What's up?"

The same question every night after I've put her to bed. "I can't stand it when she won't let me go. It's a nice feeling to be needed, but there's something awful about it, too. You know how it is."

"Maaaaaamaaaaa!"

Fuck. She's awake again. I run back down the stairs and snap at her. "What is it?"

Naturally I think she's going to complain that I left too soon, that she hadn't really fallen asleep. She often claims she hadn't completely fallen asleep, despite the fact that I could hear that she was already deep asleep.

She looks at me worriedly and whispers sleepily, "The other door is open a crack. Can you close it? It scares me." And then she adds, "My bum itches really badly."

I've done it again. So short-tempered, such raw nerves— typical of me. Once again I have to apologize to my child.

"We'll take care of your bum in the morning. How about you bathe early tomorrow before school? That should take care of it."

How do you teach kids to wipe their asses thoroughly? I feel that even at thirty-three I could be better at it, so how can a kid master it? I don't want to turn into a neat freak and constantly talk about hygiene. She shouldn't be disgusted by her own body. She should be free. More so than I am. Nobody ever talks about the art of cleaning your bum. Nobody taught me. My mother, Elli, didn't. We're all Elizabeths in our family, all the women anyway. Which is the only gender that counts in our family, unfortunately. Each Elizabeth tried to bring a trace of individuality to the name. Even if we all have the same name, at least each of us has her own nickname. She told us that she never crapped and never farted. That made a big impression on me as a child, and I felt disgusted with myself because I couldn't manage to keep myself from doing those things. She told us that her waste evaporated into the ether, through her skin, I suppose. She had learned that from her own mother, Liz, our deranged grandmother from Camden. She acts to this day as though she is the rightful queen of England. For which the name Elizabeth is perfect. She also has never taken a crap or farted. How nice for her. You can't expect to get any help in normal human functions from those two. Just have to teach yourself.

You also can't bother anyone else with such a nasty subject. Which means you just have to get creative and try to guess how other people do it. Earlier I would just wipe once, regardless of what came off on the toilet paper, and then pull my underwear back up. I just didn't think about it enough. These days it goes like this: I wipe once, twice, and then I look to see what the situation is on the paper. Usually there's still something there. So I wipe until the paper shows no sign of anything. I'm sorry, Greenpeace, but I use a lot of sheets of toilet paper that way. But at least it's recycled paper! Which is once again about sacrifice. Everything that's good for the environment entails sacrifice. Back when I still didn't care about the environment, I used the thickest, softest, whitest toilet paper I could find, sometimes it was even dyed light blue. Like a typical English girl. But I made the switch and will never go back.

Once I can't see any signs of anything on the paper with the naked eye, I do two rounds of wiping with spit. Just to be safe. Because commercial wet wipes are out of the question on both health and environmental grounds. They take a lot longer to break down than regular paper and are pumped so full of chemicals that you don't want them near your body anyway. Better not to use them. Most of them are manufactured by the worst companies, too. I spit on a few balled-up sheets and rub myself good and clean with the saliva. Then I repeat it to be safe. Wiping with wet toilet paper creates those horrible little clingy minirolls of paper that you have to pull off with your fingers. With my fingers and some water from the sink, I get rid of those. Then I use a paper towel to pat everything dry. Done. Shipshape. And the entire process thought up and perfected on my own. I've never talked about it with anyone. What a crazy world. You have to figure everything out on your own.

I should have anticipated the problem with the door to Liza's room. I'm familiar with this fear of hers, and closing that door is part of the bedtime routine. I almost never forget. Liza has two doors in her room, and the one that connects to our room has to be shut, or else she's afraid that someone or something will come through it. She sleeps on the floor. Her room is designed to look like an ocean, with a pirate-ship bed. She could sleep in the pirate-ship bed, of course, but she doesn't want to. She always sleeps on an air mattress placed on the blue tiles that represent the seawater. If you lie next to her, you also have to lie on an air mattress—otherwise you'll slip beneath the sea. And ever since I've had to lie there every night, I have noticed that you feel oddly helpless lying there on the floor, totally defenseless. From that vantage point, the door does look gigantic and imposing, especially when it's slightly ajar.

I've often worried about all the various and ever-changing children's fears Liza has. She's scared that snakes live in our apartment—poisonous snakes or the ones that strangle you. She's scared that a tiger lives in our back garden and will jump into her room through the window. She's afraid of burglars. And of people who abduct children. She's scared of ghosts, witches, wolves, foxes, badgers, skeletons, lizards. But only at night.

Never during the day. Frau Drescher says these are inner fears that children project outward. Children are afraid of the inner evil inside themselves. When they get upset at their parents and secretly wish the parents were dead, they immediately feel bad and project their evil thoughts instead onto evil animals that could attack them and hurt them. That way they remain innocent and can feel like victims instead of culprits.

My initial impulse when she first started to express all these fears was to tell her that all the business about animals in the house and garden was ridiculous. There are no ghosts, my child. Not a single person in the entire world has ever seen a ghost—at least not a person with all their marbles. But my therapist told me that is the completely wrong approach. If all I do is to constantly tell the child that all her fears are absurd—to tackle the whole thing with arguments based in reason—she'll just stop telling me her fears at some stage. But she'll still be just as afraid. She'll just carry her fears around with her silently; after all, the fears are ridiculous and she won't want to make a fool of herself. So she'll have to get over her fears all on her own, even as they become greater and less easy to control. As a good mother, I took this to heart and immediately changed my approach. Which is to say, now I take her fears seriously. By the way, it's something that I've noticed in the relationship with my husband as well as in the raising of my daughter: that the most obvious solution—even one rooted in good intentions—is usually wrong and just makes everything worse. When I look deep inside myself for a solution, I find that I'm completely off base when I go to reassure myself with advice from professionals. That's why I think everyone with a child or a husband or a wife should go to therapy. And if you can't afford it, at least read a handbook.

Ever since I've been properly instructed, I talk with Liza about things like what the witch who lives under the dresser looks like. Sometimes I peek under the dresser to have a look at her myself. She's about the size of a rat. We tell her that to her face—witches can take it. Liza and I wonder whether she's evil at all. Up to now she hasn't done anything bad despite the fact that she lives here full-time. Just like most terrorists. Some nights when the witch is particularly intrusive, I ask Liza if I should just throw her out the window. My child says okay, so I open the window and—accompanied by lots of laughter—start to feel around under the dresser. I act as if my fingers have been bitten a few times, then I get my hands around the witch's neck and back so she can't get me with her teeth anymore, wrestle her to the window, and finally toss her into the garden, telling her to stay out all night. "Tomorrow we'll let you back in, you naughty little monster." My daughter laughs and looks at me gratefully. Because now she can sleep. And I'm endlessly grateful to my therapist, because that's the kind of shit I would never have come up with on my own.

I close the door in Liza's room that leads to our bedroom. The door to the rest of the apartment has to stay open. I switch personalities from mother to whore. Until tomorrow morning when my daughter gets up and I have to be a mother again, I'll be switching between wife and whore. Although I'm really a mother again while I sleep. After all, when I sleep my ears are always vigilant, set in a sort of alarm mode for anything amiss with the child. For seven years now. Nobody mentioned that before I had a child. But for now, whore. Once the child is finally asleep and grown-up time begins, my husband and I have a date.

We're going to plan tomorrow's brothel visit. Originally, years ago, going there was my husband's idea. He wanted to sleep with another person. I had to think about it for a long time. It seemed perverse to me at first, and my initial thought sounded like something my mother would say: "Are you nuts, you chauvinist pig? That's just what a man would want!"

But as the wife of my husband, what I actually said was, "Sure, we can try that." I want to be the coolest wife my husband can possibly imagine. I want him to have that because he's given me so much. Everything he has, he shares with me. Money, time, his apartment. Everything. He would let me wear all his clothes, too, but they don't fit me. So I try to do everything I can for him as well, including making sacrifices. And I'll try to always be that way. I hope I manage it. That's the plan, anyway. But he should never notice that I consider anything a sacrifice—that wouldn't be sexy. I act as if going to a brothel with him is no big deal to me. I'm a good actor. But I get scared, too. When I say I'm going to do something, I'll do it. And that's why I get scared, because I have to do it once I've agreed.

The first time we talked about it, I immediately got diarrhea. Any kind of anxiety goes straight to my guts. My husband is familiar with this phenomenon. I just run out of the room without a word, laughing, embarrassed, and lock myself in the guest bathroom. That's probably how tonight's discussion will end, too—I know what I'm like. We both kneel on our big designer sofa. It's really huge. When I sit with my legs stretched out and my back up against the back of the sofa, my legs don't even reach the front edge. It's from his first marriage. Not only do we have a patchwork family, we have patchwork furniture. We sit there and look at each other. He knows it's hard for me to talk about these things because I alternate between my mother and my husband.

He smiles. It calms me down.

He says, "I have a plan. Do you want to hear it?"

"Sure."

I thought we were going to plan it together. But of course he's already come up with a plan. It's fun for him to think about, whereas it just gets me worried. And if I'm feeling sufficiently confident and relaxed and free that it doesn't make me worry, then it makes me anxious instead. And I hate to be anxious. You just can't win either way with me. I wouldn't like to have to be with me—or married to me. How horrible!

"We can go for a late breakfast at the place next door, Café Fleur. They have Wi-Fi—I already called to check. We'll take the laptop with us. I'll go alone to the sex shop and see which women are there. Then I'll come back and we can look at them together online."

We've done this many times before and we know from experience that the brothels are packed during the day and not, as a layman might expect, in the evening or late at night. The busiest time for upscale brothels is during lunch hour, when men pay a quick visit from their offices. Nights and weekends the places are closed because all their clients are with their families and can't disappear without arousing suspicion.

In most brothels they don't like it if I, as a woman, show up out of the blue. My husband goes in by himself first. Totally normal, like any other customer, looking around. In the price category we operate in, discretion is taken very seriously. Georg is usually taken into a private room without any other customers seeing him. Then the women come in individually, spin around once, and say their name. They usually come off bored because there's no money changing hands at this point, and they don't know until later just how much they're going to earn from us. They sometimes misidentify Georg as a con man, thinking he's just having a look before he goes home and jerks off for free. When he explains that he would like to bring his wife and asks whether that would be all right, they smile sympathetically at him and think to themselves, *Yeah, you poor thing, you idiot, a lot of husbands would* like *to bring their wives.* They've heard it many times before: "I'll bring my wife with me next time." Nobody does. He has to ask each one whether she's willing to sleep with a couple. Some are willing, some aren't. I don't know why, or what they would have against it. Doesn't matter, that's just the way it is.

My husband looks at their bodies. He doesn't like bigger girls with thick waists or big stomachs. For me a fat girl wouldn't be a problem. And he doesn't like women who have had plastic surgery. With his practiced eye he tries to figure it out during the brief introductory meetings. Aside from paying attention to their bodies, he also looks for friendliness and a good sense of humor.

At this point, things start to get interesting. He has to choose someone his wife will find sympathetic. She can't have giant breasts. He knows his wife has a breast complex. Until I got to know him, I never really thought about the size of my breasts. I thought everything about me was normal tending toward nice. This man was the first one I ever worried about losing. And as a result I've gotten myself into some impossible situations. Occasionally when he was out for an evening I would try to find out more about his past. Once I worked up my courage by drinking and then rifled through his old boxes of photos while cross-eyed drunk. I found a lot of photos of old girlfriends. They went back to when he was eighteen. He's fifty now, almost as old as my father.

My parents split up when I was five. Unfortunately my father quickly found a new wife. A bad one, at least for us kids. She ruined every moment we had with our father. I missed my father so much, even when I was with him. For me, he represented protection, security, everything. I loved him so much, with his red sports car that my mom always criticized. I loved the fact that he was rich, smart, manly; I loved that he wore socks and sandals and shorts, that he had hair on his back. That's my image of male beauty. Varicose veins and spider veins and red splotches on the bum. Sometimes I read about those conditions and their causes and whatnot. I find things online. Not with Google. With the green search engine Ecosia—for the environment.

My therapist says I have a bona fide father complex. A lot of older men have benefited from it over the years. My father's absence during my childhood ensured that my body has provided a steady supply of young flesh to old men. I'm not interested at all in younger men or men my age. Only old, old, old. The older the better. They make me feel secure and desired. And all the old men have my father to thank. But both sides benefit. A lot. Whenever I go to my therapist, my husband always says, "You guys can work on anything, just tell her not to get rid of your father complex. Otherwise you'll leave me!"

It's the running gag of our relationship. He's right. As soon as I'm over my father complex, I won't need my husband anymore. So the complex can happily accompany me to my death.

I want to take it to the grave. You can say that even if—like me—you'd never want to be buried in a grave. I will definitely not be put into the ground in a Christian cemetery. Over my dead body. In my will I wrote that whoever has to handle it must make sure that I am cremated and then that the ashes are put out with the household garbage on the regular pickup day. Right now that's Wednesday. There is no way I'm going to fall for buying and maintaining a grave site, letting my corpse leach into the groundwater and all that.

There are a lot of things I've completely changed since getting together with my husband. I question myself, my mind, my body, everything. Not sure, though, if it's because of my husband or not; maybe much more to do with the accident and the resultant therapy.

I regularly wear myself out, though my therapist is trying to train me out of doing that. In going through his private crate of photos, for instance, I had the shattering realization that Georg actually seemed to be into large breasts. And afterward I kept accusing him of this, taking him to task for it. I just can't keep my mouth shut when I'm in such a crazed state: he should just admit it! I knew it all along! No matter what he said to try to rebuild my confidence, I wouldn't believe him.

That's one of the landmines in our relationship—one that I buried in the ground beneath us and can't dig up and get rid of. There's no going back at this point. No way to undo it. My tantrums over it were horrible. Especially for him. He was at a total loss. What was I on about, what was wrong with me? He kept asking me, "Why are you trying to prove to me that I can't find you attractive? That I don't find you sexy? That I don't love you? Stop it!" I tried with all my might to turn a good relationship bad. Always looking for reasons why he didn't love me instead of listening to him or judging him by his actions—which were always the opposite of the things I told myself I feared.

He has to take all of that into account when he chooses a woman for me. The breasts can't be too small because it would be too obvious. But definitely not too big, either, so he doesn't ever fall under suspicion of relapsing. And we don't just want to sleep with the prostitute. We also want to talk and have a fun time. Meaning we're very demanding customers. Sometimes Georg comes across a prostitute he finds so nice and funny that it doesn't matter that she's not so good-looking or that she does have big breasts or has had plastic surgery. We always try to leave each new brothel as the friendliest couple ever to visit. Fair trade and organic, and a healthy gratuity to boot.

That's our plan for the next day. When we plan such an exciting outing, my mother always pops into my head and says, "Don't do it! Why do you put yourself out for your husband? Just admit that's not for you." But I can see how happy my husband is. And he thanks me nonstop. And I think to myself, *Wow, I am so easygoing. My mother can't tell me a thing.* And at some point I get turned on about the plan, too. I would never admit that, though. That's something my husband just has to pick up on and figure out on his own. It's the same with him, except that he can say it.

I would like to get past the uptightness that keeps me from being able to articulate my sexual desires. I can't say what I want. He asks me all the time—he would like to know. In bed. It would be cool for me, too, if I could just ask for whatever I felt like. But I can't. I'm mute on that topic. I just do whatever he wants to do. And I'm always turned on by whatever he does.

But there's nothing of my own in there. It's almost as if I can get turned on only by seeing how much my body and I turn him on. In therapeutic terms that's called mirroring. I get horny only when I reflect his horniness.

But I'm going to make sure we don't have sex tonight. We already did it this afternoon. I don't like to be excessive about it. We're not twenty anymore. Besides, we need to conserve energy for tomorrow—like an athlete before a big match. And besides, I don't really like having sex when the kid is home. And besides, and besides, and besides. I always find plenty of arguments against sex and few in favor. A child should never catch his or her parents having sex. Children and sexuality must be strictly divided so as not to overwhelm the child. It's not like we're Catholic priests! The child has been on the planet for seven years now, and so far we've managed to avoid her catching us at it. Not in our bed, not on the couch, not at night, not during the day. We're very proud of that. I know people who are traumatized from having accidentally seen their parents having sex. I'd like to spare my daughter that.

As we're sitting there talking about our brothel visit, I suddenly notice an intense tingling and itching on my butt hole. Is it horniness? Can't be. I've never felt it that way before. Hello, illness. Immediately I think, *Thank you, dear nonexistent God.* And: *Thank you, Mother, for saving me before tomorrow's outing.* I immediately have a suspicion about what it could be. But only a suspicion, because it's something I've never had as an adult. I take my husband's laptop—he's on the brothel's website, looking at the women who are online, which is pointless, since prostitutes do what they want to. Just because they're online, in a photo, doesn't mean they actually work there or that they'll be there tomorrow. You have to show up in person and look them in the eyes, no matter how uncomfortable it is. Looking anonymously on the computer is nothing. You just have to keep your eyes open and get through it in person.

I turn the laptop screen toward me so Georg can no longer see the screen. I change the privacy setting on the browser. Then I type "worms in children" into Wikipedia. Just a suspicion. I scan the entire informative entry until I get to the point where a quick test is described: you press the sticky side of a piece of tape to your butt hole and look to see if any tiny, thin, white, squirming worms are stuck to it. Oh God, like a horror film. Please don't let it be true. I go back to the brothel's page and click the privacy settings back to normal. Then I put the laptop down on the couch and hop up. We have a drawer in the kitchen where we keep tape, rubber bands, and glue. I go in and grab a roll of clear tape, but somehow I already know what the result is going to be. With this itching, there's nothing else it can be. I lock myself in the guest bathroom. We painted over all the ugly 1980s tiling in bright yellow, which looks very nice. I particularly like the way it looks where we painted over the grout. Like our relationship, this room will always stay the same—like everything we've done in the apartment, in fact. Frau Drescher says that love and relationships must always evolve or else they will wither. That may be true, in which case I'll change for the sake of the relationship—but I'll still never change anything in the apartment.

Since the accident I'm rigidly opposed to change. Most people change things because they get tired of them. That's why they watch cop shows, too. But as a result of what happened to our family, I feel old and troubled, and I just want peace and

quiet—and no change. Except maybe having sex with someone new. But otherwise everything can stay just as it is. Our
apartment and our relationship are set up for eternity—or at
least for life.

I sit on the toilet and pee first. Ever since I've been conscious of peeing, I pee as loudly as possible. I don't like women
who try to pee quietly. I read a book once as a kid where a man
described how much it turned him on when he overheard the
loud splashing and tinkling of his sweetheart peeing. It's possible that my husband feels the same way. Though I'd never
talk to him about it, because then the spell would be broken.
Piss as loudly as possible, crap as quietly as possible. Run the
water so he can't hear anything when I'm crapping. And air the
place out afterward so he doesn't smell anything. Which means
I never really live here. I always think of how I can be appealing
to Georg. I want to be with him forever. Which means there's
never a chance to let down my guard and feel comfortable at
home. That would be the ugliest form of letting myself go.

I'm quickly finished with my loud pee—because I didn't
really have to go—and pat myself dry. I used to often hurt my
labia because I wiped too hard. I don't do that these days. In
part because I learned in therapy to be nicer to myself—and
also to my labia. But I haven't mastered it in all areas of life.

After I've nicely wiped, it's time for the tape test. I wrap a
strip of tape three times around my fingers, with the sticky side
facing out, rip it partway through with my teeth, and then rip
it free from the dispenser with my fingers. I learned this move
from my mother. As a child, I saw her do it often. She did a lot
of things with her mouth. It made a big impression on me as
a child. I often saw her with a mouthful of thumbtacks, or up

a ladder with a mouthful of nails. And I would think, *I want to be like that, too.* And it worked. Unfortunately I became too much like my mother. It's horrible being like her. She's a very unhappy, aggressive woman, and now, so am I. Bad genes and a bad role model.

When I had to tell my family that I never wanted to see my father or mother again, they were all shocked. Which is normal. Particularly those on my mother's side—they lectured me about how I should think it over again. I told them that I had already thought about it a lot and always came to the same conclusion: my life would be better without my parents. They needed to be punished for their conduct—forever. They didn't deserve children. First and foremost they didn't deserve to have my dead brother as their child. The poor kid—all that he had to go through! He missed his father so much, far more than I did. And because my dear brother is dead, the case against my parents is intolerably strong. For his sake I must keep the flame burning.

The entire family said things to me like, "But your mother loves you so much." Yeah, I said, she loves me too much—she won't let go of me. She wants to dictate and control everything. I'm only allowed to be the way she wants me to be; otherwise I should just not be at all. I told my relatives, "She wraps her arms around me, and if I try to create even a little space between us so I can be myself, be somewhat independent, and take a step away from her embrace, I look down at my body and see that her embrace has left me battered and bruised."

"But your mother loves you so much. She was such a good mother to you." Yeah, yeah. When you were around she played the fun, creative clown, the unflappable, child-loving mother.

But when we were alone with her, she let out the overburdened beast. She just ran around screaming. She was always on edge. It happens with so many kids at home. I have trouble not falling apart with just one child! But I don't fall apart, and as a result I think I'm a tiny bit better than my mother—for one thing, I don't hit my child. I'm sure she convinced herself that she didn't ever resort to corporal punishment back then, that she never hit her children. But she did. It goes like this, in case someone wants to re-create it at home: you hold the child's arm tightly in the adult hand, and then, with all your might, you send a sort of jolt through the child's entire little body. You use the whole body as a sort of whip—you push the small, easily dislocated arm, then swing it powerfully in the opposite direction. The child's body almost rips itself free of the arm, and it hurts the child so badly that he or she can barely breathe for a quite a while afterward. I can still remember looking at my mother in disbelief after she did that to me. I could never understand how my clowning mother could do that to me.

My relatives think I'm lying when I tell them my impression of my own mother. They simply can't comprehend that she has two faces. I learned that from my mother, too: if I'm going to get upset, I always maintain total control of myself until I'm alone with my husband, at home. Home sweet home. And as soon as the door is closed, I fly off the handle. Sometimes he won't notice for the course of an entire evening that I'm furious. I save it up until we're alone, so nobody else sees the real me. That's something my mother did to us children, too. The punishment often came long after we did something bad—when there were no witnesses. The avenging angel exercising perfect self-control.

At our home we just give threats. If you don't do this or that—usually brushing their teeth before going to bed, since we don't have much more serious problems with our children—then there'll be no bedtime stories. It's worked so far.

And when I give a threat like that, which is not very often, I have to follow through. Then we start an ugly game between mother and daughter. I hate to have to do it, but I stick to it even when tears start to flow, because I've learned from books on child rearing that kids only change their behavior when they know their parents' threats will carry real consequences. In fact, I think children like it when people do as they say, regardless of the context. Of course, it's possible that I just imagine that because it's so horrible having to follow through on threats. It sometimes causes me bodily pain when I hear her in bed crying because she wants to hear a story from her mother and can't have one only because of a threat I made. It makes me feel schizophrenic. Often I just want to give in. As a mother. Or as a stepmother.

I often used to wish that my stepson, Max, would die in a plane crash. But so far, luckily—or unluckily, not sure which—it hasn't happened. You see how well wishes function. I always thought that if we couldn't get along, things would take care of themselves through a plane crash. Naturally I would help my husband through the tragedy and eventually divert him from his pain. And my daughter would help him get over his loss, as well. It would make his life simpler, too. Sadder, sure, but also simpler.

I think my desire for the death of his son is strong because I'd like so badly to get rid of Georg's ex-partner. She regularly presses his you-left-me buttons, and I'm always watching him to see whether he'll fall for it. We can never be free of that—or at least not as free as we'd be if we'd had our children together.

With my ex-husband, I always hope he'll be in a plane crash, too. Even though my daughter would lose her father, she'd get over it at some point. And I'd no longer be tied to him in this uncomfortable way just because we have a daughter together. This eternal guilty conscience, this awful and familiar pattern you always fall into—therapy-speak for repeating the same mistakes you always make in relationships.

Sometimes I even wish Liza would die. I know how it is when something awful happens to you, when you're hit by a devastating stroke of fate. And how nice it is—the attention you get, the sympathy. You can nestle in that and do all kinds of shit without anyone noticing or getting upset at you. I think you can get hooked on that unnatural level of attention you get from people and that look of concern they all have in their eyes.

You get carried around like a hero because they think, *Look how brave and strong she is*. It's nice to be able to be brave, to show you are strong. When else do you get a chance to do that? Exactly—only when fate deals you a blow. And because after it happens once you are always bracing for the next time—which will probably never come—you begin thinking it might be better if it came sooner rather than later. That way you no longer have to wait around dreading it.

Ever since the accident, my mother doesn't want to hear anything critical of her. She just closes her ears or hangs up the phone, just like my best friend. That's the advantage of such a horrible stroke of fate. You're liberated from any criticism. But I have never figured out what the terrible blow that liberated my best friend was. The two of them just want to be cut slack. Which is why, despite their megatrauma, they don't go to therapy—they can't take the criticism they would get there.

My mind and my vagina are ready for an affair. I picture the two cousins in *The Tin Drum* as my model of a nondestructive affair. They meet up regularly, nobody notices—well, okay, nobody except maybe the Jewish tin drum salesman a little bit, and the woman's son, Oskar. But otherwise the affair works great. I don't care whether it's incest or not. Cousins are distant enough that it's not disgusting. Neither one of them wants anything more than they get. They meet up regularly, have wild, intense sex, and go their own way again. They both understand that they don't want to screw up each other's life. Neither represents a ticking time bomb to the other. Neither of them says to the other, "Be together with me now!" Balance is important.

In their case, things go well because they have a familial connection. In my case, I've decided that I need to choose a man who, like me, has a lot to lose. Preferably one with a career, perhaps even a high-flying one, one that keeps him somewhat on the straight and narrow. Someone in a stable relationship, ideally married, with children, and still together with his wife and kids. I don't want any chance of it developing into a grand love affair, like what happened between me and my husband. I want to be better for my child than my mother was for me. Meaning not constantly leaving men, moving, and living a whore's life. All of which later screws with the child's head. I always say, *I am the sum of all my parents' mistakes*.

My parents' mistakes have already subsidized Frau Drescher buying her own apartment. She once asked me during therapy whether, since my husband and I often pay for sex, she also represents something that can be bought. And I answered, "Well, we can't exactly pretend that our relationship has nothing to do with money, Frau Drescher. I'm not *that* crazy."

In any event I'll stay with my husband until I die. But I'd like to get to a point before I die where I can sleep with another man openly, not secretly—be permitted to sleep with another man. The way hippies did. And not just with one other man. With other *men*. I'd like to do so with as little guilty conscience as possible. I imagine that the guilt I'd feel from doing it secretly would ruin the whole thing for me. I don't want that. I'd like to be there freely and, when I finally have another cock inside me, to be able to think, *I'm allowed. I have the coolest husband in the world, and he permits me this*.

In my fantasy, my affair would never put me under the kind of pressure that would make me leave my husband. Or move out of our home. I just want to meet a man—and he can be even older than Georg—in a hotel room, have wild, intense sex, and then go home. At home I would hope to have a tiny feeling of guilt even though Georg had given me the okay and, as a result, fall even deeper in love with him. Sometimes a bit of guilt can make things more exciting than they were before. Because you no longer take everything for granted.

I would try to rinse the sperm of the other man out from inside me, even though that's not something my husband would expect. Then I would sleep with Georg and my heart would melt from gratitude. And all because I was allowed to have more freedom than ever before and yet still retain all the benefits of our relationship. That would be so nice. Please, my dear husband, please allow me this, allow us this. You must let me go so I can come back of my own volition.

I have to be honest: this formulation originally came from Frau Drescher. Anytime I fantasize about sleeping with other men and sometimes other women, which I do constantly, as if I'm possessed, I feel guilty afterward. I'm nicer to my husband as a result and snuggle up to him. I always imagine he can see from the blush of my cheeks what I've been thinking about. But he benefits from it, even when I'm cheating on him in thought only. What would it be like if I did for real? My therapist asks me whether I could just keep the fantasies as fantasies—thoughts instead of deeds. I don't think I can do that for long. That's not the way I'm wired, or at least that's what I say now. Earlier I had hoped for absolute loyalty from my husband. How do you reverse that? Changed my mind! After seven years! Haha. And now?

In my previous relationship, it was easier because I could take care of my husband. But I fell in love with my current husband because he was so strong. So it's tougher for me now, because unlike in my previous relationship I hardly have anything to take charge of or care for. Just a child and two inseparables—our pets. Two parrots with red cheeks, also known as peach-faced lovebirds or *Agapornis roseicollis*. No man to look after anymore. That leaves just myself to deal with, which is insufferable. If I could figure out a way to take charge of myself, I'd be able to divert myself from my own depression. But as it is, I get broadsided by myself. Georg is strong and doesn't need any help, unfortunately. And I have clearly taken on the role of the kook in our relationship, which is only heightened by his feeling of superiority. But I don't believe he's as healthy as he makes out. It'll soon come out one way or the other in his therapy. He isn't going there to get over his fucked-up crazy family; nope, he's going there to be able to get along better with me.

The only thing I could help with—or at least show empathy for—is his back pain. But he won't let me do anything on that front. He understands that one of the reasons I no longer wanted to sleep with my ex-husband was that I took care of him all the time. When you constantly look after your husband, eventually he becomes your child—and you don't sleep with your own children. At least most people don't. And if there is one thing in our relationship he doesn't want to lose, it's sexuality. It's our firm belief that when that goes down the shitter, everything else also goes down the shitter sooner or later.

I hold my sticky fingertips against my butt hole and then up to my eyes. I knew it! I've caught four of the little bastards on the first try. On the Internet it says they come out at night and cause bad itching because they try to spawn on the anus. To spawn they need fresh air, just like us. Disgusting! I feel sick as I watch them dancing like they're on speed, listening to techno. Man, are they weird animals. I feel under attack—I'm a host for parasites. I hate being a mother: this is exactly the sort of thing it entails. Liza got infected by some little fucker at school, then gave it to me. Right, or the other way around. Who knows what happened?

I put down the lid of the toilet with my clean hand, sit down on it, and flush. Okay, let's think it over. There's no way I can sleep with this itching. I want to stay up the whole night—don't want to get these fucking things in our bed. Suddenly my daughter's final words of the night occur to me: "Mama, my bum itches." She has it, too. Shit, shit, shit. Are you allowed to send a kid with worms to school? If she doesn't go to school,

I can't work tomorrow morning. And in any case we can't go to the brothel. Fuck. Because of the child and because of the risk of infecting someone. I'll give them all worms. Actually quite a funny thought. Phew, what a relief! Thank you, dear nonexistent God, or rather, thank you, Mother—we're mono-theistic in our family, after all—thank you for the worms! I can't go to the brothel. And when I notice how happy I am about this, I realize what a burden these outings are on me. I'm going to go out there now and tell him we can't go to the brothel. Super.

Still, the fact that I have worms horrifies me. I envy my daughter, just lying there, sleeping, even though she almost certainly also has worms. There's no way I'm going to be able to fall asleep. I feel an intense need to be consoled by my husband. He should commiserate with me and help. Mind you, what could we do now, at nine thirty at night? No doctors' offices are open. And you don't go to the hospital for this.

I squish the squirming worms against the yellow wall. They burst like pimples. I take some toilet paper and wipe up the mess, wrap the tape in the paper, throw the clump into the toilet, and flush again. It's probably bad for the environment, but there's no alternative. I wouldn't know where else to put four dead nematodes that have come out of me. The environ-ment is just going to have to deal with it—it's an emergency.

I leave my worm lab. I go back into the living room and ask, "Does your ass itch, too?"

"Yeah, sometimes, why?" He laughs.

Ha, it's never boring with his wife. She comes up with some new crap every minute.

Breathlessly hurtling through time.

"Because if it does, that means you have worms, too." Way to bring up the subject subtly. Typical of me.

"I don't have worms. What do you mean by 'also'? You have worms? How do you know? And don't assume that I have them just because you do!"

Oh, he's pissed off. I should talk about my worms, not his. I learned that in couples therapy. He obviously doesn't want to have worms along with me.

"Just before she fell asleep, Liza said something. And now I'm itching like crazy. I just looked it up on Wikipedia and did the tape test."

"I know the test from when I was a kid. We had worms all the time when we were young."

"Us too. I thought I'd be able to keep it from happening to my own child. I mean, she's seven already and never had them. I figured we'd never get them. It's so disgusting. They move around the whole time—that's why it itches so bad. Luckily Liza is already asleep, so she doesn't notice it. There's no way I can fall asleep and let them eat me up."

"They won't eat you up. Call the twenty-four-hour pharmacy and ask whether you can get something for worms without a prescription. Tell them you'll get the prescription tomorrow and hand it in after the fact."

Good, very good. At least there's one clear head here. I call information to find out where the nearest twenty-four-hour pharmacy is, then call the place all worked up. I just can't believe it's happening to me. Fucking worms! Inside me!

"Hello there, my name is Elizabeth Kiehl. My family and I have just realized at this late hour that we have nematodes. Is it possible to get something for that tonight, without a prescription? I could bring a prescription tomorrow after my doctor's office is open again for the day."

"I'm afraid I can't dispense anything without a prescription. All too often people fail to bring a prescription after the fact."

Just as I suspected would happen in this shitty country. In other places you can just go the gas station and pick something up. Here you have to wait an entire night for the doctor's office to open. This can't be happening. A prescription for antiworm medication. What would I do with that—kill myself or someone else? Party? Overdose?

"Okay, thanks anyway. Have a peaceful night." With scores of dead and dying people lying in front of your fucking pharmacy!

I imagine myself lying awake the whole night with this itching. These creatures are moving around like crazy. They're squirming and dancing inside me. I think of my ex-boyfriend. He might have worms, too, seeing as our child and I both have them. We were never married, although we would have tied the knot if something horrible hadn't intervened just as we were about to. Unfortunately we are now bound together forever because of our child. Which is for the most part stressful.

It's good that our child isn't confronted with the strain between us. Good that she doesn't have to anticipate her parents' needs the way I had to as a child of divorce and as almost all children of broken relationships do—what do Mama and Papa want? Can I speak freely to Papa about Mama? Or vice versa? That puts a great strain on children. You know exactly what you can and cannot talk about, depending on who you are with at any given moment. My ex-boyfriend and I manage it well, though I still feel some aggression inside me. A perpetual wish to be rid of him forever. And rid of the buttons in

CHARLOTTE ROCHE

me that he pushes. It drives me nuts that we fall into the trap of behaving as if we were still together. As an outsider, my new husband always sees it. And he notices us doing it before I do. Since—because of our child—I can't really have the complete 100 percent breakup I'd like, we often fall back into those old patterns, the patterns of our relationship. Bad, bad, bad. I've been fighting that tendency for seven years. We should get along well for the sake of the child, but not too well—for the sake of my new husband, sure, but also for my sake! Patchwork families are fucking complicated.

But right now I have to figure out whether my ex-boyfriend also has worms. Whether through indirect mouth contact—me kissing our child, him kissing our child—he might have been infected with any of the live worm eggs currently in my body. I have to worry about exterminating not only the worms in my daughter but also any worms in him.

Eight years ago there was a wedding planned with my ex-boyfriend—and I would have said yes, too. That's why my ex-boyfriend is secretly my ex-husband in my head.

We plan the entire wedding and want to fly everyone to England, where I'm from. It'll take place outside London, in a pretty old hotel. Big place. The justice of the peace is coming out to the hotel just for us. The dress is being made in Germany—a huge production, actually. It's being put together from five antique wedding dresses. The tailor is supposed to cut apart the vintage pale yellow, cream, and white lace dresses and then make a new one out of a wild combination of squares from all five old ones.

And since we're working with the cloth of five dresses, I decided to have the tailor give the skirt a long Princess Diana–style train. As a little English girl, I thought the best wedding of all time was Princess Diana and Prince Charles's wedding. I looked at pictures of it hundreds of times in a children's photo book. My ring was supposed to look like Princess Diana's, too. The train of my dress was so heavy that it needed a reinforced, corsetlike harness at the waist so it wouldn't droop during the ceremony. I had to go try it on many times.

Everything that a bride and groom could need I buy in our neighborhood. New sets of luggage that for the first time in our lives all matched. That made me feel very grown-up. The makeup: light green eye shadow, pink lipstick, pink blush.

I can get hold of all the superstitious relics right here near us, too. *Something old, something new, something borrowed, something blue, and a silver sixpence in her shoe.* The old: in an antique jewelry store I buy a tiny gold and silver pendant—a silver acorn with a gold cap—on a long delicate chain. Since it doesn't match the rest of the outfit, I'll wear it under my wedding dress, hidden in my décolletage so nobody sees it. The new: the veil, which, unlike the dress, I bought new. The borrowed item I get from my mother: an ivory necklace. It's a choker with five strands of ivory beads and, right in the middle of the throat, a big carved ivory rose that looks like a wide-open vagina. The necklace is like something a prostitute in the Wild West might wear. The blue: a classic garter. I left the strange sixpence part to my relatives. They'll have to get something. Unless they forget. That would be a pity. I'll stick that in my shoe for the ceremony, since I have to, but I won't keep it in for the dancing afterward.

I think a sixpence is some sort of old English coin. And since I flip out if I have a grain of sand in my shoe, there's no way I'll be able to take having a coin in there for long.

Beautiful bridal underwear, too, all in cream. And in every shop, naturally, I tell them what the things are for. The salespeople seem so happy for us and wish us luck. You really need luck more for the marriage than for the wedding. The marriage lasts a lot longer—it's supposed to last for years, while the wedding is just one day.

On the day of our departure, I drive to the tailor's in a taxi and tell the driver to wait because I'm going to get the dress and then continue on to my mother's in the next town over. Since the dress is so gigantic, I can't stuff it into a suitcase for the flight. So my mother's going to transport it by car. She decided to cancel her flight for the sake of the dress and drive to England with my three brothers, Harry, Lukas, and Paul, along with Rhea, Harry's girlfriend. Harry is the oldest of the brothers but still a year younger than me.

I was the first! It's important to me. The oldest of the three brothers was born right after me, though. To this day it's still a mystery to me how my mother managed to become fertile and conceive another baby so shortly after the birth of the first, namely me. I fought with him his whole life and hoped every day that he would die. That always made me feel guilty, since you're brought up to love your siblings. But he was so close to me in age that I always saw him as a rival. Though I have no idea what we were rivals for. Food? Achievements? The love of our parents? All three probably.

Later I found scientific writings about sibling hatred, which said that many siblings who are born so close together end up that way. Because the firstborn—me, in this case—can't understand why suddenly he or she must share the attention of his or her parents with some completely extraneous entity that just turns up one day. It wasn't until we were well into our teens that it stopped. After we both hit puberty it was as if the hatred just completely dissipated. We were one heart and one soul. But up until then I must have wished him dead eight thousand times. I wanted to be an only child.

A big roof-mounted container designed to carry skis was added specially to the car to carry my wedding dress. It could easily lie flat in there. Like Snow White in her glass coffin. My beloved dress in a plastic ski locker.

The taxi driver is waiting outside. He's parked his cab on the sidewalk directly in front of the tailor's shopwindow and is smoking a cigarette in the sun, leaning against the Mercedes star on the hood. When I saw him sitting like that I thought, *Don't break the star*. It'll bring bad luck. Not for me. For him. Though I'm not superstitious. I chat a bit with the tailor. She wishes me luck. Again I think, *For the marriage or the wedding?* I pay the rest of the bill for her work and we lift the huge dress together and put it into an oversize garment bag already lying open on the floor. The tailor has tears in her eyes. How kitschy of the old lady. Kitsch, I read somewhere, is the renunciation of death and all that is bad. She pays close attention as we close the bag, centimeter by centimeter, to make sure none of the lace gets caught in the zipper.

We carry the dress out together to the taxi—like a body wrapped in a carpet—and lay it carefully on the backseat. I lift up the bits that are hanging out as we close the car door. It's nearly shut with my arm still in it, then I pull my arm quickly out and slam the door. We did it.

The driver and I get in and as we drive off the tailor waves after us, now openly sobbing. I have the feeling that I've taken her only dress. She worked so long on it and earned so much doing it that she doesn't want to let it go. But it's mine now. Mine, mine, mine. I'm the only one it fits, since it's a custom job. I talk about nothing but the wedding with the taxi driver for the next eighty kilometers. By the time we arrive, he knows everything. How the cake will look. How many people are coming. How many alcoholics there are on the English side of my family. That I pray there will be a fistfight. Because that's part of a successful wedding. That all my brothers are going to wear matching Hawaiian shirts—perfect for a summer wedding— that I picked out and bought for them (in different sizes, obviously). That we've ordered little baby's breath bouquets for all the guests to pin on themselves. Which Adriano Celentano song will play after we've said "I do." That the bride and groom have each made mixtapes for the party afterward. Between us we've put together nine hours of music to dance to.

The sun shines into the taxi. As we drive up to the back entrance of my mother's house, the entire family comes running out to greet me. We park behind my mother's car, already fully packed for the trip. All the doors are open and things are falling out of it. Inside are sleeping bags for all the kids, nice clothes for the wedding, gifts for us, the couple, as well as books and toys to keep the children amused for the four days we'll be in England celebrating. They'll all be staying either at the wedding hotel or a nearby bed-and-breakfast. The most important thing is that they can all reach their beds on foot, drunk, on the wedding day. Tomorrow, that is. Today everyone is traveling.

I have to go back to my hometown now, in the same taxi, to catch my flight together with my future husband and his twelve family members. I see that the roof rack has already been fastened to the top of my mother's car. My brothers try to persuade me to quickly try on the dress. They want to see me in it. I should say no and be firm. But I can't—I want to show them, too. I don't want to be superstitious and old-fashioned, believe in all that crap about nobody seeing the dress before the wedding. I just can't manage to stay firm. So my mother, the taxi driver, and I lay the garment bag out on the lawn behind my mother's house. It's very warm outside, and I undress down to my underwear. It's actually embarrassing in front of the taxi driver. But I don't want to be some kind of bourgeois prude and ask him to look away. Fortunately he does it without being asked. My brothers laugh but don't turn away. My mother helps me first to climb into the heavy skirt and to close the hook-and-eye closure in the back. Then she puts on the satin corsage, which covers the thick waistband of the skirt so the outfit looks like a one-piece dress. To be funny, my mother pulls the veil out of the bag and puts it on my head crooked and backward, with the long part over my face. And there stands the bride in her complete getup. Everyone is happy and says how nice it looks, the taxi driver allows himself to look again, and we all clap. Then I slip back out of the heavy thing. The weight of it really tugs at the waist. Luckily I don't have to wear it for long—I bought something short and light for dancing in the evening after the ceremony.

Once I have my pants and blouse on again, we hoist the repacked dress into the roof container and lock it.

"When are you leaving?" I ask.

"In a few minutes."

"Okay, I'll see all you idiots in England," I say, laughing, adding an obligatory, "Beat you there!" I've said that as long as I can remember when people are heading to the same place by different means of transport.

Now quickly back the whole way with the taxi driver. I'm pretty stressed in the lead-up to the wedding. I keep thinking, *I've forgotten something important*. But no, I haven't. I keep going through a mental checklist of things I'm responsible for, and I have indeed taken care of it all. Weeks of work, a wedding like this—doing and planning everything yourself.

When I arrive at home virtually all I can say to my future husband are things like, "Did you pack this?"

"Yes."

"Did you pack that?"

"Yeeeees."

Apparently he, too, had remembered everything. Prior to the wedding we're not particularly infatuated with each other, which is normal. There's just too much to think about. You don't necessarily want to marry; you'd really rather just be married. Who has ever had a relaxing good time at their own wedding? I don't know anyone. It begins to get fun only when everything's nearly over, there's nothing left to go wrong, and you can start drinking. At least I hope!

We meet all my boyfriend's relatives at the airport. That's also nerve-racking—organizing a big group of travelers. The children of some nieces and nephews of my future husband start screaming during check-in. I turn off my mobile phone shortly before boarding. I'm a good little flier, always following all the rules. The children scream even more once they're inside the plane. I just act as if I don't know them. They are sitting in the row in front of me, so it works fine. I do breathing exercises to try to stave off panic from all the commotion. I fake a relaxed smile when my boyfriend looks at me and takes my hand. I'll be happy when we have some peace and quiet at our hotel room. When we finally arrive.

Short afternoon flight to London. About fifty minutes. We land and exit the plane. We've booked a huge tour bus with a driver. He's supposed to meet us outside holding one of those funny signs with our name written on it. I've never been picked up by a driver with a sign. We took out a big loan for the wedding. So we don't have to spare any expense. I'll be very relieved if everything with the bus works out—if there really is someone standing there and we have a driver.

We collect our luggage, and as we pass the customs booth I switch my phone back on. It rings the exact second I turn it on. I can see it's my father's number. I answer.

"Hello, Papa. We just landed."

This story from back then—and what is about to happen on the phone with my father—has ruined my entire life. It still plays an immense role now, eight years later, as I sit on the couch with my current husband. My husband married a complete wreck.

Back to the worm problem.

Lying in my husband's arms, I call my ex-husband, ex-boyfriend, whatever you want to call him.

"Hello?"

"Am I disturbing you?" That's always the first thing I ask everyone I call. It's far too polite and apologetic, which is why I like it. This feigned meekness. The submissiveness.

"No."

"To cut straight to the chase, Liza and I have worms. Nematodes, to be exact. I have to take her to the pediatrician tomorrow. Which means she can't go to school. Have you noticed anything at your end?" Well put.

"Well, now that you mention it. I thought it was something else."

Please, no details! But here they come . . .

"I had this painful other thing recently, so when I felt the itching, I just figured the same thing was coming back again—though it did feel very different last time."

Got it. Dragged right into it. We were together for years, after all. Even if I can't possibly imagine it now. It's horrible when you have kids with someone you split up with. Your first instinct tells you that the fact that you once had sex together is not a reason you ever have to see each other again. But, because of the child, you can't give into that instinct; instead you have to get along passably forever, for the child's sake.

Horrible. I would rather not see anyone I ever have sex with after the end of the relationship. Whenever you see someone you've been with, you always end up thinking about it, or rather you are reminded of it even against your will. Awful. It always seems almost impossible that you were actually together, before, ages ago.

"Have a look at Wikipedia, please, so I don't have to go into detail. You can inspect your stool—they'll be squirming around in it if you have them. They're bright white and very active. They move around like crazy. Or you can hold a piece of transparent tape up to your butt hole."

Oh, God, this is embarrassing.

"They'll stick to that if you have them, and you'll know."

"I'm pretty sure I have them, too. Like I said, I had just blamed the sensation on something else. But I'm totally itchy, too."

I have to smile. Man, patchwork families are absurd. You're not spared any indignity.

"I'll try to get medicine for all of us from the pediatrician tomorrow. Not that we all have to be examined. I bet he'll believe me if I say the father and mother have worms, too. I just don't know whether a pediatrician can write prescriptions for adult medicines. At least I fit in children's clothes. It'll be tougher for you to pass yourself off as a child. Maybe you won't need to try—maybe I can get medicine for all of us. I'll call you tomorrow after we see the doctor, yeah?"

"And Georg, does he have them?"

"No, we haven't infected him yet, fortunately." A total lie. But he's sitting right next to me, so I can't say, *He says he doesn't, but I can tell from his reaction to my question about them that he's lying and is infested, too. I think the reason he's lying is that he wants to try to stay sexually attractive to me.*

"Well, that's something, at least. Okay, thanks a lot. Talk to you tomorrow."

My husband looks at me consolingly, but he can't think of anything else at this point. We'll just have to wait. Nine hours. As horrible as it is, and as disgusting as it is, it's also a little bit exciting. Because I've never experienced it. At least not knowingly, during adulthood. I ask him if he wants to see the worms. I can feel that a bunch of them are outside now. It's time for them to step out for a breath of fresh air. The thought that he should look at the worms is such a motherly thought. But he really should act like a mother for a minute and help me; he should defuse my horror at the situation. He should look at it together with me, comfort me, and tell me it's not as bad as I think. He declines.

"There is no way I'm going to look at your worms."

I immediately feel insulted. He doesn't want to look at my worms? Why not? Such an enticing offer. I would definitely say yes if it were the other way around. I'm sick, infested in fact, and he doesn't want to see the source of the misery?

"I don't think it's a good idea. I shouldn't take a look. We're a couple, married even, but that doesn't mean I have to look at every disgusting thing you get."

Yeah, yeah, yeah, I know what's coming next: the lecture about childbirth and how it's better if a man doesn't see all the gory details because it will ruin the sex between him and the mother. I've heard it a thousand times from my husband.

"It's just like when a man looks at everything up close during the birth of his children—as if he's a doctor or some-thing—and then can't cope with seeing the vagina all stretched out and torn to shreds," he says.

Men also can't take it when so much shit comes out during birth. The combination of shit and a newborn says a lot about mankind, though. That the two holes are so close to each other is proof that there's no God. He would have put them as far apart as possible—one on the foot and the other on top of the head.

And if a man can't cope with witnessing birth, sex is nearly impossible afterward if he does see it. You have to preserve the sexual allure of the reproductive organs, or else it's true what my husband says.

But in terms of wanting to show him the worms, I feel as if I'm offering something nice. And he just turns me down. I thought he'd find the fact that I have worms at least as interesting as I do. But he flatly rejects my offer, which at first makes me sad, then angry. I left my parents for a man like this? Great. I guess I'm totally alone. I can't expect help from anyone. I'll just have to deal with any disgusting ailments all on my own, with all the horrible images they leave in my head.

I want him to share the images. But he doesn't want to be burdened with them—he wants to be able to keep me pure in his memory so he can still get it up when he sees me naked. I fold my arms on my chest. I always do that when I feel crazy thoughts brewing inside me.

"Don't get angry. I know exactly what you're thinking."

I'm never able to hide it for long.

"You're thinking I never help you in an emergency. But Elizabeth, I have to tell you, having worms is not an emergency."

He's laughing at me. He's mocking me. Asshole. He's got worms, too; he just doesn't have the guts to admit it to me.

"If you really had something bad, it wouldn't matter how disgusting it was—I would look at it, I would help, I would do anything and everything. But there's no call for that here. There's no reason I need to look at your worms and then have to have that unnecessary image in my head. If I can have some input into this decision, I would opt for our love life over having that image in my head. And anyway, you *asked* me, so I'm allowed to say no."

Fucking therapy-speak. He picked that kind of language up at marriage counseling. How to draw lines. He knows he shouldn't always do what I want just because I flip out. He and I have learned that he should never allow me to pressure him. He's not responsible for my happiness. I can't blame him for my unhappiness. That's my parents' fault. What is he supposed to do about that? He's always there for me. He's nothing but supportive, but it's still never enough for me. You just can't make me happy. I can't be satisfied—or pacified, for that matter. Except by myself, and that is a long process. He's been freed by the marriage counseling, and all problems now lie at my feet. I'm clearly the aggressor in our relationship. I wheedle, pressure, pull him down with me, and he just needs not to be swayed by any of it. He needs to establish boundaries— just like he did with the worms. He needs to say, "That's your problem. Go ahead and throw a fit. I can't do anything about it, and I can't help you. You're unhappy, but you are the only person who can fix it. Either you save yourself or not. There's no way I can do it for you."

I need to stop overwhelming him with demands. I was better off before the marriage counseling, because I could just passive-aggressively try to make him responsible for everything. That would have quickly destroyed our relationship, though.

I didn't want to allow myself to feel any grief, which is why I became so aggressive. When I was fighting with my husband, I didn't feel any of the sorrow. It was nice for me. And bad for him. Now that I leave him in peace and no longer try to blame him for all the bad things I've experienced in life—things my parents did to me—I have to shoulder the burden myself and sometimes feel as if I'm about to collapse. And my husband has to step aside and watch. He can't help me. The grief that I don't wish to feel comes from that phone call, back there in the customs area of the airport.

My father says to me over the phone, "Elizabeth, you have to be very strong now."

Like in a movie. I start to hear a whooshing noise in my ear. I stand still and probably put a grimace on my face, because my boyfriend looks at me, aghast.

"There was a bad accident on the highway. A multicar collision. The Belgian police just called me. We have to assume that everyone who was in the car is dead. That's what they said."

A long pause.

"Now I have to ask you who was in the car."

"What? What? What?"

"Who was in the car, Elizabeth?"

What? Who was in the car, Elizabeth? He doesn't know? He doesn't know. They told him everyone was dead. But they don't know who was in the car? Huh?

"Don't say Harry was in the car. Say he's there with you. Did he fly? Say something!"

That's his only son. My brother, the sibling closest to me in age. I have to think for a long time. I don't want to say anything wrong. Maybe they'll die if I say the wrong names. Concentrate. Concentrate. Come on, Elizabeth, think. For once in your life.

My brain has almost shut down from shock. And now I have to give a list of names. I have to list the dead? I'm thinking. He's calling me to find out who is dead? Think. You just saw them all playing in the yard. Pull yourself together. Try to say the names.

"Mama . . .

"Harry . . .

"Lukas . . .

"Paul . . .

"Rhea . . ."

I can hear him writing it down. He's also in shock. He's afraid he'll forget the names. One he will not forget. I've told him his son was in the car.

No more? Yes? No? Is this right? Is this all the names? My head hurts. My eyes are barely open. The light hurts them.

In the middle of the exit area, my legs give out and I sink to the floor. My boyfriend sits down next to me and stares at me. He knows it has to be something awful I am hearing. All his relatives stop and look at us.

Everyone is very serious—except for the fucking kids. It gets very quiet, though I can see the children are still scream-ing. I don't hear them anymore. I never want to get up from this spot again. My body has lost all strength. I implode.

I think and think. It's difficult, exhausting, and slow to think. My brain is blocked.

"Mama is dead, too?"

"Yes, everyone. They said we should assume they are all dead."

A new thought shoots into my mind: *What happened to my dress?* It was in the car, too. Above the car. On top of the car. Is the dress dead, too? Is it wrecked? I can't bring myself to ask. I'm possessed by the idea that nothing can have happened to my dress. Suddenly I can't think of anything that could be worse. My wedding dress. It cost so much. All the fittings! I have to give the tailor a photo of me wearing it. I promised her.

This part of my reaction embarrasses me to this day. My therapist says I don't need to feel bad about it, though. Our minds do funny things when we experience terror. I just wasn't in a condition to truly understand that they were all dead. But I was in a condition to understand that my dress might be lost. It's much less painful having to deal with that than the loss of people. Your brain just shuts down, allowing only a few small less painful thoughts.

My father is also in shock. That's the reason he suggests we still go ahead and get married. He says this shouldn't get in the way. He also can't comprehend the magnitude of the situation in the slightest. He says he has to hang up so the police can reach him. Then he hangs up.

After that it's as if I'm on autopilot. My body does everything automatically. I repeat everything my father said word for word to my boyfriend and his family. They are all speechless and stare at me. Nobody says a thing. We are blocking the other passengers trying to get through the customs area, but we don't care. We stay on the floor and think. I have no idea what to do next. We sit there for an eternity.

The news my father delivered that day has left me a bewildered person to this day. It plays out in every decision. My husband bears the brunt of that, the poor man. But he benefits from it as well, because as a way of sort of making up for my psychological shortcomings, I put incredible effort into it when I suck his cock. As gratitude for the fact that he has put up so long with a wounded animal—me.

So, he doesn't take me up on my spectacular offer to show him my worms. I'll have to deal with that alone. Got it. Thanks a lot. That's the last time I make such a nice offer.

"But if my guts were hanging out, would you help me? Are you sure? You'd have a look then, yeah?"

"Of course I would. You know that. If it were really something bad, I would rescue you."

Thank you. I lean against him. Hopefully something really bad will happen to me again soon. It can't go on like this—that I keep picturing the most horrible things happening without anything ever actually coming to pass. I have a crazy sense of imagination. That just dreams up new horrific scenarios. I think the scenarios out to the smallest level of detail. I really work myself up doing that. I learned in therapy that the only time I'm free of fear is when I displace it with hypersexuality. Then I am able to enjoy life for a little while and feel as if I know what I'm living for. My therapist calls it fear arousal. It feels similar to sexual arousal. For me it's either one or the other. The one extreme or the other. Frau Drescher says I'm trying to escape my fear through sex—that it's the only feeling that can sometimes temporarily displace the fear. It is not, however, the answer to my problems. Too bad. She says I need to address the problems within myself and not transfer them outward.

I could easily have sex ten times a day. I could alleviate a lot of tension that way. But usually I opt instead to agonize over things myself. It goes like this: every night I lie down in bed and look up at the ceiling. There's a crack in the plaster.

I look at it every day and am sure that it is getting bigger. So I convince myself that it's not just a crack in the plaster but a more serious structural problem.

We live in a building with four apartments in it. Stacked one on top of the other. All of the rest above ours. We're on the ground floor. If it all comes crumbling down because it was poorly built, I'm prepared. I've played out that scenario in my head a million times. To the right of my side of the bed is a load-bearing wall. If I hear the building crumbling, I just roll out of bed and lie against that wall. Once everything has collapsed, I'll crawl along the intact support wall to the kid's room and find my crushed daughter. Then I'll crawl back to see my crushed, smashed husband. I always have my phone and a knife with a long sharp blade next to my bed in case burglars break into the apartment. I swear I'll stab them. If the building implodes, I'll call 911—and I'll be the only survivor. But as my life will have no meaning anymore without my husband and child, I'll kill myself a few days later in the psychiatric clinic where I'm placed for trauma therapy. I play out this scene every night in my head, with different endings. The fact that the house will soon collapse, however, is certain. My therapist says that people who fear their building will collapse around them actually have structural damage in their psychological "building." They project their inner fears outward on the exterior building. What's collapsing is inside, not outside.

It doesn't seem to make things any better even when I acknowledge that buildings never collapse in Germany—that everything is too meticulously built, with solid foundations. Death always seems to be lying in bed between me and my husband. I've asked my husband hundreds of times in the years we've been together whether he, too, has noticed that the crack in the ceiling is expanding. He rolls his eyes every time, then looks at it the way I look at the witch under my daughter's dresser, and says, "No, it hasn't gotten any bigger." In these moments he talks to me as if he were talking to a crazy person, in a deep, calm tone. It makes me sick when I hear my own craziness in his voice.

These days I ask him only when it's an absolute emergency, when I'm more worried than usual, because I pretty much know he's just going to lie to me and say no. It's important to note that my therapist has found that I'm not afraid of dying. I don't have a problem with death and dying as such. I'm happy to have Death nearby; he makes a good friend. No, my problem is with losing control. I just don't want to die from something I could have prevented. If I get sick and there's nothing that can be done, I would embrace death. But to die because of something stupid, something you just didn't pay attention to, is something I don't want to happen to me or those close to me. I'm always on alert to save the life of the members of my immediate family.

I sit on the couch and tell my husband that the visit to the brothel tomorrow isn't going to happen. He can see the hint of a smile on my face. He says, "You're happy about that, aren't you? Relieved?"

"Yes, you know I hate to be anxious about something. And if something that's making me anxious gets canceled, then I'm relieved at first. We'll set it up again as soon as I'm no longer infested with these vermin."

He knows just how overwhelming our brothel visits are for me ahead of time, how I get so anxious and afraid, and how afterward I congratulate myself because I've succeeded, I've survived: despite having sex with someone else, my husband is still with me! What a miracle! Woo-hoo!

The disappointment on his face is clear to see. He always looks forward to these outings. The anticipation alone makes him so happy. He's much more transparent than I am. Just like on any other night, we turn on the TV. We sit silently for a little while—he's silent because he's disappointed that the trip to the brothel is off, I'm silent because the itchiness from the worms is driving me crazy. I hate to disappoint him. He's really down now. Fuck.

We both stare mutely at the huge TV screen. My husband thinks I'm watching the show, but I'm actually ruminating secretly on the accident again. I let the scene play through my head over and over again, as if I had been there. And I have to keep repeating to myself, *Yes, Elizabeth, you have to reconcile yourself with it, because it really happened, it's true.*

I'm kneeling on the floor in the airport and searching around in my head to try to figure out if what I told my father was right. Who all was in the car. I feel blocked when I try to think of the names. It's so many! But in order to help my father, I need to know I haven't made any mistakes. I fight to find all the names. I repeat them several times: Mama, Harry, Lukas, Paul, and Rhea. Yes, I think that's right.

The mother of my boyfriend, the woman who will be my mother-in-law, goes out to explain everything to the bus driver, who does in fact have a sign with our name on it. I feel that if I say it to a stranger, it will actually become real. Or more real. I can see from afar the way the driver's face changes. At first his ugly English mug looks relaxed and happy. But as she talks with him, darkness creeps across it, and he keeps looking over at us.

The way he looks now is probably how I look, too. A contorted look of horror. No more keeping up appearances. Not a single muscle is moving. I no longer have to act anymore, there's no more need to smile anymore. No need at all. Every move now is made as if in a trance. Calm, automatic. I'm able to perform just basic functions now, nothing else.

At some point we have to get up. We load our baggage into the cargo bay of the bus. I sit in the last row, just like when I was in school, back where the cool kids always sat. The man who suddenly would no longer be my future husband sits down next to me. We proceed as planned. What else can we do? The plan was to drive everyone from the airport to the various hotels, after which we—the bridal couple—would be delivered to the hotel where the wedding would take place. But after we have taken all his family members to their destinations, I no longer want to go to the wedding hotel. I just can't take it. I have a ton of cash with me, as a good bride should, so I offer to pay the bus driver to change the plan—I want him to take us instead to see my relatives in London. Fortunately he doesn't have another job to go to, so he agrees to drive us there. It takes an hour and a half.

My boyfriend and I sit alone in the huge bus as the driver keeps a worried eye on us in the rearview mirror. I hand my phone to my boyfriend—it has all the numbers of my English relatives on it. He calls my uncle and aunt, and I listen as he relays the unbelievable news. I keep thinking he's lying. It can't be true. He should shut his lying mouth. What a load of crap. He must be nuts. He's saying there won't be a wedding. Okay. That's probably true. It's hard to rethink it after months of planning. Every fiber of my being wants to see the plan through to the end. But I can't now. We sit silently beside each other. He holds my hand. What else is he supposed to do? Nobody is taught how to act in situations like these, how to be helpful or useful. It's like men during childbirth. What are they supposed to do? They don't teach that in school. The important things. You only ever see situations like this in war movies. Five people dying simultaneously. It's like an act of war against my family. As if a bomb has been dropped on us. And still almost all I can think about is what happened to my dress. Woe is me, it's ruined.

My mind just isn't capable of much more. Once in a while I think to myself, *I hope my mother isn't dead*. I wouldn't want to live if she were dead. We're very close. Too close. I often still sit in her lap when I see her. When I was a child we were close; during puberty as far apart as two people can be; and then when the storm clouds of puberty cleared, we were once again as close as when I was a child. Fatally close. I was never able to create space from her as an adult—my options were limited to being close to her or having no relationship with her at all.

On the bus, driving to my uncle and aunt's place, I keep thinking to myself, *Fuck the rest of the people in the car. Please, just don't let my mother be dead*. I was willing to make a deal with destiny, with the devil, with God, with whomever. I didn't care: I would trade my siblings and my brother's girlfriend for my mother's life. Because I just can't live without her. Don't want to live without her. It just shows you how fucked up faith is. At the moment when the most horrible things happen, when you are weaker than ever, you start to go nuts. It's the best proof of the fact that God and faith are inventions of man. But just because people want it to be, does not make it so. It all comes from despair, from the feeling that everything is pointless and that we're all alone and lost in the world. When fate strikes, it's just a coincidence. Or human error. Every single accident. Fate if you are not found legally responsible; your own fault if you cause the accident. There are no other possibilities.

That's why I get just as pissed off at Christians as I do at women who pump silicone into their breasts. Because both are taking the easy way out. Christians just can't handle the idea of spiritual homelessness that I've dealt with, been fully conscious of, for my entire life: life is pointless, the world is pointless, mankind's existence is a fluke, and there is *definitely* no life after death. To console themselves, Christians dream up a life after death. Because they would like—so badly—for us to be more important or more unique than animals. They convince themselves that there's a heaven up there for them in the afterlife. You wish! Oddly enough it's always the self-professed Christians who flip out the most when they lose someone close to them—despite the fact that they will ostensibly see each other again soon in heaven. When you see their reaction to death you can tell they don't believe their own bullshit. And when it comes to breasts, you should just accept the ones you have and deal with it—like the pointlessness of life.

My husband is still clearly disappointed that our visit to the brothel tomorrow is off. He's sulking. This time there's really nothing I can do about it. I didn't get worms on purpose. Though he probably wouldn't put it past me.

I want to get away from the oppressive atmosphere on the couch, so I say, "I'm going to bed."

But as an adult woman, I can't simply flop down and sleep, as I'd like to. I have to wash all the coloring I put on that morning off my face, using a special cleaning substance called makeup remover. You have to brush your teeth for a good long time to set a good example for your children—even though they're not watching. Comb your long hair so it won't be all tangled in the morning. Undress, throw your dirty underwear and socks into the rattan laundry basket, and put on your slightly musty old pajamas that are hanging on the hook on the back of the bathroom door.

We try to do as little laundry as possible, for the environment—our ersatz religion. And that means wearing the same stinky pajamas over and over. We also change the bed linens as rarely as possible. As a result our bedroom smells a bit like a cave. I often think, *This is the same way the Neanderthals smelled, this greasy bodily odor*. We make sure not to stink only when we interact with others, outside our home. At home everything is subordinated to the environment. It's always a competition between me and my husband to see who will do all the things we have to do before bed in the big bathroom and who will be forced to use the little guest bathroom.

We try to do everything better than we did in our previous relationships, because we want—need—to stay together forever. So we eliminate all the mistakes that killed earlier relationships. Anything to do with bodily hygiene we hide from each other. We don't brush our teeth in front of each other, or wash, clip our nails, piss, or poop. We did those things in front of previous partners and realized it had been a problem.

I lay claim to the big bathroom and don't have to worry about him coming in and seeing me doing any of those things. Then I lie down in our musty bed. I take up a third of our double bed because I'm petite. He gets two-thirds because he's big. Even when I sleep I don't really relax. I try to stay in control— try to make sure that he has enough room, that I don't fart in bed. I think farting in bed is also detrimental to sustaining a relationship forever. He does it a lot in front of me. Before I've fallen asleep he lets them fly. But I don't want that to happen in reverse. Otherwise I might be abandoned.

I lie down in our sweaty, greasy, semen-crusted bed and look up at the ceiling. Yep. There it is, my beloved crack. I stare at it. And I imagine saving my family from being crushed by the inevitable collapse of the building. I'm prepared for everything. I won't be caught off guard by Death. No. Never again. Death lies on top of me as I fall asleep; he's there when I wake up. I can't imagine that it will ever stop. No matter how many thousands of hours I spend on Agnetha's couch. The accident and all the details surrounding it follow me, especially when I'm alone, as I am now, lying there waiting for the concrete walls to collapse and crush me.

Frau Drescher has taught me that trauma is so painful because it's like an open wound that won't close and heal. It still feels as if the accident and everything surrounding it happened just a few days ago. It's as if no time has passed since then at all. I'm trapped in that time and can't get past it. It's like a movie in my head that just keeps repeating over and over. Maybe it will stop one day. But I don't think so. I've become so accustomed to the images during the last eight years that it's hard for me to imagine a life that doesn't include this movie playing on a continuous loop. This horror movie.

The English bus driver drops us off at the home of my relatives. They storm out of the house to welcome us. They hug me for a long time and give me looks of sympathy. They're not good at it. Because they're not exactly sure what to do, either. Or what to say. I taste blood: I immediately feel happily aware of the special status you are granted in such a situation. They hold me and look directly into my eyes. They try to figure out what it does to a human being to receive news like that: *Your mother and three of your siblings are dead!* That's where my addiction to sympathy started. Endless sympathy. More than the people around you. Always granted special status. Like a saint. Everyone who sees you pictures you thinking, *I'll grit my teeth and get through it. I won't let myself get down. I won't give up.* And everyone is amazed. To this day I find it really nice to be pitied, to be treated like some kind of superbeing—so much so that I almost look forward to mourning my child and husband. Just so that doesn't sound too evil, my therapist would say at this point that I'm only trying to prepare myself for the worst so it won't be so bad if it actually comes to pass. Yeah, yeah, that could be. I constantly see myself alone in my visions of the future, with a child and a husband who are dead because I failed to protect them from who knows what.

We go inside with my aunt and uncle. And drink a lot of alcohol, in the middle of the day. First cans of beer, the big ones, half-liter cans. Then the hard stuff. What else would you expect from a family of alcoholics? But even with all the booze I remain oddly sober. It must be the shock. We sit silently around the kitchen table. What can they say? The situation just steamrolls everyone.

My phone rings. It's my father.

"Yes?"

"I have some good news. Rhea is alive."

"No news about Mother?"

"No. I'll let you know as soon as I hear anything. They said that's their information policy—tell people to assume everyone is dead, and then, if anything changes, it comes as good news. They say everything is chaotic—it was a giant accident and the injured had to be sent to many different hospitals. Some of them are unconscious, some don't have ID. There are Dutch, Belgians, English; and they have to find out who is who, who's alive, and who's dead. I have to keep my phone free."

He hangs up. Good that he has something to do. He's a man. He has yet to hear anything about his only son. My oldest sibling. But younger than me. My father at the command center of the accident. What is an "information policy"? Lie to everyone first? Say everyone is dead, even though they don't know that? Promulgate the worst-case scenario? Everyone is dead. But only maybe. What? Hope? First destroy all hope. Then a little creeps back in. They first say everyone's dead and then they inform the living step-by-step. So in the end there's a little happiness. Instead of just despair. Nice trick. The Belgian police are sly as foxes when it comes to psychology.

Rhea, Rhea, Rhea. So what? My brother's girlfriend. I have no relationship with her at all. Or barely any. Great—for her family. Definitely great for them. But not for us. Blood is thicker than alcohol. But alcohol thins your blood. Is it possible that Mother is also still alive? It's been three hours since my father's first call. It's possible that he'll call any minute and say, "They found your mother." She's alive. Or she's dead. He'll either confirm the initial news or repudiate it. Everything is still possible. Excruciating wait. Hanging on the news. Call. Papa. Call. Call.

I talk drunkenly with my relatives and boyfriend, staring the whole time at my phone. I keep checking to make sure I have a good signal. Don't want anything else to go wrong. Slowly it becomes evening. I'm not hungry but I eat something anyway. My aunt makes something warm for us.

Late in the evening, I realize that my two cousins are missing. I ask where they are. And I'm happy that something normal has occurred to me, something we can talk about. That's when you know how poorly your brain is functioning while in shock—it takes hours before I realize that two of my relatives are missing. My aunt and uncle sent the kids away when they received the call from my boyfriend. They didn't tell the kids why they had to go, but they sent them to a friend's place so they wouldn't have to deal with something so horrific at their age. They'll tell them the next day.

The phone rings. I answer immediately. I saw the word *Papa* pop up on the display even before the ringtone registered.

"I have good news. Mother is alive."

"Thank you, Papa, thank you. Where is she?" From the look on my face and the word *she,* my relatives and boyfriend can figure out that my mother has survived. Yes. That's what you say. She survived. The most important person to me on earth survived the mass accident.

"Do you have something to write with? I'll give you the number of the hospital in Antwerp. She's badly burned, but she's conscious."

She's alive, but she's badly burned? All the things you have to wrestle with in life.

"What? Badly burned? What does that mean?"

Please don't let it be Mama's face!

"I haven't talked to her directly. The doctor said her feet were burned down to the bone on both legs. And her back is broken. But she can talk, do you understand? She is conscious, Elizabeth. Call her."

"Okay, I will. Talk to you later. Thanks again."

But I'm not going to. I'm not going to call her! I can't do that. What would I say? I start to feel creeped out by my own mother. I'm unbelievably happy that she's alive, but what is there to talk about? This is when the speechlessness in our family began. Out of cowardice. My mother survived a mass wreck, her back is broken, and her feet are burned. What else is there to say? I stare at the long number beginning with the country code for Belgium. Does it go directly to her room? Do you get your own room after a multivehicle crash? We all have just basic insurance. We wouldn't normally get a single room. Everyone in my family says it would be too boring to be alone in a hospital room. Or perhaps a nurse answers the phone? Or whoever she is sharing a room with? Which parts of her body are burned again? Broken back? Where exactly? Is she in traction? Neck? Pelvis? Did they just dip her in plaster to create a full-body cast? Is her vagina full of plaster, too, as a result? I'm not calling. I can't. She's alive. Wonderful. But I don't need to call and hear exactly what is burned and how badly.

I explain to my relatives that I have her number at the hospital. But also that I'm not going to call. I don't want to. I don't want it to happen to us. A minute ago I thought the best thing that could happen would be if my mother survived the accident, but now I'm already back to complaining. I wanted her to survive uninjured. It hadn't even occurred to me until this moment that you could also survive despite getting hurt. In fact, that's the most likely thing to happen. And how ugly her injuries sound! Severely burned, a broken back. The phone rings. My father.

"Bad news, Elizabeth."

I can barely understand what he's saying. There's loud noise in the background. As if he's at a racetrack.

"I'm afraid it's bad news. The children have not turned up in any of the surrounding hospitals. They've identified all the survivors. Your brother is not among them."

Your brother? Your son, too, Papa. Not just me. You, too.

"They've cleared the site of the accident. The autobahn has been reopened. I'm here with Lukas's father. The whole area is a charred wasteland."

What? They're at the accident site? Are they crazy? They should get away from there. How can they possibly go there? What? They stopped on the autobahn and are walking around? It sounds like a racetrack. It is now. An autobahn. They should make sure nothing happens to them.

"Be careful, yeah? Be careful, Papa."

"Yes, we're being careful. Don't worry. We just wanted to see the site of the accident. We drove here together."

I know that both of them drive very fast. I don't want them to anymore. I must tell them not to. There will be no more speeding in our family.

Right, so they are not among the survivors.

"Are the bodies somewhere?"

I can't believe what I'm asking. But he doesn't seem to mind answering.

"There are no bodies. That's the odd part. The car exploded and burned beyond all recognition. We had to tell the police that the children had been in the backseat. Nothing was found—no bones, no teeth, nothing. At first they didn't believe us. They insisted that there must have only been two people in the car—the two in the front, who survived. Your mother and Rhea."

That's my father, my scientific, emotionless father. Bones, teeth. Nice! Now you can picture it all. Finally he's explaining things clearly.

"So, they're dead?"

"Yes, they are dead, but there are no bodies."

This is incredible. I want to hang up immediately so I can tell my relatives. I'm including my boyfriend now among the relatives. Because we had almost been married. It counts as having been married. If you were going to say yes. Coulda, shoulda, woulda. Even in the middle of a catastrophe, you never lose a sense of appreciation for something sensational like this—and you are aware of its interest to others.

We hang up. I repeat everything my father has just told me, word for word. It's the beginning of something that will follow me for the rest of my life: I talk about the accident in all its gory details, but I can hardly believe what I'm saying is true. It's just words. I can't get rid of the feeling that I'm lying to people about the story. Like when I used to lie about how rich my father was when I was young so that other kids would think more highly of me. I'm a con artist. A poseur. I just try to make myself the center of attention with made-up stories.

For a few hours, my relatives allow me to continue to think I'm not going to call my mother. Then they tell me it's just not an option. They convince me to call. They say I have to get through it. I have to talk to her about her burns and broken back. She's probably waiting for me to call. You can't avoid it, they tell me. What then? We'll definitely want to visit her tomorrow. What? Visit? Tomorrow? Oh, God, right, that's what you do. But we're in England and she's in Belgium. We don't have to go visit her there, do we? I hadn't even thought about that. I haven't really been able to think at all since the news of the accident. It's like my brain is sick. Like someone with Alzheimer's. Shock-dementia.

There's only one technique that allows me to get away from these thoughts and fall asleep. I have to breathe them away. In order to relax, in order to be able to get to sleep. Before I start my breathing technique, I stick one of the greatest inventions in the world into my ears: Oropax ear plugs. Oropax means "peace of the ears" in Latin. I think so, anyway. I was terrible in Latin. Georg has now come in and lain down next to me. He snores. It's because he's full of testosterone. I'm sure of it. And because he's old. With the Oropax in my ears, I am totally removed from the world around me. There is nothing but the whir of my own rushing blood. I am self-contained. The trick I use to fall asleep goes like this: I tense all the muscles in my feet, breathe out, then in, three times, very deeply, then I loosen all the muscles in my feet. Then I do the same thing with my leg muscles, my buttocks, my back, my hands, my arms. Theoretically I should carry on until I reach my face and tongue, but I never get that far. I always fall asleep by the time I get to my arms at the latest. Before I start with the breathing, I quickly cross my arms on my chest as if I'm praying. I'm practicing being dead. I look forward to my own death. Peace at last. In my head. In my body. Not that I do anything particularly stressful. But for me, just being is enough to wear me out. Once my hands are folded for my mortal slumber, I'm ready.

Wednesday

The alarm goes off at 6:20 AM, like every morning since I had a child. Horrible. And today it's even worse than usual because of the worms. Gravity is particularly strong and pulls me back into bed, and it takes all my power to fight it. I have to use every ounce of superego I have available. I went to bed too late last night and fell asleep even later. I wake up every morning in the exact same corpse pose that I fall asleep in. I don't move at all in my sleep. Georg can't tell whether I'm alive or dead. Sometimes he puts a finger beneath my nose to feel for warm breath. He's told me. He's rehearsing for my death, too.

Waking up has always been difficult for me. Even as a child I dreamed up theories about how something was wrong with the fact that everything—school, work, hospitals—started so early. It screws up your whole life. In school we learned that every person has his or her own biorhythm, but that's not reflected in reality. You learn in school that the system is wrong. And it continues regardless. Now I have a child and have to get up early again. I didn't realize during my pregnancy how long all the responsibilities would last. My God, eighteen years will drag on forever.

The morning—actually the entire day—always unfolds the same way. I get up alone and make breakfast for Liza. Either organic granola with an entire organic apple cut up in it, or cottage cheese on top of a whole-grain roll baked by my husband.

That way no additives can get inside our bodies. For myself I make a latte, which for Georg's sake I have learned to do very well. Obviously I benefit, too. Then I go downstairs and wake up the child. She never wants to get up, never. Just like me at that age. But I act as if it's important to get up in the morning and go to school, even if I don't really believe it myself. She needs to be prepared for life so she doesn't turn into a bum or a slob or a junkie.

I talk so much nonsense that eventually she gets up, laughing. I jiggle her with both of my hands and tell her in the middle of summer that it has snowed. Or I tell her it's her birthday and congratulate her while she's half-asleep. Or I tell her a large animal is waiting for her in the living room, so that she has a moment of fear before she laughs and says, "Oh, Mama, cut it out, you're so embarrassing."

It's the sentence most frequently exchanged between mother and daughter since she could speak: you're so embarrassing.

That's how I get her out of bed. Then I have to coax her upstairs like an animal just waking up from hibernation. With each step she lets her feet hit the floor with a *thwack* to show how out of it she still is. Every morning I have to fight the impulse to say, "You know what, my dear little child? Go ahead and lie back down. Forget school today. I'll lie back down, too. It's all complete nonsense. You'll make something of yourself even without going to school, and you'll probably be happier."

But I don't say that. I would love to, though. It's all pointless. I know. But I act as if the opposite were true. I have to be a good mother. Better than mine. Much better, hopefully. Though that shouldn't be hard.

She sits down at the kitchen table, eats her breakfast, and drinks a glass of lukewarm water. Lukewarm water is best for the body.

I let her eat quietly before confronting her with the worm problem. I try, as always, not to telegraph my own panic.

"Can I have a quick look at your butt hole, please?"

"Why?"

"You said it itched yesterday. And I have worms. I want to see whether you have them, too."

"Okay."

We go together into the guest bathroom. It seems odd to me to conduct the examination at the kitchen table.

I don't let on, but I'm appalled. They're everywhere.

So yes, she has them. Just as I suspected. She and I are infested. She won't be going to school today. We will go to the pediatrician this morning. It's a bit embarrassing, but I hope her doctor will be able to give me medicine, too, so I don't have to go to my own doctor's office as well. My husband, who is just coming upstairs as we are leaving the apartment, asks me to get him a prescription, too, as a precaution. Sure. As a precaution.

"You don't have to go to school today. We're going to the pediatrician."

"Huh? Why?"

"Because we all have worms. You and me for sure, and I hope to get medicine for Papa and Georg as well."

"Oh."

"Yeah, having worms is no big deal. Everyone gets them. Maybe after the doctor's office you'll go to Papa's place if he's not working today."

"Okay."

Brave kid. She doesn't protest. Either she likes it equally well at both our places, or it just never occurs to her to play one of us against the other. Maybe because we try to shield her from everything. We never fight in front of her, we never put pressure on her. We separated parents never raise our voices at each other, at least not in front of her. Despite the fact that there are definitely grounds to do so on both sides. Again, we are doing much better than my parents did.

In therapy I've learned that the most important thing is to make clear to the child that he or she cannot do anything about the split. I missed my own father so much when my parents split that I convinced myself the whole thing was my fault. My parents had no experience with therapy and never saw any need to read a book about dealing with a child of a breakup. They just stomped around in our heads, egotistical as they were, without a thought about protecting our little souls (regardless of the fact that there is no such thing as a soul!).

"Mama, do I really not have to go to school today?"

"You're not allowed to go to school with worms."

"Yay. Cool."

We are already in the car on the way to her pediatrician's office.

We go there without an appointment. It's the best way. Just sit in the waiting room until we get a chance. If someone is late arriving for an appointment, we're there.

Fortunately the pediatrician doesn't need to examine us. He believes the good mother and the super tape test. We get a children's prescription and three adult prescriptions, enough for the whole damn patchwork family. The doctor explains that the itching should stop after the first pill, and that the pill on the second evening is just insurance to make sure any remaining worms are knocked out. He says Liza only needs to be held out of school today. By tomorrow, she won't be contagious any more. I call my ex-husband from the doctor's office and let him know I have medicine for him, to take care of the itching. I also pressure him to take Liza now so I have the rest of the morning alone with my husband. He agrees, and I'm immediately in a better mood. Worms will soon be gone, child will soon be gone, things are looking up.

As we walk out of the office with a bag containing the four batches of medicine to combat our nasty parasites, I tell him over the phone everything the doctor told us about how the stuff works. The beastly itching will stop as soon as you take the first pill. You have to talk about that kind of thing with your ex-husband just because you have a child together. Man, the images that go through your head as a result. I know what his butt hole looks like, even if I'd rather not anymore. Unfortunately, I now know what it looks like when white worms are hanging out of a butt hole. And unfortunately I also have sufficient powers of imagination to combine these two images and create a coherent vision. It makes me feel angry at my ex-boyfriend. Angry that I know what he looks like naked. That he knows what I look like naked. That he knows how I moan when I come. I'd love to erase his memory. I'd be able to get along with him better then.

It's also hard to shake the feelings of guilt for leaving him. I destroyed his family. He wanted to have a family with me and our daughter. But I said, "No, I don't want that anymore." He just had to live with my decision. And that results in regular outbreaks of hostility, which we hide from our child. He's in therapy, I'm in therapy, and an important reason both us do that is so we can help our child deal with our breakup.

Therapists say that you're allowed to leave if you fall in love with someone else or out of love with your partner. But morally speaking, and from the point of view of the child and the abandoned partner, it's never cool. I used to feel so bad about it that I wanted to wire him money as some sort of replacement for me—I thought he should at least be well situated financially. It took my therapist many years of hard work to cast such crazy thoughts out of my head. *Of course*, my ex-boyfriend thinks, *if she wants to leave I have to let her leave*. But he's having a decision about his life made by someone else, and he has to deal with the fact that I'm throwing our daughter's life into chaos as a result, too. Everyone has the romantic image of Mama and Papa staying together forever. Kids especially, but also abandoned partners. I thought that way as a child, too. The governing principle once you have a child with someone is: just stay together forever. And even I, a product of a broken relationship, broke this cardinal rule—at the very moment Liza was born, I was already pretty much separated from her father.

I convince myself that this is the one thing that makes it a little better for the child: she has no conscious memories of what it was like when her parents were together. I was permitted to experience what it was like to have a normal family for five years as a child. Well, I guess you couldn't say it was sound, not in any adult sense. But as children we didn't see what was happening behind the scenes. No fights or suffering for us. The only suffering came from the breakup. That's when everything started to go downhill. That's when the sadness in my life began. The ever-expanding cracks that never healed. I cling to the idea that my daughter, on the other hand, suffered only a virtual sort of loss. She knows intact family life only from other children whose parents are still together or from books and movies. When we talk about the fact that her mother and father used to be together, she just laughs. Since her birth, she has only ever known me together with my current husband. I think in her child's imagination she figures I just decided to get pregnant by a neighbor, for the sake of good genes or whatever. Her father lives in the immediate vicinity to make it easier to shuttle her back and forth. Everything is set up to spare her as much pain as possible.

My parents didn't do that for me. I had to move constantly, switch schools, lose friends, deal with new situations, and block out the past anytime my mother pronounced another man dead. It was always the same pattern: Mother moved with us children into some man's home, a substitute father. Be nice to him, he's your new dad. For two years we'd put on a family show, then the sex would disappear, the love would disappear, we'd move out, and he was pronounced dead.

And the man was always at fault in the breakups. Then all the kids, including the ones added along the way, were out of there; next would come a subsidized apartment in public housing and an impoverished mother. Then a new man, everyone into his house, family show, and so on and so forth. As the oldest child, I lived through that cycle four times. In retrospect I'm bitter about the fact that my mother followed her libido, without ever looking back or thinking about what was being lost. I try to control that in myself. Mostly for the sake of the child. But also for the sake of our relationship. It's damn tough. But when you have kids you have to keep yourself together—so the children can put down roots. I have no roots. I don't have a family home where my parents live, no hometown I can visit. My daughter does. She's been in one place for her entire life. And we'll stay in one place for her. I can't imagine what that's like for a child because I never knew any stability. I find it difficult to stay in one place, to stay with one man. I knew only the opposite: run away.

Whenever I have such evil thoughts about my mother, I also have to admit that it wasn't always like that. Then I'm sitting in my aunt's kitchen again, afraid to call my severely burned mother.

Okay, got it. Not calling is not an option? Grit your teeth and get through it. I go into the living room and sit on the couch next to the phone. I look around and see out of the corner of my eye that my boyfriend, aunt, and uncle are trudging after me. Family! How horrid. The living room is decorated the way the English decorate. A bit lacking in taste. The denial of death and everything bad is evident in the wallpaper, the carpets, the upholstery. Everything covered in little green tendrils and pink flowers, here and there a bluebird or a squirrel.

Motorized drape pulls in the recesses of the windows. Glass figurines on the fake mantelpiece. And in every household of my entire family—both my mother's side and my father's— there's one of those clocks that sounds the top of the hour with bird noises instead of a jingle. Whoever invented that type of clock must be very rich.

They all come in, sit down, and watch me. I like this special role—the lone sufferer. What must be wrong with me for me to like being in this position?

We've lost three children, like in a war. Three in one family. Unless my father calls again with a different report. Otherwise we have to go on the assumption that it's three. Before, there were five children of my mother. Now only two. If the information doesn't change. Is that why she had so many children? I always thought it was low-class. Five kids. Like cats. Out of proportion by today's standards. But maybe my mother suspected there would be an incident like this. Have a bunch of kids so a few are left even if three die. Maybe there was a master plan. Perhaps she's not as low-class as I thought. Maybe she's just better at math than I am.

I dial the number without considering in advance what exactly I will say.

"Hullo?"

She's English and always answers the phone with a friendly English hullo.

"Hi, it's me."

We recognize each other's voice. We have the same voice. When I speak to her on the phone, it feels as if I am talking to myself. Our voices are mirror images. She always used to say this when I was little: "You are just like me. Everyone says so."

How can anyone become someone else? Only by killing that person.

"How are you, Mama? I was so happy when Papa said you were alive. That was the most important thing for me."

Right. Fuck the rest of them. She would probably rather have died if her sons could have lived as a result. But there are no deals to be made. Just coincidence and misfortune.

"I know. Yes. I'm alive." She says this in a strange voice. Has she gone crazy? She sounds very . . . not the way she usually sounds. She's speaking in a different voice. Higher. More shrill. As if everything that happened were hilarious.

"Are you in pain?"

"No, they are giving me painkillers. I burned my feet. I can see it, but I can't feel it. And a vertebra in the middle of my back is broken. Ha."

Wow, she's laughing. She has gone crazy. But I guess that's the very least that would happen after something like this. My own mother is crazy. Or is it just the drugs? Hope so. Painkillers. Psychotropic?

"I don't want to stay here. I told them they need to take me home. They are going to drive me home tomorrow. They're overcrowded here anyway. I'm going home in an ambulance."

"Mama? Are you serious? You can be transported? You'll be home tomorrow?"

"No, not home, you dummy."

Jesus, why is she talking to me like that? She's never called me a dummy before. This word isn't even a part of her vocabulary, as far as I know. She's also speaking to me in German, which she never does. Normally I speak German to her and she answers in English. Normally. But nothing is normal right now. Nothing will be normal again after today.

"They are taking me to the hospital near our house. You know the one I mean? Where Lukas was born."

But Lukas is . . . better change the subject.

"Yes. Aha, that one. Then we'll fly back to Germany tomorrow. So I'm able to be with you."

"But you have to get married. It's no big deal if we're not all there."

"Yeah, we'll get married and then fly back."

My boyfriend looks angrily at me. I press my lips together, open my eyes wide, and shrug my shoulders.

What am I supposed to say? I want to get off the phone. I'm not going to argue with a crazy person. Get married. Sure.

"See you tomorrow, Mama. I'll be there. I'll take care of you tomorrow."

"Have fun tomorrow," she says in a quivering, distant voice. She's aged years. But at least she's high on Ecstasy or something.

I hang up.

My eyes are only half-open. I let out a long, deep sigh. The tension of the last few hours and, most of all, of having to talk to my crazy mother on the phone dissipates. I'm no longer the main focus of pity. Unfortunately. Now that my mother has survived, we all have to look after her. I won't be taking care of myself; I'll be taking care of her. Hold everything. In my head I have to go back and reorient myself. No more taking; giving.

My head starts to spin. I'm drunk. Finally. I want to sleep. One more call. I need to rebook the return flight for tomorrow.

In English I say, "Good evening. We have an emergency. We're a large wedding group. The wedding was supposed to take place tomorrow. But there's been a massive accident on the autobahn. My three brothers are dead. We need to fly back tomorrow to visit the injured in the hospital."

They give us two seats in a plane going first thing in the morning.

My boyfriend's family will have to wait another day for a return flight. He calls and explains it to them. They'll have to kill time in England, in the country near the eastern coast. All they have with them are nice party clothes. Nobody thought about having to attend a funeral. I don't believe in funerals anyway. Load of nonsense. We don't believe in Christ, after all. We believe only in Coincidence.

They'll just have to go for walks or whatever it is people do when a wedding is canceled. I can't take care of them. They are all still alive. They are adults and they'll just have to figure things out for themselves. There's nothing else I can do.

We lie down in the guest room. Here everything is dark purple, even the toilet paper in the bathroom. We stare at the ceiling, wiped out from dealing with the good and bad news. We don't say a word. Then we fall asleep. There's nothing either of us can do for the other. I noticed that the first day. It's every man for himself.

That's when it started. Working through everything alone. The various ways of mourning. The disgust at the other person's mourning. Grief doesn't bring you together. It splits you apart. We aren't holding together, we're pulling apart.

We are awoken with tea at our bedside.

"Morning. Wakey, wakey!" Everyone in our family says that when they wake someone up. "We have to leave for the airport soon."

Headache. Fucking alcohol. Can't someone invent something that you drink with alcohol to eliminate the hangover? Mankind is still super primitive, when you think about it.

Neither of us showers. In a situation like this, you have to stick to the basics. We stay in the same clothes we fell asleep in and eat an unhealthy English breakfast. Toast with salty butter and marmalade that has more sugar than fruit. Sweets for breakfast. Disgusting.

My uncle is usually a funny guy. In every family photo he's holding a can of beer in one hand and flipping the bird with the other. He's laughing loudly and belching. You can't tell that from the photos, obviously, but I know he burped in each picture because I'm usually standing next to him when we take pictures. And in the photos his mouth is wide open. He is able to belch on command and always manages to burp as the flash of the camera goes off. Not everyone can do that. Today, however, he is silent as he drives. He's most likely thinking of his big sister, my mother, who lost three children yesterday. Yesterday? Yes, yesterday. My sense of time is totally off. It'll never get back to normal. That's what happens with a tragedy like this. It opens a wound in your soul, even if there is no such thing as a soul. How should you describe it? Your heart? Your psyche? In any event, it creates such a huge wound that you are never able to believe any time has passed since the tragedy. And the wound never heals. It hurts just as bad today as it did in the car that first day on the way to the airport with my almost husband and my uncle.

He drops us in front of the airport. We check in and sit down in the boarding area. My phone rings.

It's a number I don't recognize. It could be my mother's hospital, or my father calling from a Belgian phone booth. Who knows.

"Hello?"

"Hello, am I speaking to Elizabeth Kiehl?"

"Yes."

"This is Herr Paulsen, from the newspaper *Druck*. I'm sorry, Frau Kiehl, to have to tell you this. You're going to have to be strong. There's been an accident and three of your brothers are dead. A comment, please?"

I take the phone away from my ear. I don't say a word. I'm smart. I want to react correctly. When do you ever have a chance to say that? My boyfriend asks who it is, what's going on. I have a strange look on my face again. I must look weird, given the way he is looking at me. We are sitting next to each other in the waiting area. I have to think. I put my finger in front of my lips so my boyfriend doesn't say anything more. This beast, this evil incarnate, will not get any more information about us. I look at my phone—he's still on the line. I can't believe what is happening here. I'm more outraged than I've been in my entire life. The rage is just as great today as it was in that moment. A newspaper, a person, who makes out as if he is doing a job, takes the liberty of calling me in this situation. And to top it off, he thinks that he is breaking the news to me, that he is the *first* to tell me. Getting me on the phone for a story to publish, based on violating the lowest moment of my entire life. This pig is trying to do the work normally reserved for the police or, in my case, my father. But not to be helpful. To make money.

I stare at the display on my phone. The person on the other end hears nothing except my boyfriend whispering at regular intervals to ask what is going on. It's freaking him out that I'm taking so long to answer. This is how they get their stories! Every day something new. That's how they fill their pages. At that moment I knew I wanted to stay on the side of goodness and fight evil. These are evil, depraved people. All of them. They profit daily from this method of work. No decency, no morality, no respect for people's grief. No respect for pain.

I'm the type of person to get revenge. And I'll definitely get revenge for this. Of that I'm sure. Revenge against the people responsible for making this phone call. Revenge against the people who make money from this sort of call. The ones who've gotten rich off it. Who probably present themselves as good

Christians. They've stepped over a line. And this isn't the end of it. This invasion into our lives and our grief for the sake of a story had only just begun. An enemy was born. And so was an embittered warrior. A woman warrior. Track them down and smoke them out of their holes.

I push the glowing red button as if it's the trigger for a bomb.

Call ended. It's what every single person should do when these vermin call. That would quickly take care of the problem. Cut them off, shun them. That would be a peaceful solution. There wouldn't be any more stories about dead children, cancer, alcoholism, divorce, bankruptcy. The only reason there are things to publish is because so many people talk to them. Why doesn't everyone just shut up?

Just hang up. Like I did. It wasn't tough. Open your mouth and you have no one to blame but yourself. "No comment" will still get published. You've helped them even by saying that much. It's easy to do the right thing if you stop to think about it for a second. Every single reader who buys a copy of that newspaper and gives a few cents to them every day is complicit in the phone call made to me that day. The only things that truly speak to them are numbers in the red—the only feelings they have are in their wallets.

I explain to my boyfriend what just happened. That they found out about it. That they got hold of my number somehow. I'm not in the phone book. Someone who knows me personally must have given them the number to be able to make the call. Of course I'll never find out who it was. That's not something people brag about—selling somebody out, throwing someone to the wolves at a time when that person really needs peace and time to recover. I curse whoever it was. Though I don't know the details, I know the accident was the result of some sort of human error. Accidents are always the result of human error—that's why they call them accidents. The phone call was something purposeful. Which makes my rage that much greater. And now it's a race against time, to try to stay ahead of other calls. I ring all my relatives, and they all express their condolences. How do you reply to that? Thank you? Same to you? Why don't they teach that in school? In German, when relatives of yours die, people say to you, "Deepest sympathy," to which you're supposed to answer, "Deepest sympathy to you, as well." Sounds too stiff. I decide to say, "You, too." It's a bit less formal. Not so ponderous, not so stiff.

Once that's taken care of, I explain to each relative that I've just been pestered by someone who probably considers himself a journalist but whom we will refer to henceforth in our family as the rapist reporter scum. I tell them that they should just hang up without saying a single word, not even "no comment." That anything they say can only hurt us and play into the hands of those who want to exploit the situation. I get everyone in line. Our family is going to be threatened. Our peace is going to be threatened. Our grief is going to come under attack.

It's finally quiet on the airplane. I hold my boyfriend's hand and, for the first time in my life, worry that I could die in a plane crash. Not my boyfriend. Just me. I think how awful it would be for my mother. She can't lose another child before she herself dies. Three is enough. I consider myself my mother's property now—I have to make sure I don't go missing. Not because of me, my boyfriend, or our life. That, at some point, with luck, will be okay again and halfway normal. Because of my mother. My mother can't go through anything bad again. I have to make sure of that.

I grip his hand tightly and stare at the EMERGENCY EXIT sign two rows in front of us. I run through a water landing in my head—how I'll hop over those two rows to be the first one out. I don't mention anything about the plan to my boyfriend. It would be too difficult for us to do it together. I have to stay unencumbered, flexible. Have to be the first one out so my mother doesn't have to deal with an even bigger body count. Because of the accident, I've learned how quickly life can end, and I want to keep that from happening. I don't want to live for myself. I live for my mother now.

I'm cold and covered in sweat when we land. I was sure for the entire flight that we were going to crash. In my head I'd already said my good-byes to everyone. I wrote my will in my head as well, despite the fact that I have virtually nothing to pass on. With our new wedding luggage, bought for happy times, we drive to the hospital my mother mentioned on the phone. There we meet three fathers, each of whom has lost his only son. Meaning that on the fathers' side of the family there are six grieving grandparents. My leftover sister is also at the hospital. I have to keep going over who is dead and who is alive. I can't get it through my head. My fourteen-year-old sister, Emily, and I are alive. There's just two of us. Dead: Harry, twenty-four; Lukas, nine; Paul, six.

We hug each other in front of the hospital. I laugh because I'm so glad to see them. We've already expressed our condolences on the phone. They all say how sorry they are that the wedding had to be canceled. My sister, who is also standing there in front of me, was also invited, of course. She was going to fly over to England today. Right. The wedding was supposed to be today. Today. If the worst thing ever to happen to us hadn't put an end to everything. I hope it remains the worst thing ever to happen to us and that nothing worse comes along. I look at my watch. I would have been married four hours from now. I look at my boyfriend from the side. I can't believe it—all that planning for nothing. I love him. Will we try it again? Or stay unmarried forever? Fear starts to creep up my chest and take my breath away as I imagine having to plan another wedding and then having to find out I've lost more family members traveling to it. And in my family weddings always involve traveling. People have to come from all over the place. Or I guess we could just do something by ourselves. Then nobody would have to come—and nobody would have to die on the way.

It's the middle of summer. We sit down on the lawn in front of the hospital and wait for our mother. I'm worried that she may look badly disfigured. What do people look like after a mass accident? No idea. I'll just assume the worst. Two of the three fathers went to look at the cleared accident site yesterday. They have a lot of new information about how it could have happened. From what they say, together with the information from the two survivors—my mother and Rhea—and the police, I will eventually assemble the following mosaic image of the accident:

They left right after I tried on the wedding dress—which I wasn't supposed to do. I'm not superstitious. But after something like this, it takes a lot of work not to become superstitious! Since I tried on the dress, I feel responsible for everything that happened afterward. And they drove only because my dress was so big. So actually I'm directly responsible. You don't have to be superstitious to see that. My oldest brother let his girlfriend sit in front because he's a gentleman. They're having fun in the car. Singing songs, the kids constantly asking questions about the wedding. My mother explains to them that they will all be wearing the matching shirts we picked out together. It's very hot that morning and they take their shoes off during the drive—boat moccasins with little tassels, they look as if they could have been handcrafted by Indians. I saw them on their feet before I left my mother's house. She drove the speed limit in Belgium: 120 kilometers per hour. She hadn't had a drop to drink. And she never talked on the phone while driving with the children in the car. That's important for the retrospective question of responsibility. On the day of days—that is, yesterday—my mother is driving through Belgium with the boys and my oldest brother's girlfriend, on their way to the Eurotunnel. There's a lot of traffic on the autobahn, but it's moving. On the opposite side of the road, she can see a traffic jam building. The driver of a tanker truck full of gasoline doesn't notice the traffic slowing in front of him in time. It could be that he fell asleep at the wheel for a second or that he just wasn't paying attention. Maybe he dropped a cigarette in his lap and burned his balls. But he, too, was sober. He's heading full speed into the stopped cars. Without braking. The drivers at the back of the traffic jam see him approaching in their rearview mirrors. But they get lucky. The truck driver jerks his steering wheel to the left just before he hits the line of stopped traffic. The tanker clips a full bus, and the two vehicles—the tanker and the bus—shoot across the median strip and form a wall across the other side of the autobahn in front of the oncoming traffic. Which is right where my family is driving, in the slow lane. "Lucky Man," by the Verve, is playing on the stereo of my mother's car. Cars plow into the bus and tanker, flipping them on their sides. The passengers in my mother's car see the wall they are suddenly headed for and start to scream. Impact. My mother doesn't even have a chance to hit the brakes. Three inches. Between the gas pedal and the brake pedal.

Silence. For a long time. Rhea, my brother's girlfriend, is the first to regain consciousness. The airbags are lying on the dashboard. She doesn't look to her left. She just sits there. She can't hear anything. Silence. Just a whooshing noise in her head. Everything is in slow motion. She opens her door and wants to get out. She collapses. She can't stand up because her legs are smashed. She lies on the ground next to the car and crawls a few meters away from it on her stomach, like the sick gorillas in the mist in that movie we had to watch when we were way too young, in the hope that we would become animal researchers or environmentalists. She reaches the grass of the shoulder and lies there. She turns her head from right to left and watches what is happening around her. She sees lots of cars driving around the mess rather than stopping to help. I don't want to belong to a species capable of that. There are lots of dead and lots of injured. The families in the tour bus have kicked a hole in a window and are crawling out one by one.

At some point after Rhea is out, my mother wakes up. She also sits there at first. That's what happens in an extreme state of shock. You don't do anything. You're limited to the most minimal things. Your brain doesn't function right. Your heart beats, but nothing more.

She sits and sits. She wonders about the silence in the car. She doesn't turn around. She doesn't look at her children. She's not a mother anymore, not capable of taking care of her children. She can't even save herself. She's like a badly injured animal. She doesn't look over to the right, either, where Rhea was. Though that would be an easier motion than turning her head around to look at her children. She just sits there and tries to comprehend what just happened. For several minutes.

Someone rips open the door. It's the driver of another car snared in the accident. Not the cause of the accident—he died instantly. This other driver puts his strong arms under my mother's arms.

It's the only way he can carry her. She's too heavy for him. The contents of the tanker are spilling out; hundreds of liters of gasoline now form a gleaming puddle beneath all the wrecked cars. Some flames have broken out from short circuits in the Belgian street lamps knocked over in the median strip. The other driver drags my mother like a sack through the flames on the ground. Everything is burning now. Everywhere dense smoke and the stench and screams of death.

He lays her on the side of the road with all the other injured and dead.

She says to him slowly, "My children, my children are still in the car."

He turns to go back to get them.

But just then everything spews into the air in front of him. A huge explosion.

She knows she has lost her children.

She saw them go up in flames. With her own eyes.

There is another explosion and another. The gas tanks of all the cars are blowing up, one after the next.

The people who were able to escape from the tour bus give my mother first aid. They douse her feet, which are burned to the bone, with cola, Fanta, and apple juice, to cool them. The doctor later said that it helped a lot. It would have been much worse for her otherwise.

In my mind, the worst thing of all is that none of us knows whether my brothers were still alive when they went up in flames or whether they had already been killed by the impact. It sounds macabre, but that's the way it is. I've hoped for eight years now that the impact was intense enough to break all three of their necks and that they weren't still aware as they were being engulfed in flames. The question haunts me daily. During the day, and at night, in my dreams. I'll never know. There will never be an answer. Because my mother didn't turn around. Frau Drescher says it could be that she did but that she lied to us all to avoid having to describe what she saw. Or what she saw was so bad that her brain erased it so she wouldn't become even crazier. Brains know what their owners can take and what they can't.

We sit in the sun and wait for my mother. My horror-movie mother. I'm terrified to see her. I'm afraid my pretty mother is no longer pretty. She's usually so well kempt. But not now, I'm sure. Don't give yourself hope, Elizabeth. She's almost certainly going to look awful, and you can't let her realize it. You can do it.

A nurse emerges from the hospital building and beckons us to come in. Mother has arrived. She has her own room because of the severity of the accident. I knew it. Because she's lost three children, she doesn't have to share a room with some random idiot. Great. Thank you, dear hospital! The nurse tells us that my mother has been here for a little while and has been examined. The doctor will want to talk to me soon. With me? Why? Oh, God, what does he want from me? We'll see.

Elizabeth, you have to be brave. Things are going to come at you that you don't understand. My knowledge of this kind of stuff is limited to things in movies Mother showed me. Maybe that's why she showed them to us? So I could get through all of this and help her in this situation? It's possible. Can't put anything past her. She always seems to have a master plan—an evil one, but a plan nonetheless. The nurse whispers to us in front of the door marked 322 that we shouldn't be surprised if she acts a little strange. Huh? Stranger than usual? They have her on strong psychotropic drugs, so she doesn't understand that she has lost her sons yet. She hasn't realized yet. The drugs ensure that the blinds are drawn in her head and that comprehension of what's happened seeps slowly into her consciousness only a few days later.

She doesn't know yet?

Aha. Good to know. Man, this is all crazy. There are drugs that make it as if my brothers are still alive? Why can't I get some, instead of only my mother? I don't want to go into the room. I don't want to deal with a burned mother. It's all too much for me.

Nobody says, "Come in." She's lying there, very small in the big bed, sleeping. Good. I can get used to the view first without her seeing from the shocked look on my face how shitty she looks. Her entire face is laced with bloody cuts. Aha, must be from the windshield. All the cuts go in one direction. As if Freddy from *Nightmare on Elm Street* had said a quick hello.

She has a swollen black eye and a stitched-up wound on her head. From the steering wheel or dashboard, no doubt. But the worst thing—something I hadn't anticipated at all—is that her beautiful, long blonde hair has been fried into short, thick, charred dreadlocks. The heat. It hadn't occurred to me. Hair evidently melts the way you would expect a plastic wig to. It will all have to be shaved off. There's no way it's ever going to look right.

She opens her eyes and smiles at us. The look on her face is pained. Her eyes are open wider than usual. Like a hunted animal. Yes. I can tell that her subconscious already knows what happened.

She says, "What can I say? I don't know what to say. What are you all looking at? Cut it out. Did you get married, my child?"

She smiles like a crazy person.

Everyone in the room visibly tenses as she asks the question. My leftover sister and I—that's what we are, leftovers—go over to her bed and lay our heads on her chest, gingerly, so as not to cause her pain.

"Yes, Mama, we got married."

Why not? She's on drugs, so I can tell her what she wants to hear. It doesn't matter. I can always say she misunderstood because of the medicine.

"I'm happy for you." She looks at my boyfriend. "For both of you. I'm happy for both of you. Now you'll have to quickly have three children."

Aaah. Help. I thought she didn't know yet, or didn't know anymore, because of the drugs. It would appear they don't work perfectly.

I stroke her hand. It's also covered with cuts, like her face, also from the windshield. Her whole body appears to be battered.

I look her in the face again. Her eyes are closed. Her breathing is agitated.

We all start to creep out of this room of horror. As we sneak out on tiptoes, in exaggerated slow motion, we can't resist giggling. We quickly turn around to see whether it's woken her up. Nope. On we go. Out of there.

In the hallway we meet the attending physician. He looks at me the entire time he speaks. I'm the older of us two remaining siblings. And my mother is no longer together with any of the men present. That means I am the next of kin and the contact person for all the shit coming down the pike.

"Frau Kiehl, we've given your mother her own room since it will be a difficult awakening process when we slowly reduce the psychotropic medication and she realizes, step-by-step, that she has lost three children. She was driving the car. Even though she isn't legally responsible for the accident, she will blame herself. It's possible that it will be so bad that she will try to kill herself. Please stay with her day and night for the next few weeks and make sure she doesn't attempt to take her own life."

Got it. I have a new job. My heroic duty: keep Mother from killing herself. Will do, no problem. I can handle it.

"We're going to place another bed in the room for you to use. That's the psychological situation. Now the bodily situation. Her feet are extremely badly burned. She has to be brushed every second day to avoid the formation of scar neoplasms. They would affect her range of motion later on. She'll have to deal with incredible pain. When we brush the open wounds with the rough bristles we'll put her under general anesthesia. But afterward it's going to be bad for her. Once the anesthesia wears off, we won't be able to suppress a hundred percent of the pain. It's going to be very unpleasant for your mother, and it would be good if you were with her at these times. She won't be able to get up for a long time—for one thing because of her feet, of course, but also because of her broken vertebra. The vertebrae will have to grow back together, and until they do we'll have to keep your mother still. We believe that one of the children in the backseat must have been launched through the front seat and caused the fracture of her spine with his skull."

Now here is a piece of evidence. This means that at least one of the children, you would think, was already dead before he was burned in the flames.

Or at least unconscious.

"That's what we have at our end. If you have questions, please feel free."

We all look at one another and shake our heads.

Thanks. See you later.

I want to be alone. I tell the relatives—which since yesterday includes my boyfriend, too—that I'm going to walk the two kilometers home. Alone. To go and pack some things so I can stay overnight at the hospital. They should stay here and keep an eye on Mother. I take off. Out into the fresh air. I march along the sidewalk as if I'm on the run. This feeling will never leave me. I do everything quickly so I have as little capacity as possible for painful thoughts. I'm moving into a hospital. I'm afraid of spending the night there with my mother. I don't want to be there when she becomes lucid again.

I picture her opening her eyes and screaming, grabbing onto me, crying, begging for it not to be true, for them to come back, for us to turn back time so she can set off a few minutes earlier and pass the site of the accident before it happens, for my dress to be a little smaller and more modest so I can fit it in my suitcase and we can all fly together. In a safe plane. She grips me tightly and pulls me down with her into madness.

Out of love, I go with her, down, down, out of life. Into darkness. I hope it happens during the daytime, when others are around. I shudder at the thought of the gaps in her comprehension closing and her realizing three of her children are dead. I suspect I'll need help. I'm not going to get through all of this alone. Why does she get medication while I don't? I'd love to be medicated into peacefulness. I need to find a therapist. I'm falling apart. And now I'm going to spend weeks and weeks looking after my suicidal mother. I'm out of luck. She's suffered the greater sorrow. Out of all of us. I just lost my brothers. Which is worse? Losing your children, of course. And the men have each lost only one son. Which is worse? Losing three children. None of us were there, either. Which is worse? Being there. So we'll focus our efforts entirely on the mother who has lost three children. Nobody can complain about that. It's also why we won't get any drugs. Simple as that.

I don't want to talk about the whole thing with my boyfriend or the three assembled fathers. Or with my own father. I want to talk to a professional. Somebody who has studied the shit I'm going to have to get through. Somebody who can help me deal with it. So that I come out of it a tolerable human being. So that I survive it. With these thoughts in my head and my purposeful gait, I reach home in record time. The place where I live with my boyfriend is nearby. Thank God I don't have to go to my mother's house. Three kids' rooms are empty there now. Forever. That's where all the relatives who are coming from England will have to sleep. All the people coming to support us. Now, to support my mother, not us! It's like the wedding, only the other way around. We were all there, for a happy occasion. Now all of them are here, for a tragic occasion. Wedding, funeral.

My mother will probably leave the rooms exactly as my brothers left them. The way they always do in the movies. Then my mother will sit around on one of their beds each day, hold a baseball bat in her hands, and cry. Except that none of my brothers played baseball. The whole family is against all things American. We're anti-American. We're against war, the death penalty, obesity, Monsanto, Exxon. In our family, America represents only bad. Yeah, yeah, all the things that go through your head. A wedding and three funerals. And I'm right in the middle of it. I cannot fucking believe it.

I run into our apartment and pack the essentials. My body is working surprisingly well given all that's happened. It is acting as if things will go on as usual. I'm functioning; my body is doing things and following orders. Well, yes, though not much more than that. My brain is trailing way behind—it's still somewhere in England. Or is it still in Belgium, on the autobahn?

I think back over all I know about the accident, going over it all until I feel sick. Until I feel almost as if I was there but was unable to do anything. I couldn't help. My little brothers! Nobody saved them. I just watch the images in my head and imagine with horror what it must be like to be burned alive because you haven't been pulled to safety. Because people drive past or exit the autobahn to avoid being caught in a traffic jam. Because they don't want to be late to some unimportant appointment. For that they leave children to die in tin cans filling with flames.

Who knows? Maybe if more people had helped, they could have been pulled out of the car. Dead or alive.

At least then we would háve had bodies for the funeral. What are we going to bury now? I hadn't thought about it up to this point. I envy everyone who loses someone and has a dead body to touch. To better understand. So the crippled brain can understand the person is dead. Life will not return to this life-less corpse. Never. Look at it, touch it. The body is stiff and yellowing and as cold to the touch as a dead chicken from the freezer. I'd love to have that. Having to say good-bye without a body is playing tricks on my brain. I don't want to accept the inevitable and instead try to fool myself into believing that if no bodies have been found, it's still possible they are alive. Maybe they saved themselves. Got out of the car before the big explo-sion and ran into the woods. Who knows? It's possible! Rhea managed to open the door and crawl out. Maybe they did, too, before my mother was taken out.

They are living in the forest in Belgium, with all the animals that have yet to be brutally run over by the car owners of ever-advancing economic growth. The accident took a lot out of them, of course, and they've been crazy since; they can't remember any-thing about the accident or their life before it. My oldest brother is the leader and looks out for the littler ones. For the child who had been sitting behind my mother—I don't know which one it was—the big brother cobbled together something out of leaves and branches for him to wear during the day since his skull was fractured by the impact with my mother's seat back and her hard backbone. But it slowly grows back together thanks to my brother's serviceable headgear. The little brother frequently has bad headaches as a result, though. The three of them figure out that if he chews the bark of a certain tree, however, it relieves the pain. They eat berries and sprouts, like the Indians, living in harmony with nature. They are naked and dirty and have long hair. Since the accident they've all lost their voices and communicate with looks. They understand one another perfectly, though—they are survivors. What else do they need to communicate? They've leaned a long tree limb against the trunk of a tree and then collected hundreds of smaller limbs and leaned them against the limb to create a big lean-to, where they sleep. They cover the lean-to with soft moss and leaves so it's watertight and warm in their shelter. They pad the floor with dried moss. And they have everything they need to live. They drink from a little brook that runs through the woods. They gather berries of a certain type. One of them tries a few while the others watch to see whether the tester's face changes color or his skin or pupils show a reaction. If he gets sick they know that type of berry is poisonous for people, and they help him throw up with the aid of a stick they find in the woods and use just for this purpose.

When, using this method, they find berries that are edible in each season, they collect far more of them than they can eat and dry them in their lean-to for the winter. One of them must stay with the berries because the birds and squirrels are direct competitors for the same food. Whenever my brothers fail to be vigilant, their food stores are pilfered. The animals of the forest are smart enough to realize it takes less energy to steal than to gather their own.

They've set up a monetary system between the three of them. If one of them finds something interesting and another wants to buy it, they need something to exchange. So they came up with their own currency. I'm sure the idea came from my money-crazy oldest brother. They creep out near the autobahn at night and collect shards of broken glass from bottles thrown there by people in cars. Their favorite is blue glass. Blue shards are the most valuable in the country where they live. Next come green shards, then brown, and the least valuable shards are clear. They polish the jagged edges down using rocks so that the pieces can be held comfortably in the hand. The noise made by rubbing the glass against stone is almost unbearable, and they laugh uneasily about it and hum loudly; they don't know the name of it, but the song they are humming is "Lucky Man," by the Verve.

With the rounded shards of glass they pay one another and hoard their treasures. That's how they live, day in and day out. Life is a bit more trying in winter, but they prepare for it. The skull of the one who was behind Mother—why don't I know who it was? This piece of information is missing from my mosaic. I can't ask anyone else who was there. I've cut off contact with the two survivors, Mother and Rhea. In any event, the skull heals slightly askew. My brother can feel the bump of bone through his long, dirty, matted hair. But he's happy that the headaches stopped after a few years.

Yep, that's the way it is in the Belgian forest. And nobody can prove otherwise. Because nobody can show me the dead bodies. Because there is nothing left for the funeral.

Or is there no funeral when there's nothing left after a flaming inferno? Really, we've already conducted the cremation—there on the autobahn. We've just done without the crematorium. And nobody collected the ashes. Right? Did they just blow away? Where? Or did the ash stick to the tires of a car driving past or to corpses—in open wounds? In the hair of the firemen? Did they wash my brothers down the drain with men's shampoo after they finished putting out the burning cars? Were the ashes swept up when the sanitation workers cleared the accident site? Just before they reopened the road? Together with the glittering shards of shattered windshields, scattered pieces of clothing, bandages, and medical tape, panels of cars, forgotten stuffed animals and kids' toys? Everything in a big pile in the emergency lane. And then the carefree drive continued for those stuck in traffic during the cleanup.

Since the accident, I'm the only one who drives. That is, I never let myself be driven by anyone else. I feel as if everyone else drives worse than I do. I haven't become a nervous driver since then. Not frightened or tense. Just very careful. I drive defensively, always on the lookout. I try to anticipate all the craziness of other drivers. It's up to me to get everyone in my car safely to their destination. A task my mother was unable to accomplish. It's my duty. If I am a passenger, I can't take it for long. Every time we go on vacation, I drive the entire way, regardless of how many hours the trip takes. And anyone who doesn't like it can't come with me. I convince myself that I pay more attention than anyone else because I know just how quickly things can happen.

I count all the dead animals along the road. They are like my brothers: innocent little creatures. Anyone who drives is potentially complicit in the deaths of other people. Since the accident, I notice all the signs of other accidents. I'm haunted by accidents. Not just ours, but all of the accidents I see evidence of. The places along the autobahn where the police have sprayed paint to mark the scene of an accident, the scrapes and dents on people's bumpers, the long skid marks on the asphalt. I see it all and try to imagine who died and whether someone left children behind—which makes it worse. The rules of life must not be broken. And one of them is that parents die before their children. That is the correct order. And everyone should die a natural death. Meaning they should fall asleep and their heart should just stop beating—once they've reached an advanced age. For me, cancer at an old age is okay as well. Alzheimer's, Parkinson's—hey, we all have to die of something. That's just the way it is. But children should not die before their parents, and definitely not in a car accident, car catastrophe. Ripped from life. Without any good-bye. That is brutal. On an ordinary trip on the autobahn I usually count about four dead barn owls, two hawks, one fox, and two cats. I don't really care about domestic animals. They belong to someone. They get fed. They are not stand-ins for my brothers. But the wild animals pull at my heartstrings when I see them lying there dead. They are proof to me that driving is wrong. That the whole thing is wrong. The fact that we've built autobahns through the forest in order to get to places faster strikes me as a huge mistake. The animals were there first. They run around in the woods and don't know how to get across the street alive. Six lanes of cars racing by. Some of them going more than 200 kilometers per hour. I always hope that they will wrap themselves around the support beam of an overpass—without hurting anyone else—before they gash a huge hole in some family because they are so damn important and in such a hurry. Speed kills. People and animals. Though I care less and less about people. Most of them deserve the worst. I feel sorry for the animals. They haven't evolved to the point where they understand that some cars drive too fast. Sometimes I'd rather die than live among these people- and animal-killing speed demons. A momentary lapse of concentration, a slight oversight, and *boom*, it's too late—a catastrophe that destroys an entire family. I hurriedly march back to my wounded mother in the hospital. I have a duty: to take care of her.

I arrive at my mother's hospital room totally out of breath. Maybe I overdid it a little, walking so fast in the bright summer sun. But since that day, I stay in constant motion. Sitting around hurts. Having time to reflect hurts. Staying on the run makes things bearable. Later on, when I go to yoga classes, I love doing all the poses and getting my heart beating until I am more body than mind—that feels good. But when you're supposed to relax at the end of class, I get up and leave instead. The instructor can't expect that of me—to lie there as if nothing bad ever happened. It's always the accident. It still follows me eight years on, and even now I cannot tolerate moments of peace and quiet because the images of my brothers flood back into my mind, images of the hellish pain they must have endured before they died. Then comes the unbearable guilt about the fact that I am alive and they are not.

Mother is sleeping. I sit down on the bed in which I will spend the next few weeks sleeping. Like an old woman I hold my handbag in my lap. I hide behind the bag. I'm afraid of my mother; I'm afraid of my dead brothers; I'm afraid of feeling guilty for being alive.

When I fall in love with something, I feel bad that they no longer can. When I celebrate some success at work, I'm consumed by guilt. They had their entire lives ahead of them and would certainly have enjoyed many successes and had a lot to celebrate. But they never will. While I can. And that suffocates me. If I make a lot of money I can celebrate it only halfheartedly. My brother, the oldest, the one closest to me in age, loved money. He always missed his rich father—whom my mother, as always, left for the next man, for whatever reason. My brother loved money—as I did—because for us it represented our father.

My most vivid memory of my oldest brother is when he and my mother went to the bank to withdraw a sum of money my mother needed to buy a used car. She wanted to buy the car in cash. My brother begged my mother to let him take the money out of the envelope. Five thousand marks. Smiling, she let him. He spread the bills into a fan in his hand and fanned himself. He insisted that my mother take a picture of him. And he hung a print of that photo above his bed. Standing there with a massive amount of money in his hands with a wide grin on his face. We gave him a hard time about that picture. But he never backed down about his love for money. He was Mr. Bling in our family. Though I'm probably just as obsessed with money as he was, I can hide it better. Which is probably why I gave him a hard time about it. Because it was something about myself I didn't think was good. It's looked down upon in our society to be obsessed with money. Despite the fact that the entire fucking system is built on it.

When we were allowed to see our father and he took us out to a restaurant—something that seemed ridiculously extravagant to us at the time—my brother, my dead brother, would make a scene until he was permitted to see the bill at the end of the meal. My father tried in vain to teach him that it was bad manners to want to know how much the bill was when somebody else was paying. But my brother never gave in. For him, it was important that my father had a lot of purchasing power. He always looked at the bill, and from the sound he made you could tell he thought the sum was sky-high. Then, once appeased, he would look at our father with wonder in his eyes. I always rolled my eyes and acted as if I thought the whole thing was embarrassing. But looking back now, I'm sure I would have demanded to see the bill, too, if he hadn't done it for me.

Sitting on the bed, I feel as if I'm in prison. I get short of breath. It's all too much. These fits of short breathing have followed me since the day of the accident, too. The accident is the defining moment of my life. I describe all the minute details of that day to everyone I've gotten to know since then—everyone who has come to mean anything to me, that is. That way everybody knows how significant the accident is to me, my life, my psyche, my character, my fears, my worries.

A nurse enters the room. She puts a cup with a pill in it on the nightstand next to my mother's bed and whispers to me that she needs to take it to make the transition to general anesthesia easier. Okay, I'll see to it. She's about to be taken to have her leg wounds brushed. Right, that's what they call it here. Some kind of euphemism. What the doctor described to me earlier this afternoon—ripping off the healing scabs to avoid the formation of scar neoplasms or whatever they are.

All the things you have to deal with when you've barely flown the nest.

I sit there and stare at my mother, waiting for her to open her eyes. A new fear starts to well up in me. All of a sudden I notice the IV tube in her hand—there's a cannula attached to the back of her hand. I see the fluid dripping slowly, but there are also air bubbles in the tube. They're going into her vein. Obviously. Otherwise the fluid wouldn't serve any purpose. But can't you die from getting air in your veins or in your blood? Isn't it a method of killing someone you see all the time on TV shows—a way to murder someone without getting caught? I ask the nurse as she's walking out whether it's dangerous for air to be going into her vein. My mother's not a balloon. The nurse laughs and says you'd need a meter of air uninterrupted to cause problems. I thank her, though I bet there's a meter of air in there already, even if it is broken up. I'm going to keep an eye on it. I'm not going to let my mother die now from some screwup in the hospital. I'm going to have to watch everything like a hawk.

The nurse's laugh wakes up my mother. I stand up, put my bag on my bed, and go over to her. I hold out the cup with the pill in it and explain that she needs to take it before she is put under. They're about to do the thing with her feet. She starts jabbering about how they shouldn't mess around with it, they should leave the bandages alone. I tell her with my usual directness that they can't leave it alone. That otherwise the dressing will be stuck to her feet. That it has to be refreshed every two days. And that the scabs have to be rubbed off. It sounds awful, but she has to get through it. Our roles have reversed. I speak to her as if she were a child and I were the mother.

She listens to her daughter-mother. She pops the pill into her mouth and looks up at the ceiling. She has changed so much. Unbelievable. I can hardly believe it's even her. Did my old mother get burned up in the car with my brothers, perhaps? Did she go with them somehow? Is it possible? Has she lost part of herself? Or is it just the drugs? We will see. Time will tell. The nurse comes in again and pushes my mother out of the room on her bed. She bumps into the door frame. It annoys me. "Please be careful, okay?" She pushes the bed the rest of the way out. Treat my child properly!

I'm alone. I hate being alone. I walk around the hospital looking for my relatives. More and more are arriving by the hour. Soon the entire family will be here. Just three brothers missing. Otherwise we could get married right here. They tell me they've ordered pizza for us and that they want to eat in Mother's room. And they have plastic bags filled with cans of beer. From the gas station on the corner. Nice. Finally, anesthesia for me. We dance on the graves of my brothers with pizza and beer. Food, finally. I'm hungry. Yes. I notice now how hungry I am. I guess I am still here—at least I feel the sensation of hunger. The relatives sit on my bed and on the floor. It's fun to be with all of them. Because we're all together, which is rare, and today was supposed to be the day of the wedding, it almost seems like the wedding reception. Just a little change of plans: it's in a hospital. As if there was a minor hiccup and we had the wedding here in the hospital as a result. We laugh and sing. We are like chickens whose heads have been chopped off, running around for a last few minutes before the news of the accident sinks in.

The accident finally put my family over the edge. The family was already screwed up, wrecked, probably beyond repair, but the accident was its death knell. Nobody kept in touch with anybody else afterward. That's the way psychology is. Crazy.

When Mother returns, we're already tipsy from all the beer. She is still asleep at first, but as she slowly wakes up and the anesthesia wears off, the fun is quickly over. She has horrible pain. She screams and shakes, says she's unbearably cold. We all scramble around and manage to get four additional blankets. But it doesn't help. She's cold inside. There's nothing we can do on the outside. She says the same sentence over and over again: "My feet, my feet, they need to leave them alone!" This is what the doctor meant. There are some types of pain you can't entirely control with drugs. And she's going to have to bear that type of pain every two days for who knows how long. I think she's going to go crazy. And I am, too. I'm just like her. We are the same. Your pain is my pain. Mother. I have to take care of you. Take care of you. Maybe I'll just let myself be totally absorbed by you. I don't want to be myself anymore anyway. I don't want to be just myself. I want to merge into you, be absorbed into you. Maybe that way it will hurt less for both of us.

After an hour of anguished screaming that feels like an eternity, she finally quiets down again. She falls asleep out of exhaustion. The relatives have lost their buzz amid all the horror and have to drink themselves back into a haze.

The day slowly comes to an end. The first day of a new life. A life full of fear and guilt. A new life informed by the irrefutable fact that death will soon come to take us all. Every last one of us. And that sheer luck is the only thing that allows you to cheat death for a while and survive. But do I even want to survive? Life is an ordeal. And it hangs precariously from a fine silk thread. Above, a silkworm clings to the ceiling; hanging several meters below am I, wrapped in the thread coming out of the worm's ass. That's the way life looks to me since the accident. For eight years now. And I've aged at least thirty years in those eight.

The relatives head for the house, where there are now three empty rooms, and, knowing them, drink the rest of the night away. They leave me with this thing that used to be my mother, alone for the night in the hospital. It's like a horror movie. We're preprogrammed to think of things that way because of my mother's obsession with movies.

For a long time I can't fall asleep because I'm thinking about what I will do if she realizes what's happened while I am alone with her. I can imagine that she will pull me down into the abyss with her, that she will go crazy and grab hold of me, and that I will sink into the same madness as hers. The ticking time bomb called Mother. I must have fallen asleep at some point, because I am awoken the next morning by my boyfriend.

The moment the accident happened, our love was finished. No couple can withstand something like that. On the way to their own wedding.

He has a copy of the local tabloid in his hand. Has he lost his mind? We are upstanding people with morals! For the most part, anyway. And when it comes to newspapers, always. He seems distraught and motions for me to join him out in the hallway. The mother creature is still asleep. I swing out of bed and walk out with him still in my pajamas. It's clear that it's something to do with the accident. Obviously. What else? I brace myself. But for this, there is no way to prepare yourself.

He hands me the paper, open to a particular page. The pigs have somehow gotten ahold of a photo of the accident site and printed it across an entire half page. I stare at the burned-out car. The contorted steel frame in which my brothers died. I never wanted to see that. But in that second it is burned into my brain forever, thanks to the paper. I don't blame my boyfriend. I need to know what everyone else is seeing. The scene of the crime, photographed for public consumption. What's newsworthy about this image? To me, this is grave robbing. They have stolen something from our family—private thoughts, private images. What the burned-out car they died in looked like is nobody's concern. Nobody's. It's of concern only to the police and, if anyone else, the next of kin. That car is something sacred to me, the final resting place of my brothers. And those pigs have desecrated it. By making it public they have forever besmirched the memory of my brothers. They have violated our family. Nobody should have seen it. You are bad for our country. You act as if you are Christians when you are in fact the opposite. Society should reward you with the utmost disdain for your work. I know that now. I have felt it with my own body. When you humiliate and violate someone who is so wounded and disoriented, you breed your own terrorists. I will get my revenge.

I don't say a word to my boyfriend. I retreat back into myself and swear revenge. I'm not going to drag my boyfriend into it. They will get what's coming to them. I swear to myself there in the hallway that I will not rest until I have killed them for this. After I have stared dumbfounded long enough at the wreck of my mother's car, I notice other details that make me even angrier. I have that rage bottled in a tiny decorative glass vial stored deep inside my heart—the liquid inside is dark green—waiting for a chance to strike back, to return them the favor for what they did to me that day.

There are huge letters on the page. I can't decipher them because I am apoplectic with rage. I am too angry to read. Flames flicker above the giant letters. Some graphic designer did that in the editorial offices yesterday, right after our accident. He sat at his computer and, with his mouse, added flames to each letter. And then he placed the letters above the huge photo of my mother's burned-out car. Come along now, fire. I hope he's proud of his work. Every day I hope that person gets cancer of the hand—of the hand used to operate the mouse that day. Maybe he will get it. I keep hoping so.

That was the first and only day I allowed a relative to throw a single cent into their greedy maws or didn't berate the person afterward for doing so. My boyfriend looks at me oddly. My dear boyfriend. He is totally overwhelmed by the situation.

He can tell I'm cooking something up, but he can't possibly fathom the scale of what I'm envisioning. I fold up the page until it is very small, then go into our room, and put it under the pillow on my bed. It will always be a reminder for me. And sustain my rage until I strike. I will be a hero. I will be a hero. I always wanted to do something heroic. Nice. Now I know what it will be.

The second day of the end of my life has just begun. I share the hospital breakfast with my boyfriend—a coffee and a gray piece of bread topped with a slice of cheese. The nurse says unfortunately they can't bring three breakfasts—everything is accounted for. No problem.

We all take turns keeping watch over my mother. The English relatives want to relieve me. They notice that in focusing on my mother I am underplaying the extent of my own sense of loss. While taking a turn on watch, however, my uncle commits a fatal error. He thinks, *Okay, my sister*—that is, my mother—*is asleep, so I'll go get a quick breath of fresh air, stretch my legs, and grab a cup of coffee from the cafeteria.*

This is a reconstruction of what followed, as I was unfortunately not there to stop it. I would have beaten them black-and-blue, the pigs. Nobody was there to protect my burned, bewildered, pumped-full-of-drugs mother from them. A camera team sneaks into the hospital with their equipment camouflaged with flowers. They go unnoticed by the doorman, somehow find out where my mother is, enter her room, and wake her up. They then maliciously lie to her. Their story goes like this: "We're terribly sorry that you lost your children in the accident. A truck driver was at fault. We're doing a report against trucks on the autobahn because they cause so many problems." With that, they have my poor mother hooked. She sits up in bed and thinks—half-asleep and disoriented as she is from the atrocious accident—that she needs to give an interview to try to prevent any further such accidents. We all know that journalistic ethics are not the hallmark of those types of TV news shows—they are pure blood porn. My mother, an Englishwoman in Germany, never paid much attention to TV in this country and has no idea what these shows are like. She trusts their motives are honorable.

She lets herself be filmed, with cuts and burns on her face, with her wild charred hair, with her knowledge that her boys are dead buried deep in her mind and suppressed by drugs. Before any doctor, clergyman, or relative had a chance, this camera team took the liberty of talking to my mother about her dead children. The doctor had told me it would be many days before they would let anyone talk to her about it. And then they just break into my mother's room and fuck her in her broken soul. And I don't stop it. I put my trust in my uncle and he failed me.

When I return and hear about the invasion, I shout at my mother. "Why did you do it? Why did you speak to them? Why didn't you ring for someone and have them thrown out? Those rapists!"

She says, meekly, "They said they wanted to use their report to prevent more accidents like this from happening in the future."

"Of course they said that—so you would spread your legs for them to fuck you, goddamn it."

I saw the report. Of course there wasn't a single word about measures to prevent accidents on the autobahn. Obviously. Not a fucking word. It was pure emotional porn. Our mother taught us decency. Resist the impulse to gawk, never gloat over the misfortunes of others. Everyone has the choice: be a decent person and don't do these things, or be vile and give in to your lust for lurid things—at the expense of others.

I push away thoughts of the accident. I really need to be careful not to brood over it. It messes me up. And I get demonically aggressive. That's what Frau Drescher says. These days I concentrate on my family. I am done with my mother—outwardly, anyway. I've closed that door. Internally I'll never get rid of her—that's what Frau Drescher says.

Because I hate the way my mother lived her life—particularly before the accident, when I was a child—I obsessively try to be boring and bourgeois. Or stay boring and bourgeois. But without any role model, I have to teach myself how to be that way. Every day I enter new territory, since my mother sent me off without knowing how to stay in one place, how to put down roots, how to stay with one man. How to work at something. To invest yourself in something. I want to provide this knowledge to my child. People say that without roots you can't blossom later on in life. I can't blossom. I'm living proof of that saying. I'm fearful because I have no roots. I'm fearful because I have no past.

What I want for my daughter is for her to have such boring, bourgeois parents that she puts down roots in a home where she thinks, *Man, they're so boring*. And then she can fly the nest. And be happy. And once in a while come home to see her boring, bourgeois parents. For that purpose I forbid myself to do lots of things I'd like to do: taking drugs, drinking myself stupid, fucking around, partying, and, first and foremost, dying. Maybe once she is able to get by without me. I should never have been allowed to have her. It was a huge mistake. It was clear to me even back then that I would go out by my own hand. But I wanted a child as a replacement for my ailing mother. I wanted that so badly. And now I am totally devoted to her; I love her above all else. Even though she has ruined my life and sucked all the vitality out of me like an egotistical baby bird. And makes it incredibly difficult for me to check out. To fulfill my plan. When is the right time? When does a child no longer need her mother? Or no longer need her too much? When can I kill myself and perhaps take a few others with me?

*   *   *

After I've dropped off my daughter at her father's place and distributed the antiworm medication—with explicit instructions about how to use it—I have to drive quickly to therapy. But not too quickly. Never faster than the speed limit. Whenever I'm behind the wheel I think about the way my life would be affected if I hit someone while I was speeding—how all the relatives would get the news from the police that their family member was dead because of a woman who was on her way to therapy, which she attends to get over a car accident in her own family. How, because she was trying to make her appointment, she stepped too hard on the gas. And how, like it or not, I'd then have to go to the funeral if I had managed to kill the person or to the hospital if he or she were not quite dead. And how I wouldn't know what to say then, and how the pressure would be easy to see on my face, how I'd have to struggle not to laugh because the pressure to put on a sad face would be so extreme that I'd nearly crack.

So I drive slowly and keep an eye on the speed limit signs. Now the signs are my friends, instead of enemies conspiring to keep me from getting places on time. Speed limit signs help me avoid ever having to look into the eyes of that grieving family. I think a lot about the things we discuss in therapy. Therapy defines my life, and I need the support it gives me. I see myself as a little hydrangea bush that needs to be regularly pruned by my therapist. Otherwise I'll grow and crowd out everyone else—with all my barely controllable fears and psychological dysfunctions—and choke out all the life around me, including those who are dear to me. Basically I'm hostile to life and always try to prove to myself that everything is horrible, that nobody loves me, that I have to do everything on my own, and that I'm all alone in this horrible world. That it would be better if I made an early exit. At least then I'd piss off fewer people.

On the way to therapy I try to figure out what I want to talk about with Frau Drescher. I try to arrange the time and topics so I'm not suddenly surprised when the hour is up.

I sought out Agnetha immediately after the accident. I enjoy thinking back on how I came to meet her. I was allowed by my health insurance to choose a therapist. In my mind it was clear that it had to be a woman. You're allowed to try out five different therapists before you have to decide on one.

For eight years now, I've gone to see her three times a week. Without her I wouldn't be alive anymore. I've wanted to kill myself twenty times during those eight years. Of course, just once would do the trick if you did it right. Without her, my husband would have left me a hundred times—he must have thought I hated his son, given the way I used to treat him. She has improved so many things in my life. Ever since I've been with her I have this horrible fear that something might happen to her. Obviously my concern is for selfish reasons. I don't want to have to spend years and years explaining everything to someone else just to get back to the point where Frau Drescher already is. Her brain is a giant psychological-story-processing machine. Like a giant painting that I've been working on for three hours per week for the last eight years. Plus I like her. That's another reason nothing can happen to her. I like her even though I don't know a thing about her.

I know nothing. A while back she canceled a few sessions, something that in the eyes of a patient is intolerable as it is.

Her justification: she has to have an *operation* soon. I nearly passed out. An operation? Of course, she has cancer. Otherwise they wouldn't call it an operation. Got it. Probably uterine cancer. Why else would they call it an *operation* rather than, say, a procedure, or surgery? She doesn't have to say another word. She has uterine cancer, I'm sure, 100 percent sure. She's going to die a wretched death, and I won't even be able to visit her in the hospital to continue my sessions. So that she can at least leave me halfway cured before she herself bites the dust. That sounds selfish, but that's the nature of therapy. There's nothing I can give her. I'm not allowed. I can't even bring her a piece of homemade cake. A therapist can't accept something like that—it could be poisoned. No gifts, no invitations to my birthday parties. I've tried it all.

It's no secret that I go to her. All my friends know about her. And still she never comes to any of my parties. Too bad. And I've never seen her on the street, the way Tony Soprano accidentally ran into Dr. Melfi at that Mafia restaurant and the doctor had to lie to her husband about how she knew him. What an idiotic move on her husband's part even to ask. He makes it difficult for her to keep her vow of silence, or whatever you call it. He must know that every single person she says hello to and he doesn't know could potentially be some nut from her practice.

I don't know whether Frau Drescher lives in our town. She never says anything about herself and yet she even knows exactly how I get myself off, when things are going well sexually between me and my husband and when they're not. It's very unfair.

"What do you mean by operation?"

"Nothing bad, don't worry, Frau Kiehl, it's really nothing bad."

I'm sure she'd say that even if it were something awful. Anyway, you often don't know if it's something bad until after they cut it out and test it. The results often come much later. But in the meantime she still has to appear steady, unperturbed, and calm. She'd never break down and say, "Yes, I'm so afraid, I'm really worried that my four overweight children will be left with only their other mother, and she's such a terrible mother. It was a mistake to use her brother as the sperm donor for my artificial insemination. We only did it because we thought that way the DNA would be as close as possible to hers." She would never talk to me like that, unfortunately. But I secretly know that her life is just as I imagine it. I can sense it. The poor woman.

I'd love to be her best patient. I would subvert my own identity if doing so would fulfill the desires of others—people like my husband, my therapist, my child, the neighbors, my friends. The waitress at the café. I'd subvert my own identity until there was nothing left of me.

I drive on. It won't be long until we get rid of our car. When I drive the car on winter mornings, I gawk at the fumes spewing out of the tailpipes of the other cars and wonder to myself how this is still permitted in this day and age. All the people are alone, driving their own car to work, all causing smog and traffic. Always just one person in each giant car. Sometimes I can't control myself. If the children aren't in the car, sometimes, against the protests of my husband, I hop out at a red light if there's a gas-guzzling Jeep in front of me and walk up and smile at the driver's window. They think, *Oh, a nice woman who probably wants to chat me up because I drive such a cool and luxurious car that shows what big balls I have*. Then, when the person rolls down his window, I tell him how outrageous it is, an affront to man and nature, that he drives such a wasteful car that uses so much gas.

The people inside those cars must be fucked in the head. And I don't think you can change the world if you let every asshole do what he wants without punishing him somehow. After I die my husband will get rid of our car—I put it in my will. We want to be a good environmentally conscious family, even when I'm dead.

As soon as I can see the high -rise as I'm driving up, I work myself into a state. Agnetha has a reserved parking space for her patients with a big sign that reads DOCTOR. That's just great. It's so embarrassing. Everyone knows you're nuts when you pull into that spot. Even after all these years I still feel ashamed when I park there. But I've never said anything to her. Even though you are supposed to tell your therapist everything. She always says it's important for our relationship. Yep, we have a relationship. Which is something unusual for me. The only reason I've never said anything is that by the time I get to her couch this particular embarrassment has been displaced by a thousand other things. Right, exactly, you lie on the couch in her office, as if she were Sigmund Freud. Except that she's better-looking and friendlier to women than Freud. I spend most of my time with my husband lying on the couch, and I spend all of my time with my therapist lying on the couch. I never anticipated that the couch would be the central piece of furniture in my life.

I step into the elevator, go through all the fears that used to put me into a cold sweat. I used to often reek of the sweat of fear because I had so many phobias. But I've found a deodorant that totally stops my underarms from sweating. Normal deodorants have a little aluminum chloride in them to stop perspiration. The one I found is all aluminum chloride. When I apply the roll-on directly to my skin, it itches and stings badly. But if I put it on my fingertips and then rub it under my arms, then there's no skin reaction.

I ring the bell and her automatic buzzer lets me in. Hello, *Guten Tag*, greetings, the awful handshake, looking each other in the eyes, and finally I lie down and gape at her picture of the devil. And fidget with my fingernails. I'm nervous. Always. But I would never bite my nails, because then everyone would be able to see I have psychological problems. Chewing on my cuticles is also something I'd never allow myself to do. That would offer too much insight into my psyche.

"We wanted to go to the brothel today, Georg and I. But I realized last night that both Liza and I had worms. Liza didn't go to school. And I figured I'd better also cancel the trip to the brothel. And Georg was so disappointed again. You know how often I've backed out—out of either cowardice or anxiety. We don't need to talk about the worms. They're dead. We went to the doctor this morning and all got medication. Problem solved. When I go home after this I'm going to tell Georg we can reschedule our little sexual outing.

"What I'd really like to talk to you about is my paranoia about being followed by newspaper reporters. Because they hounded us so much back then, I still feel as if they're following me. I'm going to surprise Georg with the news that we can go ahead with our trip to the brothel. But every time we go I'm always so afraid that someone will manage to snap a picture of us—ugly and naked, with fat tummies, fucking away in a threesome. Even though they wouldn't be able to publish something like that, I can't stop imagining it happening. Luckily I'd at least be doing it with my husband, not behind his back; otherwise I'd have the additional worry of the photo destroying my marriage. Those assholes from the tabloids swarmed us from all sides after the accident. The TV crew that snuck into my mother's hospital room—I've told you about it a thousand times. I dream about a producer from one of those shows—someone with blood on his hands—having a stroke or something and feeling with his own body what's it's like to be thrown to the wolves of his business. See what it's like to have someone sneak into the hospital and publish photos that show you in a really unflattering light."

"Frau Kiehl, it's almost as if you are evil. You need reparations in the form of at least one of these people undergoing the exact treatment they inflict on others."

"Yes, exactly. I've been turned evil. Very evil. You know what I dreamed about recently? I was practicing something in a rental car so Georg wouldn't know about it. I took the car out into a field in the middle of the woods and practiced wedging a brick against the gas pedal to get the car to go on its own. The idea was to figure out how to be able to jump out of the car and have it keep going. I dreamed that I spied on the publisher of the paper that published that photo. Eventually I knew where he lived, where he went out to eat, when he came and went from his office. Everything. And I knew about an annual meeting he had—he and his closest colleagues went out drinking at a certain bar after a yearly audit of the profits. That's where I decide to do it. I sit in the car a few meters away. The entire car is full of gasoline. I've painted three little faces on one of the gas cans on the backseat—one has freckles, one has slightly jug ears, and one has glasses. Just as the people from the paper are getting out of their car in front of the bar, I step on the pedal and race toward them. Sometimes I dream that I stay at the wheel, just to be sure my revenge scheme comes out perfectly. Other times I dream that I manage to jam the gas pedal down with a brick and jump out—because I've practiced it so many times."

"You're not going to do that. In reality you don't want to die, Frau Kiehl. You just feel overwhelmed occasionally."

"Yeah, yeah, I don't give a shit whether or not I die. It's just that I can't die because I have a fucking kid. That's it. It's not practical to have a child when you want to rid the world of evil and end up six feet under. Maybe when she's eighteen. Maybe then."

"No, you'll still have your husband."

"Yeah, great. But he can look after himself. And besides, he'd be proud of me. At least I think he would. New topic. I think it's terrible that my husband is still afraid of me—afraid of the me I used to be, before your help. Isn't it possible that I want to cheat on him because I like the idea of a fresh start? With someone I could show a different side to—the person I am now? That's it. That's my great desire, I think. To be fucked by somebody who has never seen me throw a tantrum, someone whose life I haven't made a living hell because of something embarrassing like having sperm in his sock. To have sex with someone you haven't already weighed down with a ton of relationship baggage."

"It's certainly possible that's the source of your desire. But I think you would feel differently afterward than you imagine you would feel. You'd be plagued by guilt. If you did it behind his back, he'd be able to read it in your body language. Your husband would sense it. That kind of thing changes the way people interact with each other. And you know what I think about the idea of going down that road."

"I know, I know. But we could manage it. I firmly believe that allowing each other to be with other people would work. We'll make it happen at some stage. I'm totally convinced it's just a matter of adjusting your way of thinking. Georg isn't there yet. But I'll get him there some day. Do we still have time?"

"Yes, we still have more time."

"Good. I wanted to talk to you about something stupid. I've wanted to bring it up for ages. But I haven't gotten up the nerve. Out with it, eh?"

"Of course. Out with it. You know everything stays within these four walls. Nothing is ever mentioned elsewhere. Confidentiality—you know all of this."

"Yeah, okay, so we were on our way home from some family celebration when I was young. I was right at the age when the glandular tissue starts to grow beneath your nipples. Twelve or thirteen, I guess. I was sitting unsuspectingly next to my uncle and he drunkenly put his arm around me like always. Up to that point everything's fine. But then his hand wandered down from my shoulder, down to my breast. And he pinched my developing little milk gland between his big pointer finger and his big thumb and rubbed it back and forth between them. As if he were trying to squeeze a big zit. At first I thought it was just accidental that his hand landed there. But I quickly realized that what was happening was definitely not right. He shouldn't be doing it, and the fact that he was gave me a bad feeling. I never told anyone, not my mother, not my siblings, not my husband. You are the first.

"And, you know, another incident just occurred to me, something that happened on the playground. The boys all wanted to kiss the girls. And it was somehow understood that if they wanted to kiss a girl they had to pay. The currency of the playground was little individually wrapped chocolates. One chocolate, one kiss. But a long kiss. Is that prostitution? Is that preparation for marriage?

"I can imagine that the only reason my stepmother stays with my father is for financial security. I can imagine a lot of marriages last only because of that. But that's nothing more than prostitution, is it? And dirt-cheap prostitution, if I can say so, not paid by the hour and not paid in cash, but in food and cleaning materials. If she's really lucky she'll get some inheritance and be free. But let me go back to my own situation. I mean, first and foremost I want a husband who can take care of me. No matter how much I earn, he needs to have more. How feminist is that? Not at all. I always find myself trying to picture what others are thinking—our neighbors, friends. And I imagine that they all think I'm only with my husband because of money. I can't even bring myself to challenge that notion. It's possible that I'm letting myself be fucked for the money. But also for life experience. Whoa, wait! If it's still better than ever between us in bed, maybe it's not about the money? Money is just a stand-in for potency. And potency in bed is definitely an advantage in a man. As you can see with us—seven years, for God's sake. It's incredible. My whore of a mother never managed that. Just yesterday I had the hottest sex in the world. She didn't manage that either, I'm sure. But now I've strayed far from the original topic of abuse."

"Yes, and it says a lot, Frau Kiehl."

"You mean my mind does that on purpose? Quickly changes the subject, changes direction? Fine, then let's go back to it. Something else occurs to me: I protect my child against her father and stepfather. Against the potential threat of sexual abuse. I was raised not to trust anyone when it comes to pedophilia. The greatest danger for children is from their own family. Forget the few strangers in the park who kidnap children—that's as rare as winning the lottery. Except the other way around. You'd have to have bad luck of the same magnitude for that to happen to your family. Much more probable are the threats within your own family and immediate circle. Which is something people still don't understand. Usually it's men, just as it is with murders committed in a jealous rage—always men. Men make the family a dangerous place for women and children. Though it's rare for women to be the abusers, in our family it's the other way around. In our family the female is definitely the most dangerous—especially for the stepson. And when sexual abuse takes place within a family, even the mothers look away and don't want to admit the truth, don't want to admit their husband or some other male relative is abusing a child. That won't happen to my child. I always creep silently around the apartment. When my husband and daughter have arranged to do something together, I act as if I have something I need to do at the other end of the apartment. Then I sneak as silently as an Indian into the room where they are to catch them in the act. Trust is good, but when it comes to abuse, it's worth checking up. Even though I am totally sure my husband would never do anything to my child. Lots of other mothers have thought that, too, and fallen into the trap. That will not happen to us.

"Up to now, for the first seven years of our relationship, nothing objectionable has ever happened. But it's possible that Liza could still develop into something that would create a pedophilic streak in him, causing him to strike. As my daughter's protector, I must always be on the lookout and always be ready to sacrifice my relationship for the good of the child.

"So there's that on top of it all. Like a sentry, always ready to sound the alarm. I inherited all of that from my mother, probably because she had some shit of her own she never worked through. Fuck. New topic, okay? Liza is going to her grandfather's next weekend."

"To your father's?"

"He is no longer my father. I prefer to say 'her grandfather.' But he's already forgotten a lot of her birthdays, too. And she hasn't even been around that long!"

"And Liza has yet to notice the problem?"

"No, she hasn't noticed at all. She keeps asking, 'When am I going to Grandpa's house?' We answer nicely, as if it's the most normal thing in the world. We only talk nicely about those idiots. Oh, yes, that's so nice, you're looking forward to seeing your grandfather, my little dear?' I always think afterward that my tongue's going to fall out from all the lying. But I am still a thousand times happier to hand her over to her grandfather than to her grandmother."

"Which is to say your mother." She laughs. Her mild laughter. I love her. I'm so thankful for her. She wouldn't believe it.

"Yes, of course, Frau Drescher. You want me to say 'my mother,' but I'm not going to. All right. Anyway, when Liza is at her grandmother's I'm deathly afraid for my child. I think the whole time that she won't bring Liza back. Anytime the phone rings I think it's the police calling to tell me about a terrible accident. To my mind she drove my brothers to their death, and I worry constantly that she will do the same with my daughter. It's horrible that because of you—well, okay, also because of my daughter—I have to let her go to her grandmother's at all. Fuck therapy. Fuck all these demands.

"The only reason I put up with it is so my daughter can have a grandmother. Because you say that's the way it should be. It's really tough for me. I keep thinking that she's so angry with me because I have a child, a little child, and all of hers are dead, that she's going to get revenge by killing herself and taking my daughter with her. That happened once in my family—that a mother took a child with her. Or tried to. It's something that's still in our bones. The great family drama that's buried in our genes, you might say.

"As far as I'm concerned, you can't put any craziness past the women in our family. Actually I'd like to make my dreams into reality, too. It just seems right to me. But my head is probably fucked up. Almost certainly, in fact. Do we still have more time?"

"Yes, we have a few more minutes."

"Don't you think it's incredible that my husband has a vacation home right where the accident took place? Of all the places in the world. And that I have to drive the exact stretch where my brothers died? Me at the wheel and my entire family in the car. It's fucking weird. Of all the men I could have fallen in love with, I fall for one who owns a vacation home there. Fucking hell. Is it a sign? And if it is, then for what, and from whom? I keep forgetting that I'm an atheist!

"When we are on the way to one of our monotonously similar vacations in Belgium and pass the spot where my brothers supposedly died, I always look for charred patches on the road surface. I look for dented guardrails, crosses. Don't see any. Never have. I look. Every time. I look in the woods, too. I look for naked, deranged survivors. The desire is always strong to grab the steering wheel and spare us all from continuing our long, strenuous lives. It's the same feeling —though much stronger—that I get when I'm out on your balcony, Frau Drescher, looking into the depths, eleven stories below, and a voice inside me says, *Jump and you will finally have peace—even from Frau Drescher*. Interestingly enough, it's the same feeling I suspect my mother of having when she's driving my daughter someplace in her car. It's the same as with my husband. I constantly suspect him of wanting to cheat on me—or used to, this was earlier in our relationship, these days I'd be fine with it—despite the fact that I actually want to cheat on him. I can admit this now after years of individual and couples therapy."

When Georg and I got together, it was intense. He told me everything about his sexuality. He was merciless about it. I listened and looked and practically fell to pieces at first. It was particularly overwhelming when he showed me all the hard-core sex photos he'd collected from the Internet. I wanted to act as if I were cool with it all. I wanted him to think I was relaxed about it, and I also really wanted to be relaxed about it myself. But I'm not. It really got to me. All these shots of women and their inner labia. He didn't want to have another relationship where he hid everything from his wife. I could understand that. It's the same with going to prostitutes—he wants female absolution. He wants his sexuality to be guilt-free. That was difficult for me at first. A bit much for little Elizabeth.

"He's often admitted that it was a major mistake to let me in on his fantasies. Over the years I've gotten used to knowing all about them. I think now I'm nearly at the point of confronting him with *my* true sexuality. For all these years I thought it was extraordinary that he knew exactly what he wanted. And I had no idea. But now I do know what I want, and there's no way he can deny me. It's comparable to all his porn flicks and prostitutes, right? My desire to sleep with other men. Lots of them. The only difference—and one that will hurt him—is that his fantasies always include me. He wants me to go with him to the brothels, for us to re-create scenes from porn movies, look at photos together. In my fantasies about other men, he has no role. It's all about me. I notice this more and more—between my legs, obviously, but also in my head. Maybe the next seven years will turn out to be me overwhelming him with the discovery of my own wild sexuality?

"By the way, I made a secret appointment tomorrow with a notary. I'm going to write Cathrin out of my will, since I am going to cut her out of my life. Soon she will be my ex–best friend. What if something happens to me tomorrow morning? Or, hell, right now, in your damn elevator? A helicopter could fly into the building any second, too. And she'd still stand to inherit something from me. That no longer works for me. I want my ex-husband, my husband, my daughter, and my stepson to get everything. My parents will get nothing more than their statutory share, and my husband should make sure my sister gets something, too."

"Yes, I know all about your will. I hope you have taken me out of it again? I am not permitted to inherit anything from you. We've already discussed that it's not acceptable for a patient to leave anything to a therapist."

"What about the other way around?"

"Very funny, Frau Kiehl. But that's also not allowed. If you haven't changed that yet, you can kill two birds with one stone when you go there."

"I took care of that ages ago. What do you take me for? When you tell me to do something, I do it immediately. I constantly think that I'm going to die. So my will has to be ready. In any event, I have a secret appointment again tomorrow. Georg doesn't know about it. You know my dream scenario for after I'm no longer around—that Liza will be raised together by her stepfather and father. That would be good. And I don't mean that the way you probably think—that my husband wouldn't get together with another woman. I've told him time and time again that I want him to find another woman as quickly as possible. I hate dead people who are so self-important that they forbid their widows or widowers to find someone else. Even from the grave they expect loyalty from their partners. I think that's terrible. I've told my husband that he can bring someone new to my funeral if he wants. He'll need to be consoled. Christians, go forth and fuck. The only people I know who get upset about people finding someone new after the death of their partners are Christians. They're awful, Christians. Awful. I think people should find someone new fast. As soon as possible."

"I know, Frau Kiehl, I know. Why are you changing your will secretly, without telling Georg?"

"Well, because he always bitches about the fact that I spend so much time thinking about death in general and my own death in particular. You think so, too! He always says, 'Yes, Elizabeth, but you're not going to die.'"

"Yes, it's true. You're not going to die anytime soon. You are generally healthy. And the chances of something happening to you like what happened to your brothers are extremely low."

"That's what my husband says. That I have my head in the sand. Maybe, but I still have an appointment tomorrow, right after my appointment with you."

"All right, the time is now up, Frau Kiehl. I'll see you tomorrow. Have fun at the brothel regardless of what I think, okay?"

It makes her horny, doesn't it? I'm sure it does. My husband always says *she* should be giving *me* money for all the stories I tell her. Other people would pay to hear such salacious stuff. True, but they wouldn't have such clever responses.

I sit up and straighten my hair. Sometimes I have therapy head. That's when the hair on the back of my head looks like I'm either an alcoholic who fell asleep during the day or like I've just been lying on a couch in therapy. And although I try to be cool about it, I don't want everyone to know I go to therapy. I adjust my hair, grab my handbag, and look Frau Drescher in the eyes. "Thank you. See you next time. I'll tell you everything then." I let go of her hand quickly after a handshake. I talk to her about everything but can never see her while I talk. Then I'm always somewhat surprised at the end of the session when I see her again, as my impression of her has changed a bit since I last saw her, at the beginning of the hour. And touching her hand just doesn't work, though you have to shake hands in Germany. And I would never bring it up with her, despite the fact that we are supposed to be able to talk about *anything*. But where would that lead us? She'd think I was crazy.

Into the fucking elevator and home to Georg. I'm looking forward to being able to tell him that we can go to the brothel after all. Now I just have to fight through the eleven-floor ride in the elevator. I can hold my breath, the way I do when I'm scared. Then I'm free and on the way home.

On the way home I feel euphoric. I use therapy and my therapist as a garbage dump. It's all about managing to stay together forever with my husband.

The only music I listen to in the car is Jan Delay. Other than Elvis, he's the best in the world. Not just musically. Politically, too. That's important to me. He fights the tabloids. He's a member of ATTAC. I listen to him rather than Elvis because I can't stand Elvis anymore since I cut off contact my father. He taught me about Elvis when I was still a kid. Even before Jan Delay he was the best in the world—even if he was a cretin politically. And it tears my heart in half when I hear Elvis these days because it reminds me of my love for my father. So Jan Delay will have to do.

Using the power-window switches, I put down all the windows so everyone can enjoy the sexiest politically correct music in the world. I pat myself on the shoulder mentally, since once again I've done something good for my mental health, for the well-being of our family, for my psychological well-being. The well-being of my marriage. As always when I drive, Accident sits on my shoulder and watches me and my life.

The funeral has to be arranged. It threatens to be hilarious. At least one mentally unstable burn victim, three grieving fathers, seven grieving grandfathers and just as many grandmothers, relatives and other people you never liked, and they all want us to scoot over and make room at the side of the grave. Why are we even going to go through with it at all? I always thought our family didn't care what others thought—that we didn't believe in all that shit. I was always proud of the fact that I came from a totally atheist family. Nobody on my mother or father's side was baptized. I think it's fantastic. We pass the tradition of non-believing down from generation to generation, using emotional pressure just the way religious people do to pass down their beliefs. You can't just leave the field to the missionary impulse of Christians without a fight because you're too tolerant. Nope. You have to keep a body count. For every convert you get a star. As a reward. That's what I was trained to do—turn men away from their Catholic families. And it works well, usually by getting them hooked on love and sex.

All the relatives gather in my mother's hospital room. The fathers are there, and my father has his new wife with him. I say new wife because that's how she feels to me. She doesn't belong here. In my opinion she's disqualified. She married my father shortly after my mother left him. She put herself between my father and us, a classic stepmother. And the way she did that was textbook stepmother stuff.

I was five and my now dead brother four. She considered us fundamentally bad. She always put herself in direct competition with us for our father's love. She refused to accept that he loved us unconditionally. She always wanted to prove that we weren't worth it. That was hard enough for all concerned. But on top of that, she also thought we ate too much. She always skimped on us, thinking that they could save money by letting the kids go hungry. She always thought we were too much: too loud, greedy, gluttonous, egotistical, spoiled. And she let us know at every opportunity.

The worst thing about my stepmother was that she always ruined the rare and valuable time we had together with our beloved father. After my parents split up, we were allowed to see him only one night every two weeks. We missed him so much. Our rich papa, with his red sports car and his cool job in a toy factory. But she was always there. I never saw him try to do anything to protect us from his new wife, either. We wanted that so badly. A sign. A sign of love from a father to his children. Against the crazy wife. Never. He always tried to stay loyal to all sides. Shame.

Except for this one time. A few days after the death of his only son in the accident. They are all in my mother's hospital room. We had to put together the death notice. To let everyone know about the death of my brothers. Death notices are something that's no longer necessary in the era of phones, e-mail, and fucking tabloid journalism. This death notice and the invitations to the funeral had to be dated way in the future, because the police had yet to release the bodies. What bodies? Funny. It was all so grotesque. None of us believes in cemeteries, life after death, prayer, any form of Christian ritual. And suddenly this! And everything goes out the window. Unfortunately there's no alternative atheist version. So, like idiots, we put a notice in the local papers along with an invitation to a funeral in two months at the local Christian cemetery. They nabbed us after all.

Whenever someone dies, the absurd list of those who survive the dead person plays an immense role in the notice. The need to address that at all when someone has just died is ridiculous. Crazy. But with us it plays a huge role, too. Out of protest, I want to be listed last. It isn't allowed. This has nothing to do with anybody's personal will. I have to be at the beginning, along with my mother and my other leftover sister. Mother doesn't want to be listed next to any man, since she is separated from all of them.

And when we get to the list of fathers and their new wives, my father makes the following monstrous statement: "I don't want my wife in the notice at all. She hated Harry. She is not allowed to be listed in the notice."

She is there in the room. She hears this with her own ears. Everyone pauses to let this unbelievable statement sink in. I have to smile inside because I know that my dead brother would have agreed. And that he would have been pleased about this sign of love from his father. Too bad he never experienced something like that while he was still alive.

My father was right. She did hate Harry. Even more than she hated me. Perhaps because he was closer with my father. They looked exactly the same, too. My mother's genes went into the girls. I look and am like my mother, unfortunately. My brother looked and was like my father. The stepmother accepted her exclusion from the death notice. There wasn't any room for negotiation anyway. Not given the steady voice with which my father made the statement. What amazes me is that they are still together to this day. He's still with the wife he didn't want listed in the death notice of his son because she hated him and let him know that all the time—a little child, who had nothing to do with the botched family situation, who got no mercy from her, ever, until it was too late, because he was dead. Her attitude was set in stone by her absence from our family notice of his death.

They are still married! He lets her stay at his side, set for life. He lives under one roof—in one bed—with the enemy of his dead son. Unbelievable. That alone is sufficient grounds never to have anything to do with them. The rest of the list of remaining survivors was drawn up appropriately, though with a pathetic patchwork family like ours it took a lot more space than usual to list all the fathers, grandmothers, and grandfathers —practically a whole page.

Because of this experience and because of the horrid Christianization of the subsequent funeral, I wrote a will that did some good after my death. I filled out an organ donor form and always carry it with me. I put everything up for donation: labia, clitoris—whoever gets it is going to have some fun!—my eyes, my nonsmoker lungs, heart, dark nipples—they can take *everything* out of me and give it out to the needy. And second, the thing with my ashes going out with the household trash. Even if it's against the law. It's in my will, so my next of kin will have to pull it off somehow. I'm against graves and funerals, against sending out letters and worrying if you've forgotten someone, against individualizing funerals with photos and music, and most of all against having a grave site where someone has to leave flowers. You can think of dead people without an ugly carved stone marker in the ground. I reject all of that. And for the same reason, I swear *never* to visit my brothers' graves. What a load of crap. Graves and everything that goes with them. Notices, gravestones, envelopes and invitations, paying for a cemetery plot, appetizers, cakes, the term *funeral feast*, rotgut coffee in giant thermoses, black clothes, people reading from a pulpit, falsely hyping the dead person and leaving out any negative attributes. Fuck you and your dead. I won't go along with it. Not one bit.

I managed to get away from the hospital one single time. And I was able to sleep at home with my boyfriend. My aunt took over the duty of making sure my mother didn't kill herself. For one night. And for the first time in ages we had desperate sex. All I could think while we were at it was that I wanted to live. *Fuck me back to life!* It was the only time I ever really abandoned myself with him. And our daughter must have been conceived that night. We had tried for four years prior to that. When I had seen him for the first time I had thought to myself, *I want to have babies with him*. It ended up being just one. In part because I'm shocked at how much work and worry it is bringing up a child. And I know why it worked at that moment. I was already thinking in the hospital that I had to give my mother a new child. She had lost three. Everything that she had to care for was dead, gone. We needed a replacement. Right. That's the way I thought it out in my traumatized head sitting there in the hospital. And naturally, because that's the way life goes, after four years of sex without protection and trying to get pregnant, it happened at that exact moment. The oyster was open. This one last time for my boyfriend. It never worked during peaceful times, but as soon as we were on wartime footing, *boom*, it worked.

Then our love fell silent. And the first thing that went bad was the sex.

The birth of my daughter is therefore inseparable from the accident. I can think of dates from that time only with difficulty. It makes my head hurt. It's as if that period is bounded off with a fence. Whenever someone asks me when my daughter was born, I can't recall at first—because I hate to think back on that time. It always comes to me like this: when was the accident? She was conceived then, so she must have been born in the year following the accident. So whenever I think of her birth, I first think of three dead children.

I hated the way Stefan mourned. He receded into himself. He got lethargic and fat. He gained twenty kilograms in a very short time. He also got on my nerves because he seemed most upset about the death of the younger ones. While I was saddest about the oldest. The two things didn't fit together. Obviously our love was put to an impossible test and failed miserably under the pressure.

I pull into our parking space in front of the building. When you buy a parking space in front of your door, you have to admit you are buried alive. Because you think you need a car but don't feel like having to find a spot for it each day. I want to get rid of our gasoline-burning car as soon as an affordable four-seat electric car is available. That's pretty much the only thing we're doing wrong as far as the environment, but I usually focus on what we're doing wrong instead of being proud of what we as a family are doing right. I hope Georg is home. It's not often that we can surprise each other. We've been together and married for a long time. You get used to each other. You don't feel as if you have to do much to try to seem interesting to the other.

I unlock the apartment door with the same hand motion as always and when I step inside I call out hello far too loudly, as I always do, so I can figure out where my husband is. He calls back and I place him in the laundry room. I sniff the air and detect our laundry detergent. It smells of lemon and nuts.

He is an absolute sex machine, pumped with testosterone, but he can do all the household things better than I can. He's hanging the washing to dry right now. I go downstairs and thank him for doing it. You should do that once in a while: even when other things start getting taken for granted, I shouldn't take his household skills—which far exceed mine—for granted. He smiles at me drowsily. It always embarrasses him when I thank him for something like this.

"Where were you for so long?" That's a snippy tone for him.

"What do you mean? At the pediatrician and then Frau Drescher's."

"With Liza? Why didn't you bring her here before therapy?"

Uh-oh, misunderstanding. He was waiting for us. In my rush I forgot to tell him. Now I know why he's acting funny. He was worried. Death always stalks us, even while we're hanging the washing. It's true.

"I'm sorry. That's right. You thought I was going to bring Liza home before therapy. I left her at Stefan's—he was able to take her earlier than I thought. I should have told you. I'm sorry."

"I wanted to go out, take care of a few things. I was waiting around like an idiot. I tried to call you many times."

Crap. Reproach. Mood in the shitter. I was hoping to surprise him with happy news.

"My phone was on silent. I was in therapy. Did you think something had happened to us?"

"Yeah, no."

"Well nothing happened to us. My sieve of a brain just forgot to tell you about the change in plans, okay? Forgive me. Okay?"

I hug him and kiss him on the big scar on his cheek—my favorite spot on his body, where the cancerous skin was cut out before we met each other. That spot shows how strong he is.

Not even cancer can mess with him. Or an accident. Or me. He's a seawall able to stand up to the harshest surf.

"I have a surprise for you. The doctor gave us pills that kill the worms as soon as you take the first one. Mine are already gone, and if you take a pill yours will be, too."

"I don't have worms. How many times do I have to say it?"

I have to laugh. "Yeah, fine, then take one as a precaution instead, and then we can plan our visit to the brothel and go tomorrow morning if they're open. What do you think? Liza will be with Stefan for the next two days and we can have a nice child-free time."

"Do you really want to? I always have the feeling that you're pleased whenever it gets canceled."

"Yes, that's true. I have to get through it, for you. But you know that I get into it, too, when I'm lying there with my legs spread and she's licking me. I mean, there's no alternative, really, it's a simple mechanical fact. Should we do it? It'll be a way to put yesterday's stupid worm night behind us."

Still holding me with one arm, he reaches down with the other—without even noticing it himself—and scratches his ass. I've got to give him one of these pills. I would love to feel as comfortable in my own skin as he does. He does lots of things he doesn't notice because he's not as mercilessly self-aware as I am. It must be nice.

He smiles with anticipation about our outing.

"Come on. I'll just finish up and we'll go get lunch."

I sit on the couch and try to breathe calmly. According to Frau Drescher, I need to practice this now and then. Otherwise I just hectically do things to flee the accident, myself, and my nonexistent grief. It's going to come sometime. And for that I have to learn to deal with downtime.

I hear Georg shuffling around downstairs and it gives me a guilty conscience because I'm not helping despite the fact that most of the laundry is mine. I breathe and close my eyes. The first thing that enters my head is a mosaic of images from the accident. My paranoia about being followed, related to the papers. The fear that they could get a photo of me and my husband screwing a prostitute. It comes from the way they hounded us back then when my brothers died. After the television team broke into my mother's hospital room we had to assume that, like it or not, the same pigs would disrupt the funeral as well. They had tried to get pictures of the dead children from all kinds of sources. Luckily everyone held tight. We had to pay for the security guards who sealed off the cemetery and patrolled inside and out to keep any photos from being taken. All to protect us from those pigs. That you have to deal with that on top of everything else leaves you maniacal with rage for the rest of your life. They created a lifelong enemy. When someone is murdered in a crime show, the cops always ask, "Did he have any enemies?" In the case of the heads of the newspaper publishing companies, their wives will have to say, "Yes, Elizabeth Kiehl." How they even have wives is a mystery to me. Shouldn't all women stand together and refuse to let the men who pull the strings at those papers have sex? Then they'd change their ways pretty quickly out of emergency horniness, no matter how much money they were making from their evil stories.

The bodies, or rather the urns, weren't released until long after the accident. The urns of the three dead children sat in a little concrete room in the cemetery the day before the funeral. You could say good-bye there. But good-bye to what? I went with my favorite aunt.

I looked at her mischievously and asked, "Should I pick one up?"

"Sure, why not?"

She's cool. You can't shock her with anything. My favorite aunt. I first lifted up the urn of my oldest brother, Harry. I shook it with both hands. Then the second. Then the third. They were each a different weight. The urn of the twenty-four-year-old was the heaviest, the nine-year-old less heavy, and the six-year-old the lightest of all. How could that be if there wasn't anything left of them? My aunt and I came to a chilling epiphany: if there was nothing left of them in the burned-out car, what were they supposed to have burned in the crematorium? If there was anything in these urns that had to do with the accident, it was charred padding from the backseat upholstery. What else could it be? They had the backseat dropped off and chipped what they could off of it. They were told how old the victims were by the police, looked at a table to see how much ash someone of a given age would render, and then dumped who knows what into the urns. Wood ash, ashes of other people who were overweight and didn't completely fit into their own urns.

What exactly was in those urns? One day, when I'm feeling very strong, I'll find out. I'll drive to the facility where my bodiless brothers were supposed to have been cremated. And I'll collar an employee there until I get the truth. It won't work right now. I can't do it yet. I'm not in the right state. I can't handle it.

I can only vaguely remember the day of the funeral. It was eight weeks after the accident. Maybe a certain level of realization had crept in, the shock that was a long time coming. Mother had arranged everything from her hospital bed. I remember that far too many people came to fit into the minichapel at the cemetery where we were sitting. The entire schools of each of the dead boys. Including the teachers. The parents of school friends. Neighbors. Sports teams they played on. All the fathers, all the grandparents. Friends of all the dead. Friends of all the survivors. Far too many people for a funeral and way too many for one head to deal with.

I didn't know most of them. And of course all of them were absurdly wearing black. What's the fucking point? In the front of the chapel hung huge photos of my three brothers. I didn't think the shot of my oldest brother captured him well. I have no idea who said what. Everything went by as if I were in a daze. Funerals are almost all the same. How can you distinguish them? Except for the photos at the front. I don't remember anything from the chapel except the photos. And outside the only thing I know is that we had to walk ridiculously slowly behind the fake urns. Very slowly, the way they always make you at a funeral. And I can remember that I kept having to keep whispering to myself, "Don't laugh, don't laugh, don't laugh, Elizabeth." The pressure to put on a stupid mourner's face (something else you don't learn to do in school) was so extreme that I had the feeling things could easily slip into a completely opposite expression.

I felt watched. Everyone looked for the craziness in our eyes. Yes, but you won't find it—it comes only later! I can remember one thought as clear as day: *What's keeping the three boys? We're putting on this big production and they're late! Such cheek. Typical of them.* I looked for them everywhere. And that has continued to this day. But I still look for them the way they looked eight years ago. I can't picture them any older.

I pushed Mother in her wheelchair. She had a release from the hospital—discharged at her own risk, as they so nicely put it. She was pumped full of who knows what to numb the pain in her back, in her feet, in her heart, in her head. I pushed her in front of me and all I could think the whole time was how I wanted to get away, how this was her show, no question about it. All the fathers whispered to me beforehand, "Hopefully she won't want to sit beside the grave afterward and shake everyone's hand."

I couldn't imagine beforehand how many people three dead boys would attract, but when I saw them all, an entire cemetery full, I also desperately hoped she wouldn't want to shake everyone's hand. But as a result of the medication she was unfortunately like someone who'd been bitten by a tarantula. All the close relatives left as soon as the pointless vessels had been put into the holes in the ground. Obligations met. Then began the freestyle portion of the program. My no longer recognizable mother and I—her wheelchair slave—stood for hours at the open wounds in the earth and let all those who wanted to shove their way past us. "Sincere condolences." Next, please. "Sincere condolences." Thanks. Thanks. Thanks. Thanks. Blah, blah, blah. At some point I became convinced that people were getting back in line because it was all so funny, again and again. The line of supposed mourners wouldn't stop. What a fuck-up. I'm never going to another funeral.

The entire cemetery and all its paths broad and narrow were filled with children. It seemed fitting. Grave full of children. Cemetery full of children.

Eventually it was quitting time for us grief workers and we were allowed to go back to the peaceful hospital in an ambulance.

I breathe deeply, feeling pressure on my chest. I have to get rid of these agonizing thoughts. How can I do that most effectively? Displace them with thoughts of sex, the usual mind trick. At least it works.

Good. Now I've told him that tomorrow we'll go to the brothel. But he still doesn't believe that I like the idea. I can't really understand myself sexually. He and I sometimes have to really force me to do things. For the last few years I've really had to have my arm twisted to have sex in general and sexual adventures with third parties in particular. My therapist says lots of women do that. She calls it "suppressing a tear." Meaning the woman can't just go and have sex; instead, beforehand, there has to be a little fight so that the man has to jump through some hoops. For instance, he has to overcome the woman's reluctance by begging or by seduction or whatever—who knows?—and then open up the oyster little by little. That's exactly the way I am. If I know sex is unavoidable, I pick a fight to try to create a delay or even a cancelation. Or I confess to him that I don't feel like it. But when he won't leave it alone and pushes the right buttons, which are all in my crotch, then I get into it regardless of whether I wanted to before or not. At that point I want everything. But at first I'm always fighting it. Must be pretty stressful for my husband. He'd like to be seduced by me sometime. But that won't work. I set the roadblocks.

I do the same thing before every one of our brothel outings. I fight it. And as soon as I'm there, I say to hell with my mother and find myself in the middle of an orgy, happy as a clam. Can you call three people an orgy? When we first started going to brothels I had a big problem with jealousy. There were images that got burned into my brain and were hard to get rid of. They kept causing fits of jealousy in my head. Images of my husband kissing a strange woman very long and deep. Yeah, well, since *Pretty Woman* I always thought they didn't kiss; they only fucked. Yeah right! They kiss all right, and how. Forever. And images of my husband spending an eternity licking another woman. Try dealing with that at first! But eventually you get used to it and realize that there's no risk whatsoever—or, perhaps let's say, little risk. But really none whatsoever. We've already been with eighteen women. I've written down all of their names. And written notes about how it was with each. So I won't forget. Grace, Amanda, Dina, Lumi, Lotus, Vanessa, Vivienne, Olga, Tina, Michelle, Melissa, Samara, Nesrin, Mira, Samantha, Jule, Ira, Diamond. When we picked Vivienne out on the Internet and went to her place, she accidentally introduced herself as Vicky. She laughed and quickly said, "I mean Vivienne." They all use false names, obviously.

At the beginning, with the first few women, I drank way too much because I was so anxious. I could barely remember anything afterward. And sometimes, embarrassingly enough, especially given how expensive it is to go as a pair, I had fits of jealousy during the act itself and we had to break it off in the middle. That was very embarrassing for my husband—it takes a while for the erection to subside, and then to get dressed, and then you're standing in front of the brothel in bright daylight in a bad mood. I'm sure he had imagined it differently. But so had I.

It was worth it for me to keep at it, though. We kept trying. Me for the sake of my husband, as a gift, a show of love.

Few people still believe in God or go to church anymore, thank goodness, but for some crazy reason we still believe—or hope, at least—that monogamy can work. For the first few years I was so worried that I might lose my husband that I built a horrid prison around him. I constantly accused him of cheating with every woman under the sun. Friends of ours, coworkers of his, strangers on the street, anyone. It was as if I was suffering from some kind of delusion, trying to convince him that he didn't like me and wanted to constantly go out, fuck other people, fall in love with someone else. My therapist says I fight my own desire to cheat by taking it out on my husband. I'm fighting something in him that actually exists only in me. She's said that for years. Rationally, I can follow her argument, but it doesn't sink in emotionally. That is the challenge of therapy. When you talk about things constantly, they eventually take hold in your gut, too. And then you feel liberated. A switch has been thrown. It's as if the therapist has removed a big tumor. You are freed—the problem is recognized not only rationally but also emotionally. And soon after, it's gone. That's why I love my therapist more than anything and forever. She liberates me and my husband from huge problems that could screw up our life.

I kept making visits to prostitutes until it was all good. At first I understood only rationally that they didn't want and weren't going to take away my husband. Little by little I came to realize that in my gut, too. And now I am free. At least in that area. Jealousy has never been entirely licked. In the truest sense of the word. They lick me, too, though not as well as my husband does. But still. Through repeated exposure, I'm not frightened of them anymore. I've worked through that. And nowadays I even send him to the brothel alone. I'm certain that you can apply the same principle to swinger clubs, having sex with other people, partner swapping, anything: if you just try it a few times together with your partner, later on you'll be relaxed enough to send your partner off to fuck someone else on his or her own. I realized it's not good that he always wants me there to offer him absolution. Of course, he is treated better when his wife is with him. Then it's not the typical sad relationship between the john and the hooker. They're not such mercenaries, the way they are when men show up on their own. But at some stage I had an epiphany and thought, *I'm fine with letting him go there alone*. And I no longer felt any pressure to screw up my courage to go every time.

To remove the pressure on me, I had to conquer my jealousy and send him there alone. Afterward I felt a strong sense of desire for him for the first time in a while. Really strong, and right between my legs. I was throbbing down there when he came home from the brothel in broad daylight. I was all lovey-dovey and horny. I tried to analyze it later with my therapist so I could get that immaculate sensation between my legs more often. And it goes a little something like this: because I was able to let go, because I didn't need to worry anymore about what happened, because I gave him freedom to sleep with someone else, I felt more free myself. I highly recommend it. Afterward we had the hottest sex of all time. Open, free, wild. I had to stake out my territory again. Poor guy—he had to deliver again immediately.

Something happened in my head that I hadn't anticipated. I started a virtual scorecard for sexual favors. As in, I did this and this for you, so now you'll do this and this for me. I hadn't realized at first that I wanted these things. And suddenly, after eight years, I had to admit Frau Drescher was right about the fact that I wanted something different. He always set things up for his own desires. And I never put any stock in any of my own. And suddenly, *boom*, there they were. My own cravings and desires. Things that I had suppressed for so long without even realizing what they were or that I was suppressing them.

I would like to sleep with other men. Lately I think, *Why should he constantly get to feel other bodies, have sex with other women, but I don't get to be with other men?* The problem is that he lives out his fantasies with prostitutes, in part because the situation can be controlled. Generally speaking, nobody is going to fall in love with anybody else in that situation. When I say I want to sleep with other men, he suggests male prostitutes. We've researched it online. But that's just not an option for me. They all look too gay. They wear it on their sleeves. Whether the prostitutes are male or female, the market is for male customers. Meaning the male prostitutes are probably gay. It's hard to imagine a heterosexual man having sex with another man for money. It's improbable. Unless he needed money badly. Really badly.

So I refuse to do the same thing my husband does. And as brave as I am, I've revealed to him that I also want to have sex with other men now. And—I really dropped a bomb with this part—with real men, men we know. That's my fantasy—to sleep with friends of ours. Preferably with men from our immediate circle of friends, married men with children. Now my husband just has to agree to it. It's obvious that he won't go with me for these affairs. He refuses to touch other men. I think it's funny, since I touch other women to fulfill his fantasies. But, oh well.

It's also nice to keep things uncomplicated, at least in this one small way.

Earlier, in other relationships, I often cheated on my partners. Because it's such a rush to let someone else see you naked and touch your naked body and all that. Otherwise you just don't feel anything anymore. I'd love to have another cock in my mouth, just for the hell of it. A little variation is good. Without it everything goes to pieces. And even though I felt guilty about it back then, the feeling I got was stronger than the guilt—the feeling that I was attractive, I was desired. And you immediately put more effort into things with your own partner afterward. Out of guilt. Your partner benefits from the feelings of guilt.

And now, since this epiphany, I am attempting the impossible. I want my husband to allow me to sleep with other men. I will convince him, I'm sure of it. I'll pull it off. After all, at the moment, the score is eighteen to nothing. And my husband is smart enough to realize that, too.

Georg is still shuffling around in the laundry room. He always insists on doing things right, whether he's working on my vagina or the dirty laundry. It's nice to lie here and think. I think about our life. Our life together. All the things he has to deal with because of me. I always let everything out. I can't hide anything from him. Whenever I'm feeling bad, which is often, he must think I always try to restrain myself so I don't burden him with my problems. I'm getting better at it, but everything that's already happened can't be undone. It's there between us. He has to think about all of it when he looks at me, when he sleeps with me. All of that goes with me, I'm afraid. Awful.

Suddenly I think of an embarrassing thing I did to him once.

Once I found a sock in the laundry basket that was full of sperm. I'm sure it was sperm—I can detect it from ten meters away. And without thinking about it I went straight to him and started complaining. I must surely have been possessed by my mother. She spoke out of my mouth and wanted to destroy the relationship between me and this fantastic, sock-fucking man. I had no idea how embarrassing it would be to him to have to talk about it. I learned only years later. Now I'm embarrassed I brought it up, too, but I just couldn't help laying landmines at our feet back then. Without any regard for the damage they might do. The sperm-filled sock landmine sits beneath our relationship and I can't figure out a way to go back and erase the tantrum that put it there.

That is in fact the biggest problem in our relationship. All the psychological problems I bring to it. I wanted him to have super-human strength. I wanted him to be above all the dirty things other people did. I thought that if he was going to replace my parents, he would have to be perfect. If I keep tabs on him, he'll stay with me, I thought. And then he goes and cheats on me with a sock. Jacks off into it instead of into me. Why wouldn't he just ask me if I felt like having sex? I know why he didn't ask. Because I'm always depressed. And when I'm not depressed, I'm aggressive. Nobody wants to seduce a woman like that. A stinky sock is more attractive than that. It was one of his socks, not mine. He didn't even want to fuck one of my socks.

The worst thing is that I understand. I've made so many mistakes in our love life. In my desperate fight to hold on to him, I almost destroyed everything, time and time again. Then

in couples therapy he learned that I am the problem, not him—
that I am the source of all the problems in our relationship.
That I need to give him some peace. That he can't make me
happy. That he needs to step back from my problems as much
as possible. Which is difficult to do when I'm standing in front
of him with a sock full of his sperm that his wife and worst
enemy has dug out from the depths of the dirty laundry pile. Is
that borderline? When you kick mercilessly at the one thing you
care most about, namely your relationship with your husband?
When you can't think of anything worse than him leaving you
and yet you constantly do things, day after day, to make him
want to leave? Make him *have* to leave, just to save his life from
my twisted soul.

Why does he stay with me? Why does he let me treat him
that way? How can he sleep with me after that kind of thing?
We're head over heels in love with each other, that much is
clear. Most importantly he adores me, because he's still with
me despite the fact that I've shown my ugly side over the years.
My therapist has now managed to get me to fight my wars internally rather than taking them out on those around me. To get
me to that point, though, things first got much worse. But my
husband has his peace now. He didn't deserve all the tantrums,
the hatred, the rage, the disappointment over things he couldn't
control. My parents are the only ones who are to blame. And
the truck driver. And the newspapers.

Up until recently I opened up so many wounds with my
behavior that he still looks at me distrustfully sometimes and
expects a tantrum when we discuss certain things. He's totally
afraid of me. It will take years before this fear dissipates. My
therapist knew that right away. She said that you can't just undo

things. She basically issued a gag order for all my problematic topics at home.

I think it must be quite impressive when I throw a fit. I've poured boiling milk on him, lifted a one-hundred-kilo table and tried to throw it at him. I've thrown everything at him and inflicted bodily pain on him.

In the movies it's often portrayed as evidence of a passionate relationship when a woman throws things around. But in reality it's evidence that a woman is psychologically damaged.

One day, not long after the sock incident, my husband and I rented six porn films. It's always embarrassing to me as a woman to go into the porn section of the video shop. Though I do feel very powerful. If I said "Boo!" the uptight men standing around in there trying to act normal would all run away. At the same time I hear my mother, who is sitting on my shoulder and bothering me. *Aha, look at this, the poor oppressed woman has to go with her oppressor to rent films of oppression or else he will leave her.* All of that goes through my head when I wander around looking for a movie with a good cover. Many of the fetish films are out of the question for us. We're not into eighties stuff or porn with heavily pregnant women; no violence, no Lolitas. No amateur stuff where the razor burn is clearly visible on all the ass cheeks. What we like best are things stylistically similar to Andrew Blake films. On that day we rented six of his movies: *Water, Aria, Girlfriends, Playthings, Wild,* and *Wet.* He seems to have a thing for the letter *W*.

That night we managed to watch only one. We watch porn films to get ourselves into a kind of flushed state. We forget everything around us—it's like taking some sort of sex drug. There's something very relaxing about lying around watching

other people have sex—as long as you manage to turn off
your jealousy, as I was able to that night. We have wilder sex
than usual either during or after watching porn. That's why
we watch it.

I had to be away the next night for work, and my jealousy
bug kicked back in. I thought, damn, he's going to watch the
other films alone and lie to me about it when I come home.
And then he'll watch one of them a second time with me even
though he's already watched it without me. And while we're
watching together, and having sex together, he'll have to be careful what he says to avoid spilling the beans. This was during a
period when, because of low self-confidence, I couldn't stand
the idea of him watching porn movies alone. That's the way
the stupid, narrowly defined rules that I established for us as a
couple worked. I tried to establish rules to make things better
than they'd been in previous relationships. I thought at the time
that if he jerked himself off, with or without a movie, it was the
beginning of the end. I was like a member of the Taliban, and
he still sees me that way to this day. I put so much energy into
it back then that he may not lose that image of me for a long
time. Maybe he never will.

I had a devilish plan. I casually got him to promise to wait
until I got back before watching the other five movies. That he
wouldn't watch them without me. That was the first step. Then,
I waited until he left the apartment in the morning. I plucked six
hairs from my head and put them on a white piece of paper. I
have long dark hair that's easy to see against white paper. Then I
checked the order the movies were stacked in. I felt like a secret
agent out of a movie. I opened one DVD cover after the next
and stuck in a strand of hair. I lifted each disc off the plastic

star in the middle and ran the hair underneath the disc. Then I pulled the tip of the hair through the middle of the disc and created a loop, which I clamped by putting the disc back onto the star-shaped holder. If he took out a DVD, the hair would definitely fall out. I tried it out to make sure. Took out a DVD, put it back in, and looked for the hair. It was gone. I was proud of myself even though I knew what I was doing was wrong. I think I also realized it could just lead to chaos and despair if I confirmed my suspicions—my suspicions that behind my back he would break my iron-fisted rule. I probably got that from my mother, too—no idea why I thought it would be a betrayal for him to shoot some sperm when I wasn't anywhere nearby. It's nearly a Catholic stance, this rule of mine! Terrible. It's a self-fulfilling prophecy. Leaving porn films lying around in a man's apartment seems to me now, in retrospect, like leaving a bone in a wolf's den and telling the wolf not to chew it. Obviously it's not going to work. Maybe I didn't want it to work. I wanted to test whether I could trust him until the end of my life, whether he was a liar or coward, whether he had the strength and will to tell the truth later if the hairs were missing.

I stacked the DVDs back up on the floor and wrote down the order. Actually the order of the movies on the stack should have been enough of an indicator—if they were in a different order when I got back, I would know what that meant. There were three different checks: the order the DVDs were stacked in, the hairs, and the confrontation. I would carry out my mission with ice in my veins, like an avenging angel, with no mercy for the love of my life.

I stuck the little piece of paper with the list of how the movies were stacked deep in my wallet, left, and came back the next day. I was anxious, like a hunter who has set a trap. Except my odds of success were far better than a hunter's—my trap was guaranteed to be closed around its prey, my husband.

He wasn't home when I got there. Home sweet home. I dropped my bag in the front hall and ran with my jacket still on to the corner of the living room where the stack of DVDs was—to have my suspicions tragically confirmed. You can't trust anyone. You can never put your life—or your heart or anything else, including your pussy—in the hands of others.

I could see immediately that they were stacked in a different order. I pulled out the scrap of paper with the list on it and checked: they were indeed out of order. Completely. Nothing was the same—not in the stack of DVDs and not in our relationship. Without even realizing it was so wrong, he had haphazardly restacked the videos. How stupid does he think I am? Breathing quickly, I opened the cases and held them up to the light. If a hair had been there I would have seen it. Every one was gone, in the first case, the second, the third, the fourth, until the last—even in the one we had already watched the hair was missing.

It shocked me more than I had expected. I sat there on the floor and thought. I knew he was a sex maniac, but this bad? I didn't know it was so extreme. He watched six porn films while I was gone? In one night? Or during the day. Crazy. I had fallen for him because of his unrestrained masculine sexuality. To piss off my mother I'd fallen for the most Neanderthal-like, sex-obsessed man I could find. And he had fallen for me to piss off his mother—me, an anti-Christian, the opposite of Catholic, so un-Catholic that I practically took things full circle and became Catholic again. We were together because we wanted to upset our mothers. And it worked well. But what now? This much sexuality was too much even for me.

I had to calm myself down and think about how to bring it up with him in a way that would cause as much permanent damage to our relationship as possible. And I would give him one more chance to come clean, just to prove to myself that things truly weren't going to work out with him.

In my delusional state—there I was, shooting myself in the foot and trying to rob myself of the love of my life—I felt deceived, betrayed, and all alone. Even so, I offered a friendly greeting, perhaps exaggeratedly so. We're still together. I need him to feel secure for the moment.

"So? Did you manage to wait for me to watch the films?"

"Of course. What did you think? I promised. And I kept my word."

Sure.

"You didn't have a quick look at one or two out of boredom?"

"No, really. I just told you. Why are you being so weird about it?"

He senses that something's lurking. He's panicking. But he has no idea how I could know it. Did he have the sound up too high? Did I have a spy out in the hall? Did I have him tailed? Is there spyware you can install in a TV? That's the kind of thing my mother always did to her men. It occurs to me that I must have inherited my distrust of men from her. Shit. Yep. Her old video recorder had a special function. She could go to bed and while she was sleeping, the VCR would record the channels her boyfriend watched and for how long as he zapped between the channels that showed naked women at night. But what is a man supposed to do, when his girlfriend is so screwed up? And yet I followed her in acting like a hard-ass prosecutor when it came to male sexuality.

"I'm asking because the stack looks as though it's been changed around from the way it was when I left yesterday, unless I'm misremembering things."

I give him ample opportunity to tell the truth. I keep asking him, giving him chance after chance to come clean, until I'm not able to control myself anymore and am about to throw a fit because of all the cowardice and lying. Though in secret I know up to that point in our relationship I'd never presented myself as the type of person to whom he could comfortably tell the truth. When you constantly throw fits and castigate the most loved person in your life, then you have nobody to blame but yourself if you get lied to out of fear. I spread fear and terror in our relationship while at the same time condemning my husband, who has gotten caught trying to avoid all that.

"Ah, that's what you mean. I was vacuuming up and knocked over the stack of DVDs. The things you notice! My sweetie. And then you automatically think the worst of me— that I would watch the movies without you. Don't worry. When I say something, I stick to it. You can trust me. Don't look so angry."

That would have done it if I didn't know, 100 percent, that he was lying—if I didn't have other evidence to rely on. It's really scary when you know someone is lying but he does it so well that you would believe it if you didn't know otherwise. That's how you get tricked.

I stare at him with squinted eyes.

"What is up with you? Is there something wrong? Don't you believe me?"

"That's it exactly! I don't believe you! You disgusting pig. What if I told you that I know for a fact that you watched *all* of the movies, maybe not all the way through, but you watched them all right. *All of them!* Every single one. I set a trap for you. You disgusting pig. How can I trust you? I can't live with someone like that. Someone who doesn't keep his word and then when he's caught just keeps lying to my face! How is that supposed to work? I know you watched the movies, you disgusting pig."

"What are you talking about? You set a trap? What? A trap?"

I run out of the room. He comes after me. When people are newly together, they play those games. Always imitating things they see in the movies whenever something extreme happens. Where else would you learn to act like that?

You don't actually want to leave. You just want to test the person to see if he runs after you. Then you can stop running.

We fought for days over all the lies. In couples therapy it became clear very quickly that I was the asshole in that situation. I set a trap, and that was worse than his lying.

My distrust about all things sexual is deep. Maybe that's why things work so well in bed? Maybe it has nothing to do with his virility or his money. Maybe it has to do with his sexual energy, which I find so hard to control—though I actually benefit the most from that energy. Because he manages to make me come every single time we have sex. Or is that just because of me? That's what he says. He says it has nothing to do with him but rather with my ability to let myself go completely—at least when it comes to sex. In his mind that's why I come so hard and so consistently.

It's great how long I've been able to sit here and breathe and think. I listen to things in the apartment. I'm slowly getting hungry and want to get going. There's still clanging coming from the washroom. I won't interrupt him. I'm happy for it to get done. It's amazing the way our relationship has changed in the last seven years. The way we—or really, I—have changed. He hasn't needed to change nearly as much as I have. He doesn't bother anyone the way I do. He's much more at peace with himself.

Earlier I clung to him like some kind of lunatic. Then I decided I couldn't be so dependent, because I was worried things would fall apart. I gradually got stronger and now I think I could live without him. Suddenly things are at the other extreme now. I wish he would cheat on me so I could cheat, too. Maybe he could cheat with the pretty babysitter or some friend of mine. Perhaps I shouldn't try to pick out the woman for him to have an affair with. That's what Frau Drescher would say, I'm sure. I'm not sure how I should confess to my husband that I want to sleep with every man I meet. I love him and I love having sex with him. But I want more. Nobody could do better sexually than he does—his handiwork with my vagina, that porn-film diddle-diddle he does to my clit that makes it almost explode. I just want to have another body between my thighs. Monogamy can be such a prison sometimes!

I hear him unfold the drying rack in the washroom. That thing is unwieldy. Does he really have so much laundry to hang that he needs to put that thing out, too? Interesting.

How can I explain to him that all the men I've had crushes on for a few days or weeks in the last year are obviously not a threat to our great love? Or is that playing with fire? And much more dangerous than it seems to me? I think that if I could sleep with them, my infatuation would quickly dissipate, would be manageable, and the magic would soon wear off.

He finally comes upstairs and smiles at me. "Ready to go?"

"Sure. Just let me go grab a sweater."

I wipe away my thoughts. I'm going to have to address them again soon, though.

We lock our apartment with several locks. Safety first. We walk to our regular Italian restaurant, called Alberto. Everything we do is well rehearsed. Food, sex, the routes we take, everything. I need to be pacified, not agitated.

Georg and I take the same route to the restaurant as always, crossing the streets at the same places. We don't talk much. Those days are long gone. Sometimes I hold his hand, but then I let go because it seems ridiculous to hold his hand. Sometimes I think we're too old to be holding hands.

When it comes to relationships, my therapist says that every single day you are together has to be voluntary. But for years, unfortunately, I've brought coercion into our relationship. I now realize that I fell in love with my own image of my husband. Then through a painful process I had to admit that he wasn't actually the way I saw him. And he had to go through the same process. And we have stayed together anyway because I still like what's left even now that all the illusions have been dispelled. It was someone else, but someone good for me—and good to me. Then I began to want to change him so he'd be more like me. My therapist has told me a hundred times, "Frau Kiehl, what do you want? If you ever managed to mold him so he was like you, you would despise him immediately and that would be it for your relationship." I had to learn—again, through a painful process in therapy—that I need to leave him as he is.

A few times along the way we say hello to someone we know. We know a lot of people here in the neighborhood. It's important to us to get along with most of our neighbors—for the children. That way when they run around in the area, everyone knows to keep an eye on them. Like in a herd of animals, everyone needs to help protect all the kids. We look into our regular café next to the church and wave to the barista, who's a friend of ours. Then we continue on in silence. The way it should be between people who have been married for a long time. Everything in our relationship is starting to fall asleep. Why should we be any different from any other couple? He says more and more often that I've become deaf to the frequency of his voice. He speaks to me and I don't react. It's not intentional, I just don't hear it. My brain has determined that anything anyone else says is more interesting; plus my brain knows I can always ask later if I miss something he says. The same is true of him. I often catch him not listening to me. The insatiable curiosity about what incredible things the other partner might have to say is completely gone, and has been for years. The air's gone out. It scares me. Help, I want out! I would love to rescue our love or, at the very least, save myself from this life.

At Alberto we go to our regular table. Luckily it's free. We have another table we use when our regular one is already taken.

We sit next to each other in the window and watch people walking past. We don't talk much. We've already told each other all the stories of our lives. As always, I order spaghetti with shredded mixed vegetables and lots of chili pepper. I've recently discovered a new god for my monotheism: Jonathan Safran Foer. I love him and his book *Eating Animals*. It plays a huge role at every mealtime. My husband sometimes gets jealous of authors. Up until now he's had no other reason to get jealous. I read nonfiction books. And I become a fanatical follower of the writer of whatever I'm reading. I wanted to become a vegetarian, which is why I read Foer's *Eating Animals*. Maybe my husband is right to be jealous when all I talk about for weeks and months is Jonathan Safran Foer. He is my God and his book my bible. Monotheism, like I said. My husband wants to be my only god. He says, smiling at me, "You shouldn't have any other gods but me." But when I can concentrate on doing something good, like becoming a vegetarian, I feel better. I don't have to spend so much time thinking about my own fucked-up self. I can focus on another challenge. Like worshipping Jonathan Safran Foer.

The food comes quickly. Not many people here today. It's also pretty late for lunch.

What other people think of me is so important to me that I am easily capable of being strict and compelling myself to give up almost anything by using the following trick: I simply tell everyone that I'm a vegetarian now, which forces me to do it for the rest of my life or else I risk looking stupid. It drives me to succeed. But I'm disciplined enough that I don't eat the things I've sworn off even when I'm alone—I'm like an alcoholic who's dried out. I figure that if I allow myself to be weak even for a little while, it will only make things more difficult going forward. So I'd rather just go ahead and bite the bullet.

After the meal we joke around with the owner's family and then pay the bill, which is always the same price—for two vegetarian dishes and a big bottle of mineral water.

We take the same route back home to our apartment. Georg takes off his pants once we're inside, emerges in his cowboy underwear, and tries to master the chaos my daughter and I create in the apartment on a daily basis.

I kill time because without my daughter in the house I don't really have anything to do. As a result of our fucked-up patchwork family, I constantly have to deal with the reality that she's at her father's place. Good for her and good for him. Shit for me. But I should be quiet. The taking-care-of-everything machine can idle in the driveway for a while; the selfish woman I was prior to having a child can give herself free rein. Act like a kid again.

I watch my husband. He's very organized, much more so than I am. He learned that from his mother. Even though she hates women, she taught her son how to run a household—probably so he'd never have to be dependent on a woman. So he can do everything better than I can. My mother didn't teach me how to be a housewife, so no man would ever want to be with me for my domestic abilities. It worked. He's with me because he loves me, not because of anything I can do—except maybe blowing him. That probably plays a role. Definitely, in fact. But that's the only thing.

It's a constant theme of discussion between us: cleaning up. For the sake of love he tries to accommodate me and I try to accommodate him. Meaning I try to be less messy and he tries to put up with more messiness. We try to work at every aspect of our relationship in order to make the impossible possible: staying together forever. We both put in an insane amount of effort to get each other to come. He always makes sure I come multiple times almost every time we have sex. I can only ensure that he comes once because then it's done—men have somewhat diminished abilities when it comes to orgasms, after all.

He looks a lot like my father. He looks like an old man, which is the beauty of him. I buy him things that make him look even older because I think at this point it wouldn't be bad if he were a bit older than he actually is. Frau Drescher says I should stop further indulging my father complex. When I look at my husband, I should see my husband and not my lost father. But I can't, at least not yet. I've already thought about the idea of taking a much, much older lover in order to free my husband from my father complex. That way we could simply be man and wife instead of father and daughter. It sounds like a good plan to me, and I'm sure it would sound good to my husband and to Frau Drescher. Even if it would take my husband a long time to accept. But he would eventually. Sometime.

I have a lot of problems, but one thing that isn't a problem: I am perfectly comfortable sitting around while someone else cleans up around me.

My husband wears good 1960s old-man clothes and has a big cock that is visible through his pants—just like my father's was. It makes him very comfortable in his own skin, the way my father always was. Being rich and well endowed makes a man extremely laid-back. No neuroses about your image. You don't have to pretend to be something you're not. Don't have to posture. Don't have to shift attention by fighting, like Sarkozy, for instance. My husband is a genuinely strong character. Even when he's taking care of all the household chores. I love him madly. I would do anything for him. Except be faithful, of course.

He's in the kitchen now, emptying the dishwasher. This is one of the things he always handles. I almost never do it. It's always been taken care of on the few occasions I go to do it. Now that I think about it, there's no way I could have known when we got together that his cock would fit so perfectly inside me. But then again, who knows? I trust our animal instincts—maybe

I could smell it? How well he'd fit inside me and hit my G-spot every time with the crook in his cock. It couldn't be just blind luck. I believe in coincidence and animal instincts—it had to be one or the other. Frau Drescher thinks the existence of the G-spot is a question of faith. There are many contradictory theories about it and there's been no conclusive research to show where or even whether it exists. Fine. At least there's one thing I am happy to believe in that is impossible to prove.

The biggest challenge for me when we got together was the stepchild. I had nothing but bad experiences with stepparents. For the sake of my mother, and at the flip of a switch, I either had to love them or, when she fell for someone else, act as if they were dead. My challenge with my stepson, Max, who is the same age as Liza, was to do things better than my stepfathers and my awful stepmother had done. It quickly became apparent that it wouldn't be so easy. Right from the start I was mean to the child and jealous of the unconditional love his father had for him. I kept thinking: he doesn't love *me* that way. Not that way at all. Suddenly I understood how my hated stepmother had felt. I was like a man who beats his wife. I don't want to do it, and I apologize every time it happens, and promise to change my ways. But I never manage to change. Because my emotions, my complexes, my feeling of being small, my fear of loss, my hate, rage, and grief are much greater than my ability to change or stop.

All of this hit me when I saw my stepson. I vowed to try to stop. I knew that the great love of my life would leave me sooner or later if I couldn't stop. But for years I still couldn't control myself. I was inhumanely hard on my stepson. Because I'd never experienced it any other way. I can clearly remember that thought going through my head: *Why should he have it any better than I did?* Why? I was always friendly and forgiving with my own daughter, the way you are with your own child, your own genes. But with Max I set completely different standards. He could never please me. I was cold and mean and snippy to him. It was so bad over the years that the little guy became scared of me. When his father had to go away for work and he had to stay with me, he looked at me with panic in his eyes and started to cry. He clung to his father and didn't want him to go. I could tell something was wrong, really wrong, but I couldn't suppress it for longer than a couple of days. Then the evil welled up in me again. I didn't enjoy being like that, but I was good at it. Mental cruelty. If there's anything I'm good at, that's it.

We had a set of stacking cardboard building blocks, each block open on one side so it could be slotted into the next. The size difference between the blocks was minimal, so that if you didn't insert them in order there would be some left over that wouldn't fit. They were very difficult for a small child to stack together correctly. He couldn't concentrate on the game out of fear. I would say to him, "You can't do it anyway." And he couldn't. Ever. He fumbled around with the blocks and looked at me, totally panicked. I never had to do anything physical to him. A look was enough. I stood over him as he knelt with the blocks on the floor. I glared at him. For an eternity. It was horrible. He would cry, snot and tears running down his face. I just had to stop the game early enough so that his eyes weren't red from crying when my husband got home. When Georg was back, Max and I acted as if nothing had happened. "I played with him and tried to keep him busy. But he wasn't so good at the game." That was the explanation I had at the ready. But I never had to explain anything. My husband had an idea that something was wrong, but he could never have imagined how awful his beloved wife was. The only thing he knew was that his son didn't like to be left alone with me. But Georg never asked anything. He probably did everything possible to avoid leaving me and my stepson alone in the house, though.

Still, I couldn't stop. I saw the stepson as a foreign body. He was the product of Georg's love for another woman. That alone drove me crazy. Not only that. Why did I have to have an abortion despite the fact that not long before he had wanted to have a child—with her? He wanted to have a child with her and did have one. Like a gorilla, I wanted to kill the child from the previous relationship. This child bothered me, made our life more complicated—just the fact that I couldn't keep a lid on my hatred for the child had a detrimental effect on our love.

My husband cautiously suggested going to therapy together, instead of me just going on my own. He saw it as a chance for our love to survive my hatred for his son. We fought constantly over questions of how to bring the children up. I wanted him to be harder on his son. Naturally I thought he spoiled Max. And (attention!) I also thought the boy ate too much. In total seriousness, I tried to convince my husband that his son ate too much when he stayed with us. I was a menace to society. This child needed to be protected from me. We were in therapy together for years as a result. So my husband could understand why I constantly wanted his son's head on a platter.

Why did he stay with me and put up with it all? I still can't believe it, as I don't seem to myself to be very worthy of love. In fact, I'm truly not worthy of love in many clearly demonstrable ways. Until the therapist was able to cut some of those traits right out of me. Regardless of the specific problem, the process is always the same: talk, talk, talk, mercilessly, primarily with me. I confess to my therapist how bad I am. I beg her to get it out of me so it won't destroy our love. Implore her to help me to protect this dear, pretty, innocent child—from me. It took years. But then suddenly—from one day to the next—I was cured. The evil-stepmother-demon had been cast out. I paid a lot of money to make that happen and ran my mouth for years, railing against myself and my own stepmother. And throughout all that time, my stepson kept trying to build bridges to me. I never wanted it, but he kept offering his hand, opening his arms. That just made it worse. Didn't he have a memory? Couldn't he notice that I hated him? Max, I'm sure, was thinking, *If my dear father loves this woman so much, there must be something to it*. He loves me and wants me to love him back.

My therapist always said Max could see the emotional distress behind my lashing out at him—that he could tell I didn't want to do it. That I just didn't want to admit to myself that I love him. I really thought there was room in my heart for only one child. For my child. And that this little man-creature was going to take away my husband or create a situation that would lead to his parents getting back together. As a child of divorce myself, I know how strong the desire is to reunite your parents.

Since I got over this problem with Max, I'm even more upset at my own father and stepmother. They never tried to seek help for the situation. To this day he lets my stepmother treat me badly because of her complexes, because she's jealous of me. And she tries, as I tried to do with my husband, to get my father on her side. Yes. Except that my father, unlike Georg, never issued an ultimatum: either you change and conquer your problem, or I'm leaving you. No, he has stayed with her and allowed her—for nearly thirty fucking years—to continue to drive a wedge between us.

I did that for only three or four years. Four too many. Especially for my little stepson. And for my husband. My therapist killed me for it, too, because in order to help her be effective as quickly as possible, I told her every bad thing I did without sparing a thing.

When you are in therapy for a long time, you start to recognize things about people that they don't notice about themselves. You can't say anything, though. You can't just go around analyzing people. You haven't studied it; you're just being treated. Frau Drescher says my soon-to-be-ex-best friend has to realize on her own that she is repeating her mother's history and decide on her own to get help. Her mother was beaten by her husband, and so my friend saw women in the victim role. Now, as an adult, she keeps seeking this role out in her own relationships with men. And then she frets over each new outbreak of violence as if it were just a big coincidence that she's always with men like that. As if she weren't actively seeking out the wrong men out of masochism. Every time. In her view, all men hit. No, baby, only in your world—a world you create. There are women who seek out men who help them, who make them stronger and build them up. But you don't know what that's like. You'd only be able to find out if you did a lot of work on yourself. You think you're not as crazy as I am and don't need therapy. But if you ask those around you how much they suffer from your complexes, your rage, your aggression—they maintain goodwill toward you for now, but how long will it last?

Georg comes in smiling. He appears to be finished.

"So, what shall we do now? We're on our own—let's come up with something nice."

"I don't know. What do you feel like doing?"

I always do that. I don't like to decide on that kind of thing. Where to go to eat or for an outing or whatever—those are his areas. It gets on his nerves that I never want to suggest anything, that he always has to make the decisions. Yeah, well, that's the way it is. Though I am trying to work on it.

"No, you decide what you feel like doing, Elizabeth."

I knew that would be the response. Now I have to rack my brain to come up with something. Oh, man, it's just like in bed, when I have to pretend to come up with things I want done to me just so he'll shut up.

I pull an idea out of thin air. "Let's look at the Internet to see who is working at the brothel tomorrow for our adventure." Very courageous of you, Elizabeth, to bring it up on your own. "We can stay in tonight, figure things out for tomorrow, then order Indian and a movie."

"Perfect. That's what we'll do."

He sits down next to me on our designer couples therapy couch and puts his head in my lap. I think he, too, misses the good mother he never had. It's just that not having one didn't inflict as much damage on him as it did on me. Or perhaps he just doesn't make as much fuss about it. That's also possible.

I run my fingers through his thin hair and then softly knead his earlobes. I always do this when the opportunity presents itself. I can feel in my gut that I'm anxious about tomorrow's sex outing. *Pfff.*

We used to go to prostitutes only when we were abroad. At home we always felt as though we were being watched as a result of my being in the papers all those years ago. My life was dictated by whether they—my biggest enemy—would be able to dig anything up on me. Every day in front of the bathroom mirror I'd imagine that they'd offered our cleaning woman money—a lot of money, or else she wouldn't do it—for naked photos of us. Not to publish, just to laugh about in the newspaper's editorial offices. I still have the same feeling that I can't do what I want, can't freely decide, because they'll steal the moment from me with a camera. The most personal moment.

But we got braver and braver in picking brothels. Until we ended up in our own city. You can get used to anything. Our favorite spot is called Lulu, right downtown. The atmosphere is very intimate there. We know all the women. And female customers—whether for sex or just for a drink at the bar—are welcome. When we sit there it feels as if we are back in the 1920s. Like real bohemians. At Lulu we had a beautiful experience with a brunette. The women there always use moisturizer on their entire bodies. They have softer skin than women who don't have to earn their living with their bodies, like me. I have rough spots here and there. On my knees, my elbows, even beneath my ass—the area that gets sat upon. But not the women at Lulu. They smell great, all over, and moisturize like crazy. Our beautiful experience was with a woman named Grace. She was funny, which for us is important. And she spoke pretty good German. She was smart and, also important, nice to me. That was psychologically clever of her because I've often put the brakes on out of desperate, crazed jealousy. She reassured me, and after that she could do whatever she wanted with my husband—or rather whatever he wanted. Once she had me on her side both of them could do whatever they wanted. I was totally relaxed for once, staying above it all rather than suspiciously keeping track of every finger, what it went into and for how long.

We met Grace downstairs in the bar. Drinks there cost about four times what they do in a normal bar. And if you buy a drink for one of the women, you can easily pay ten times more than at a normal bar. Just to get the woman to talk to us. It's like tying a couple of sticks of salami beneath the chin of an unloved child to get the dog to play with him. That's the way it is in this kind of establishment. You can't just start up a conversation, convince the woman you're nice and charming, and take off with her. Nope. You have to pay for every little thing.

We bought a bottle of champagne for her. She passed some out to her colleagues so that it emptied quickly and we had to buy a second bottle. And then she started kissing me. She had warm, soft lips. My thin English lips sank right into hers. I'd never felt anything like that on my mouth. Wow. It felt wonderful. I could have done that for hours. Everything around me just melted away. And I thought, *Oh no, my husband probably wants to kiss her, too, so I should stop soon*. She grabbed my breasts there at the bar. Her lips on mine and her right hand on my left breast. Out of the corner of my eye I could see her other hand wander down to my husband's crotch. She was good at her job. Like an octopus.

We quickly went to one of the rooms above the bar. The beds are nice—made out of washable rubber. Big cubes, like plastic building blocks—a bit like sacrificial altars, too. One of those was in the middle of the room, much taller than a normal bed. I think it should become the new standard height. You can be thankful, I was told, for how great it looks compared to other establishments. But I missed my electric blankets. Maybe I can take them some other time.

She asked if I wanted to take a bath with her. Sure! You have to start somewhere—just to get over the embarrassment factor. She turned on the water and Georg was clearly excited. He already had a hard-on. It's always quick with him. Grace got into the tub first; then I did. She had put in only a little bit of bubble bath so Georg would still be able to see everything. He sat down on the toilet seat. Grace complimented me, and I her. We giggled, both still a little bashful. But things started to go quickly as soon as we kissed a few more times, long deep kisses with our tongues. I began to relax. I could do anything. Without asking her. She let me touch her entire body. In order to get at her better, I knelt in front of her. She spread her legs. I stroked her neck, her breasts. She mirrored all my motions with her hands on my body. I fingered her, though it was a bit difficult because of the water. I put my head underwater to lick her for as long as I could hold my breath. I thought about my father, who always said to me that when you think you are going to die underwater while diving, you can actually stay down twice as long again and nothing will happen.

I came up snorting, gasping for air. Georg had in the meantime locked onto her other lips. His hand massaged her left breast. Then he kissed me again. She fingered me. The ice was broken and all my remaining tension melted away. There was no more danger. The three of us lay down on the plastic cube. I could really go down on her now. Georg quickly undressed. He wanted to get into it, too. He'd let me get enough of a head start.

He never comes inside a prostitute. Must be a Catholic thing. I can't understand it, but whatever he wants to do is fine. He always wants to come inside me. I suspect he secretly thinks no other man should come inside me. Is it possible? We'll see.

The two expensive hours with Grace flew by. Afterward she left her little bag of toiletries in the room. I took it as a memento of the beautiful experience we'd had together. Stole it, you could also say.

Now I look at my beloved old husband as he lies with his head in my lap. I ask myself whether I am negating myself by doing everything for him. I can't find the answer. I wouldn't put it past myself—it's certainly possible that I could be denying myself and not noticing it.

He sits back up. Enough romance for one day.

"I'm going to go use the rowing machine for twenty minutes. Will you order the food and pick out a movie?"

He has a nice wooden rowing machine in the basement. Custom-built for his body and his back condition.

"Sure. Do you want a vegetarian dish, too?"

"No. I'll have lamb, please."

He disappears downstairs. I go to the website of the DVD delivery service. I've wanted to see *The Clearing* for ages, though he has no desire. I order it. I call the Indian restaurant, the best one in the city. All my English relatives have said it's good, which is something, because they're all very picky. It'll be forty-five minutes before the food arrives, but it's worth it. I miss my

daughter. I have nothing to do. Without children, life can be
horrible, too.

Since Frau Drescher thinks it's so important, I lean back
on the couch again and do some more deep breathing. I see
pretty spiderwebs in the upper corner of our built-in mirror.
Sometimes I'm crazy. It's my fault that the spiderwebs are there,
because I told the cleaning woman in no uncertain terms not
to vacuum up any spiderwebs in our apartment. She thought
it was a strange request, but she sticks to it.

The reason I think of that is because my daughter is learning about spiders in school. How they are useful animals. How
we humans use them. They don't do anything to us, but they
eat mosquitoes, which bother us, and ants and other things that
disturb us. And yet we don't like to have them in our apartments.
Now, thanks to my good idea, we have an intact ecosystem—
there's a spiderweb in almost every corner, and the spiders live
with us and help us get rid of mosquitoes. And it makes me feel
that I am one of the good people, not the bad, because like a
Buddhist I try to live in harmony with nature. It's going great.
I recommend it to everyone.

I have to divide the world into Good and Bad because
otherwise I'm incapable of being political. If you pay attention
to all the yeas and nays and exceptions to the rules, it drives you
nuts and you just stop doing anything. You don't fight against
things. But if you divide people into good and bad, companies
into good and bad, and so forth, then you can do something.
You have to decide what you are opposed to. What you consider
good. And then go for it. Fight against everything that's bad.
First learn to abstain from bad things, and then start trying
to get other people to go along with you. Like in the Michael

Jackson song "Man in the Mirror." You want to make the world a better place? Look in the mirror. Start with yourself. It's tough at first. But when you manage to do without something for the first time and then get used to it, you get a rush of righteousness. Environmental sainthood will be just around the corner.

The accident completely altered my personality. I wasn't like this earlier in my life. Something like that makes you lonely and weak. And after the accident Stefan was too weak himself to help me. The exact moment I fell for Georg was when he answered a question I asked: "What does a normal day look like for you?" He said, "I go to work and take care of all the unpleasant things I've written down on a list earlier in the day."

Violins, beautiful pink sunset. This was the man for me. He's a doer. Exactly what I need. For all of my problems and because of all the catastrophes that are yet to come. Murder and death, collapsing high-rises. He's the right person.

As soon as my husband and I got together, I got pregnant. In love with him the way I was, I attributed it to his strong sperm. But it must really have been his strong sperm because it happened despite the fact that I was on the pill. Though to be honest, I was drinking so much at the time that I constantly threw up—not ideal for keeping down birth control pills. In any event, we were pregnant immediately. He absolutely wanted me to get an abortion. At first I thought, *Why? We're in love and we have money and time.* The reason he was strictly against having a baby was that our relationship was still in flux. He was very clinical. Too clinical for me. It was a love child! I had hippie parents and was brought up to think shit like that. The situation was fucked up. We fought and fought. We'd just fallen in love and we had to make a decision like that.

He didn't want to lose his first son. He worried about that a lot during the initial period of our relationship. He thought it would be betraying his baby boy if he had another child right away. Pretty early in our conversations I realized I didn't want to convince him to have a baby as badly as he wanted to convince me to have an abortion. An abortion is quick and painless; a child sticks around an eternity. All I wanted, crying every day, was to hear him say, just once, that he was sorry about our baby, that it was just bad timing and that he would surely want to have a baby with me soon. But he refused to say that to me. I pleaded with him, I begged him, I humiliated myself to hear that sentence: *I'm sorry about our baby*. But he thought if he said that, he wouldn't be able to go through with the abortion. He didn't want to betray his child any further—he'd already left the boy's mother. We learned that in couples therapy: a good father doesn't leave the child, only the mother of the child. Very important! The crappy new patchwork family arrangement was apparently a little too disorderly for him.

Anyway, he refused to say that sentence. He never said anything nice at all. He just repeated one thing over and over: the baby had to go, it just wouldn't work right now. Maybe he thought it was a trap. If he were to say what I wanted to hear, something would happen—I'd hold him to it. Even though it hurt me to the point of feeling physically ill, I also realized that my own feelings weren't as strong as his—the extent to which he so badly didn't want the baby was not true of me the other way around. So he won that contest. As soon as I said I was prepared to get an abortion, he was much nicer to me again. He didn't have to put up a front anymore. The hard decision had been made and now it just had to be acted upon. We were a team again, and things were much better.

I like to think back on the abortion clinic. I've never again met such sensitive and cautious nurses. You were handled so gently that I thought to myself that it was a place I'd like to come back to often. I felt as if I were on happy pills. Maybe deep down inside I didn't want the baby, either, and I had just been shocked by the strident nature of Georg's insistence. I took it personally. Still, I am to this day envious and jealous of his ex-wife. Why could he be talked into having a baby with her but not with me?

Once, years later, he told me that he'd also thought that I wasn't mentally stable enough to have a child, much less a second one. Cheers! After the termination of the product of our love, the abortion doctor, who was very good and very nice, told us we shouldn't have vaginal sex for a while because of the risk of infection. Aha, we thought, looking at each other, just no *vaginal* sex! Because he was so thankful that I'd had the abortion—my husband, not the doctor—that we felt very close and wanted to sleep with each other immediately. We had the best anal sex—no, actually just the best sex—of all times on the grave of our unborn child. As soon as we got home.

We walked home, as it was only a few hundred meters from our apartment. My husband supported me on my shaky legs. I'll never forget the image and how nice that extremely rare feeling of being supported was, being supported in the true sense of the word. And when we arrived home, we tore into each other like animals. For sex you don't necessarily need your shaky legs to hold you. All the conflict between us was forgotten. And I think it didn't hurt so much because the anesthetic was still having some effect.

All of that is incorporated in our relationship. Incredible that we can still have sex. That we're still together. How such an ol' couple keeps going. Great!

Where is he anyway? Where is Georg? Oh, right, rowing. Without water. I feel so much love for him when I think of all that again. He's earned my company tomorrow in the brothel. I want him to have a nice life. I want to help him achieve that. With as few moral restrictions as possible!

Georg comes back with his face nicely aglow from the exercise. Finally I can stop brooding. The Indian food and movie have arrived in the meantime. I paid for both of them with money from Georg's briefcase, which he leaves next to the front door for just such eventualities.

When Liza isn't home, we act like low-class bastards. We eat on the couch, directly out of the foil containers. Georg pulls our curry mat out from behind the couch. It's an old piece of carpeting that we lay on the floor between the couch and the coffee table so it catches everything that drips. Afterward we just roll it up again and stuff it behind the couch. We put on the movie and eat. The food is too spicy for me. Somehow it hits me in the diaphragm and I get the hiccups. Georg rolls his eyes. He hates it for some reason when I have the hiccups. Who cares?

With his mouth full he says, "Oh, man, the movie seems to be about old marriages."

I answer with my mouth full, too. "So? Do you have something against old marriages?"

We keep watching. It's also about cheating on your spouse. Get the message? I'll still have to explain it to him anyway; he'll never pick up on it from a movie. Georg, can't you see that the man in the movie loves his wife above all else and yet he still cheats on her? It's possible. Love on the side. A great love can withstand it. Yeah, yeah.

The food is unbelievably filling. We eat too fast and need to take the containers away. Like a porn magazine you've already come over—you want nothing to do with it afterward. I press PAUSE so Georg can throw out the containers. The frozen image is of the actress Helen Mirren. She's just gotten undressed and is standing there with her beautiful big breasts in a skin-color bra. I stare at the frozen image.

When Georg comes back, I quickly press PLAY.

"Finally the breasts are gone. It really gets me down."

Georg rolls his eyes and pushes the PAUSE button again. The breasts are frozen on the screen again.

"Good that you brought that up again. What exactly is it again—what's the story with breasts?"

"What do you mean?"

"Yeah, well, do you want to have big breasts so every man lusts after you? Isn't it enough that I think you're attractive? Why would you worry so much that you might not get the attention of a few assholes?"

"No, it's got nothing to do with whether everyone wants me, though being thought of as pretty would be nice. And I've learned since I was little that you're only considered pretty if you have a certain bust size. I feel unwanted, unloved. I don't feel pretty. I feel worthless. It drives me crazy. I can't explain it. It's just the way it is."

"Then get implants if it's so important to you. And you might as well join a church while you're at it. Kill two birds with one stone."

"Only over my dead body will I take the easy way out. If you want to be loved for the way you are, you have to stay the way you are. If you changed yourself you would never know whether you would be loved without the implants."

"I can't hear it anymore."

"I'm working on it. Oh, man, just turn the movie back on."

For a second I feel as if I need to go check on Liza. But she's not here. I have a guilty conscience because she's gone, because she always has to shuttle back and forth between her parents. Whenever she's away—which is every week—I always vow to be nicer when she's back. Doesn't happen very often, though. She's annoying. She pushes my buttons and can drive me crazy.

During the few school holidays we spend with Liza, I try to travel as little as possible. I have little nervous breakdowns all the time with the kids. The way everyone in my family does. My grandmother used to have breakdowns. My mother had them with us. And now I do, too, with my stepson and daughter. It starts as soon as I hear the word *holiday*. If we take a vacation with the children, it's not a holiday at all. It's total hell.

Life at home, when the kids are in school, is much easier. But if you have to spend an entire day entertaining them so they don't get bored, and then they get bored, you can have a nervous breakdown, too. What happens to me is that I run around screaming uncontrollably. I watch them with squinted eyes and think the following sentences: *You are ruining my life. I can't stand it with you around. You are pissing me off.*

Really horrible, vacationing with children. But as with all of my grumbling, the opposite is true, too. Vacations without children are just as horrible. When I have nothing to take care of I immediately start to think I'm an egomaniac with no point to my life—you might as well just kill yourself if you don't have kids. That's what goes through my mind when I'm on vacation alone with my husband. I'm just an unlucky woman.

The movie is over and I'm unexpectedly tearing up. The ending made me really sad. I hate to cry. I'm afraid of crying. I can never stop. I wipe away the tears quickly. We have our usual postfilm chat. We both liked it. Then, as always, I go to bed before Georg. He wants to watch an episode of *Six Feet Under*. I can't.

Bathroom. I practice making silly faces in the mirror, faces I'll never need to use. I look proudly at my graying temples. I feel older than I actually am, and it surprises me whenever I look at myself and see that I'm still so young. I brush my teeth.

When my husband asks me what I want to do in the future, I never know how to answer. What do you want to do? What do you want to do? Hobbies? Dreams? Desires? I always think, surprised, *What? I'll be gone soon*. It would be like investing in a vinyl record at this point. I don't have any hobbies or passions, nothing that would be worth living for. I live because I have a child and a husband. For them. Not for me. Now I quickly comb my hair so it won't be too badly tangled in the morning.

On the way to bed, I wonder why people have sex in bed at night anyway. It seems so out of place. I refuse to have sex in bed at night. Because I never know what's going on. We lie there next to each other and never know if the other one wants to have sex or not, or wants to go to sleep or not. It's maddening. At least for me. And then I can't fall asleep. I'm thinking the whole time, *Is he breathing that way because he wants to have sex, or has he fallen asleep?* So I can have sex in bed only during the day.

If sex is as important to everyone as it seems, why don't people have furniture purpose-built for it? Why do you have to have sex on the site where you sleep or on the couch? Why don't homes have a sex room or at least sex furniture? I don't get it. It would make sense. I want to know exactly what the story is: okay, now we're going to sleep. As if I'm autistic. Don't try any funny stuff in bed at night.

I lie down in bed. I need to calm down a bit. I've gotten worked up thinking about the topic of sleep versus sex. Man, I can get so agitated—by myself, all alone, in a dark room, and about something so fundamental. So stressful. I stress myself out. Fuck. My therapist has offered to give me antipsychotic drugs many times. But I don't take them. I'm afraid of antipsychotics. I'll never take them. Over my dead body. Whenever I'm so depressed I want to die—which is often—I never take any drugs that will keep me from feeling that way. Anyway, I often have the impression that depression is exactly the right feeling in this world. So why should I fend it off with medication? A depressed outlook is the right outlook. I'd rather kill myself than take drugs against it. It's more romantic, more honest, more real.

As they always do at night in bed, my thoughts wander to my mother, the woman for whom I had my daughter. Whenever my mother is out and about with my daughter these days, I am deathly afraid. For my child. My entire body aches when she drives Liza somewhere in the car. I vividly picture her driving into a bridge support, either on purpose or not, and killing them both instantly. In the version where it's an accident, her subconscious jerks the wheel as they pass the pillar because she wants to be where her own children are and have her grandchild there, too. That is, she wants to be dead, like them. In the version where she does it on purpose, she wants to take revenge on me because she's so bitter that I could still conceive and she could not.

As long as she lives she'll never have her uterus filled with happiness-generating flesh. She'll never be a bacon-wrapped date. A filled praline. A stuffed chicken *cordon bleu*. She'll have to live alone in her body until the day she dies. It will be bad for her. I'm happy every time my child comes home safely. I say to myself every time, *I didn't expect that*.

In my corpse pose I muse quickly about my husband's sexuality. It's better than thinking about burned children and the aftermath.

My husband's sexual socialization couldn't have been more different from my own. He hardly ever had sex. And he never got the girl he wanted. Had a chronic shortage. And had sex with women he found disgusting because the good ones didn't want him. The kind of sex where you fuck and then want to get away fast. I never experienced any of that. I grew up able to fuck the ones I wanted to fuck. I had a crush on someone, liked someone, and then I had sex with the person. I never had anyone between my legs I didn't think was totally cool. I never felt disgusted after sex with anyone. I never felt bad or wanted to get rid of anyone afterward. Never. I could always be very proud of everything that happened. I could always show off my sexual partners. How could two people with such different sexual backgrounds fit together? I take it for granted. I've never known it any other way. For him it's still a wonder that someone would willingly put on sexy underwear for him and sleep with him, that someone would spread her legs completely, use both hands to pull apart her labia until the mucous membrane nearly rips, just so he can lick her. Everything in our life is a deal. That's the way it is. Up to now I've benefited from that. But I don't want to anymore. I want to be free. Or at least more free. And when you want more freedom, you have to fight for it. And discuss and talk, sometimes the entire night through. I breathe myself to sleep with my usual trick. Good night, crack in the ceiling, my sword of Damocles.

Thursday

We sleep in. For my husband, that means sleeping until nine. For me, until eleven. I get up and go upstairs to the kitchen, as always, and make coffee for us. It's always his second because he makes one on his own. My goal every morning is to make mine better than the one he made for himself. But it rarely works. Making good coffee is harder than giving a good blowjob. Georg is doing tai chi in the living room and I put his coffee on the floor. I'm not sure whether you're allowed to drink coffee while doing tai chi. No idea. Agnetha says it's his decision, regardless of whether I think coffee and tai chi are opposites. She says my dear husband can do with the coffee as he wants. Which is fine with me.

I take my cup of coffee downstairs to the bathroom. I have to shave myself for the prostitute. Not for my husband. Those days are gone. He's not as particular as he was at the beginning of our love.

As I shave in the bathroom, I look now and then at my graying temples. I'm very proud of them. Can you be proud of something gained with no effort? Perhaps it would be more apt to say I find my graying hair beautiful.

My husband likes me to shave for him. But if I go weeks or months without shaving, like when it's winter and I just can't pull myself together to get to it, it doesn't bother him. He's a good man, an easygoing man. The best husband. And he knows from shaving himself in the same areas how difficult it is to shave yourself in spots you can't even see. And all that trouble just for the occasional porn-film performance with your partner. For the joy he gets when he undresses me and finds my freshly shaved plum with the labia halfway closed. My inner lips are so pronounced that they protrude from the outer lips, along with my clitoris sometimes. But I would never have the labiaplasty that's so trendy at the moment. You know from the word *trendy* alone that's it not a good idea—you don't want to have surgery based on something fleeting, regardless of whether it's surgery on your breasts or the dangling inner labia of your vagina.

My freshly shaved lips are so soft that you can't even compare the way they feel to anything. I can't help fiddling with them myself after I shave—the color, that lurid pinkish purple, turns me on. Georg flips out. Even so, it's no reason to make sure I'm completely and freshly shaved at all times. Can't be bothered. He shaves himself for me, too, but also not all the time. He hates the feeling of the hair growing back in, which starts a day after he shaves. He has to adjust his balls all the time when the hair is growing in, even grabbing himself on the street. It makes me ashamed for him because I was brought up better than that and always act as if someone is watching me in public.

I look in the mirror again. I respect people with gray hair much more than people with dyed hair. I'm suspicious of women with dyed hair because they can't accept their age. Who are they trying to fool with their dyed hair anyway? You can always tell how old people are from their neck regardless of what color their hair is. A woman's throat is like a tree's rings. You can't fake it. You can also leave your hair the way it is and get used to the fact that surprisingly enough you are getting older—just like everyone else in the world. Along with the gray hair at my temples, I'm starting to get a few gray pubic hairs. What do all the women with dyed hair do about their pubic hair? Do they dye that, too?

I get the feeling that prostitutes are very finicky when it comes to hygiene, shaving, all of that. Everything is removed except for a little Hitler mustache above their clitoris. I do the same thing now. Finished! I rub moisturizer on my entire body, giving extra attention to the part of my ass and thighs I sit on as well as the skin alongside the labia. I stole that trick from prostitutes. It often comes down to skin with prostitutes. Warm, soft skin. Touching their bodies is the best part. And looking at other women's vaginas.

My body is all set. From the large underwear drawer in my dresser I pull out garters, a thong, and bra, all in black. Sometimes I feel like looking like a prostitute. Other times I go dressed like a buttoned-down housewife, in boring white underwear. Whichever. I know only these two extremes.

I put a panty liner into the black thong so I don't get any vaginal fluid on it while on the way to the brothel. I'm already horny just from getting dolled up. As a woman with a lot of natural lubrication, I have to plan ahead in order to avoid any embarrassing situations. I put the garter belt on first, with the stockings, and put the underwear on over them so later I can take off the panties and leave the garters on. Then comes a dress that's really easy to get out of when the time comes. We're naked most of the time we're there.

My husband has some particularly sexy underwear for these special outings. It's usually a bit embarrassing when men try to make themselves sexy with underwear because it almost always seems gay. But he also wants to do something visually for the women he's about to pleasure. As far as I'm concerned, he could go in tighty whities—it's manlier. But I let him do what he wants. It's part of the ritual. He's totally shaved—no Hitler mustache above his cock. Like me, he also worried about the fastidiousness of the prostitutes.

Neither one of us is the type to take charge, be the boss of the situation. With us it's always the hooker. She's the boss. We put ourselves in her hands. It's almost sickening how deferentially we treat the hookers. Maybe at some point we'll get cooler about it all, but that's nowhere on the immediate horizon. I put on only a little makeup—it'll just get smeared by vaginal fluid soon anyway. And at that point it'll be better if I don't have black-brown-blue makeup all over my face. I braid my hair.

Georg is finished with the tai chi he does for his back. I see him pass by the door in his brothel undies. It's a G-string in the back, running up his ass crack. In the front is a gold pouch for his cock and balls. Embarrassing. But he seems to be in a great mood and is whistling a tune with a beat as fast as a racing heart.

Soon we will let a strange naked body come between us. When he's fiddling with her upper body, I'm fiddling with her lower body. And vice versa. Your hands are always busy. When he's in such a good mood I have to be careful not to get jealous—it's been a long time since he looked forward to us having sex with such enthusiasm. Though if I'm honest, the same is true of me. Okay then. Fuck you, jealousy. Let me do this for my beloved husband. He's so happy in his golden pouch. At some point I shout, "I'm ready!"

He's always waiting for me, never the other way around. But he knows women have to do much more in the bathroom than men. And I'd love to see a man try to fumble his way through putting on garters. Impossible.

We drive into town and get a table at Café Fleur for breakfast. The entrance of the brothel is visible from the café.

I can't eat much. But my husband is hungry. He likes the sense of anticipation, whereas I hate it. He excuses himself and goes ahead to check things out at the massage parlor. That's what we like to call brothels. I wait in the café and continue to get more and more nervous.

He rings the doorbell and, when Summer answers, he waves to me and goes inside. He knows he has to keep his harpy—that is, me—happy. He has to try to keep me on board so that we get can through this together as a couple. Inside he takes the elevator up to the third floor. All the floors belong to Paradise, the brothel. The madam greets him there and, as always, leads him to a private room so he doesn't see any of the other customers. You don't want to run into a business associate or your lawyer or something. He sits there as the women come in one by one, clothed, and do their slow-motion turn so he can see their asses and everything. He will pick one for us to fuck. Up to now he's always chosen well. Very well, in fact. I've liked them all, found them all attractive, sexy, and nice. Been lucky up to this point—or is it that my husband and I just share the same taste in women? No idea. Who gives a shit? He tells the madam he'll be back in an hour with me. He wants the one he's picked out to be ready then. See you soon.

I stare the whole time at the door of the building until my husband comes back out grinning. What a shit-eating grin.

He sits back down at the table with me and is as excited as a little boy. His cheeks are flushed and his eyes are gleaming. I am proud that I can make this possible for him.

He babbles on and on. "She's Brazilian, amazing body, incredibly beautiful face, speaks fluent German, is very funny. Seriously, when she enters the room it lights up. There is no doubt about it. She's the one."

I try to keep my composure, but all my alarm bells are going off. Attention! Attention! Keep an eye on your husband! She's going to steal him away! I talk to myself: No, no, no. No prostitute can steal your husband from you. It's just your fear talking, Elizabeth. He's not doing this because he's looking for a new wife. He just wants to bang somebody else. There's no danger. Breathe deeply.

"Good," I say with a feigned smile, pretending to be relaxed. "Let's finish eating and go inside. Is she available right away?"

"Yes, she's waiting for us. I've booked her for the next three hours."

Oh, man, three hours? You'd have time to do every position imaginable four times over. Ah, no matter. We can always leave earlier.

He grabs my hand and looks at me lovingly and gratefully. Is that because of me or the Brazilian? No idea. We eat our breakfast and order a glass of champagne as a warm-up. We split it—otherwise everyone would think we were alcoholics, drinking a glass each so early in the day. Too decadent. We pay the bill, then take each other by the hand, and go to the entrance with wobbly knees. We ring the doorbell. He says our real names into the intercom. What do we have to hide? When you go to the brothel with your own wife, you don't have anything to fear.

Except the clap. We go upstairs, and the madam, with her long red locks, greets me. She's already greeted Georg. She leads us into their most expensive room. You always pay extra for the room if you want a special one. With all the clichéd props. Giant mirrors, sky blue canopy bed, bearskin rug in front of the fireplace, everything decorated in light blue and silver. The floor-to-ceiling windows are covered with a metallic film that's completely opaque. After all, the people who live across the street shouldn't be able to see what's about to happen in here.

We sit like nervous schoolchildren on the bed and wait. Fuck, I hate the anxiety. Hate it, hate it, hate it. Really. My heart races and skips beats. That can't be healthy. The madam closes the door behind her as she goes out. We are alone. We look at each other helplessly and laugh. Because we're so damn polite. We are extremely uncool customers. A cool customer would get undressed. It's warm in here. Set to be nice when you're naked, no doubt. A cool customer would make himself comfortable and lie down on the bed. Instead, we sit stiffly on the edge of the bed.

Finally the door opens and she enters. She looks pretty and must have put on a liter of perfume. How does a cliché become a cliché? Whew. Crazy. It's part of the show. A dense sweet scent fills the room. She dominates the space with her body, her scent, her broad toothy smile. She focuses on me and comes over to me. I know this routine. A good hooker wraps the woman around her finger; the man is already wrapped around her finger without her having to do a thing. The woman could bail out, mess things up. Not the man. The man will get through it. He wouldn't stop even if the building were on fire.

She says, "My name is Lumi."

And she shakes my hand. In a few minutes we're going to have sex and yet she shakes my hand. Funny. Germany. My hand sits comfortably in hers. I barely move. She moves my hand for me. She'd better get used to the fact that I'll be letting her move me. She has to do a lot more than we do, and for that she gets paid well. She's quite dark skinned. She has short hair, lots of lipstick, big brown affectionate eyes. She's not the slightest bit messed up. I can't stand it when they look messed up. She's wearing a turquoise kimono with a floral print in golden yellow and purple. This is an expensive brothel and the women wear nice things. Through the kimono I can see she has small, firm breasts with big hard nipples. I know the type. I have the same.

As I mentioned before, because of my breast complex, the safest bet for my husband when picking out a hooker is not to exceed my size. But it's also a little odd, because as a result I feel as if I'm sleeping with myself. Oh well, my own fault. She has long legs and a fantastic bubble butt. She's wearing tall black shoes. Man, I'm relieved. She's good. She looks good, she's nice, everything. Whew.

"You have a beautiful wife," she says to my husband. Standard. They all say that, always. They'd say it even if I looked like shit. They'd gloss right over it. This is all about service. I smile at her. Her hands are slick with moisturizer. Like I said, hookers smear themselves like mad so everything feels smooth.

She tells us to relax. She wants to freshen up, which means, I think, that she wants to wash out the sperm of her previous client. You always act as if you're a virgin in these meetings. A pure, pristine virgin. Sperm from a previous client? No, no. With a wink she floats out of the room again. A second later we hear the water running in the bathroom. We

lie back and stare at the ceiling. We hold hands. We have to
support each other in a difficult situation like this. I tell my
husband that he chose well. He's relieved. I can easily imagine
sleeping with this woman now, putting on the usual show for
my husband. Hot licking ladies from the isle of Lesbos—but
better-looking than your average lesbians. Her, anyway. In a
minute we'll twist around and into each other to form a ball
of human flesh. It will be hours before the rush subsides. It's
like that every time.

The madam comes in and gives us each a glass of champagne. Sure, fine. Then she leaves us alone again. We take
off our shoes and get into bed. Georg takes off his sweater
and undoes a few of the buttons of his shirt. I get up and look
around the room, like always. Because of my paranoia about
the newspapers, I look behind picture frames, in the fabric of
the bed's canopy—anywhere a camera could be hidden. All
clear. I laugh at Georg. He rolls his eyes. He thinks it's crazy of
me. I settle back down on the bed. Sometimes I can't believe I
manage to dull the horns of my jealousy. But I do really believe
that it will allow us to stay together much longer. Because my
husband can take care of whatever wandering urges he has in
a permissible way, a way that unites us, I hope. I hope, I hope.
So he stays with me forever!

It takes a good long time before Lumi reemerges. Man,
she must have had a lot of sperm to rinse out. Georg and I
don't talk. Now and then we smile at each other as a sort of
displacement activity. With butterflies in my stomach and heat
emanating from inside me, I take off the sweater I have on over
my dress. Lumi finally comes in. She's wearing just underwear
and a bra, one that consists only of a wire frame, with no cloth

hiding the breasts. Good for her. Cool. She's also left her shoes in the other room. She stands there barefoot and laughs.

"Who are we starting with tonight?"

"With my wife."

She sits next to me on the bed, and my husband leans back and makes himself comfortable. He's excited. He knows he's about to see the ultimate lesbian show. Lumi and I know what is expected of us. She holds my hands and kisses me on the mouth. First with her lips closed, then more and more open, and wetter. She has nice breath. I'm pleased. I close my eyes, breathe deeply, and try not to think of my mother, who is watching us—along with the feminist establishment in the person of Alice Schwarzer—and shaking her head disapprovingly.

Here we go. With my right hand I touch her soft brown throat. I run my hand down to her décolleté, one breast, the other breast. Then both of my hands are on her breasts. You never have to worry that you're taking things too fast with a prostitute. There's no such thing as too fast. I softly roll her nipples between my pointer finger and thumb. Very gently. So I don't hurt her the way my husband accidentally hurts me sometimes. I can't get over how soft her skin is and how good she smells. That alone makes the money and the trip here worth it. She lifts up the bottom part of my dress and feels and then sees that I have garters on.

"Oh, nice," she says somewhat muffled into my mouth. Our lips stay touching the entire time. We're getting wetter down below. Her hand wanders down to my crotch. She doesn't dally very long before starting to rub my clitoris through my underwear. She does it elegantly with her outstretched middle and pointer finger. I'm throbbing harder and harder; I'm so horny it nearly hurts. I look over at my husband through half-closed eyes. We're doing this for him—I think that's clear to both of us. He's pulled out his cock and is holding it tightly in his hand, rubbing up and down in slow motion. The rush has begun. Everything is permitted. I squeeze her breasts. She's already pushed my underpants aside with her finger. Everything is totally wet, and I feel humming and pulsing between my labia. With her other hand she gestures that I should take off my dress. I let go of her beautiful breasts, pull my dress over my head, and, like in a movie, am careful to shake out my hair afterward the way you do when someone is watching you undress. I kneel on the bed stretching upward, upper body stretched out, thighs stretched out, upright. She kneels in front of me the same way, and together we practically push my husband out of bed. I keep looking to see what he's doing. He's still doing the same thing, smiling and masturbating. It's that easy to make him happy. It's fun for him to watch me and Lumi. But what I'm pretending to do for show is also actually fun for me.

Lumi's stomach touches mine. That's how close together we are kneeling now. We kiss the entire time, on the lips, on the neck, on the face. And our hands are all over each other. I squeeze her ass cheeks hard, as hard as I can. Suddenly I feel Georg's hands. He is fumbling around with my hands and her ass. He moves from the edge of the bed so he's behind Lumi. He lies flat on his stomach and kisses her ass. I can see as he pulls her cheeks apart and he licks right between them. I can hear the smacking noise, too. We stay in each position for a few minutes, then switch around. Everyone always has to have something to do. With your hands, your tongue, your genitalia. Lumi is fastidious about uninterruptedly rubbing my clitoris.

I can hear smacking sounds down there—I'm producing so much fluid.

She lays me on my back and jumps up giggling. She asks what we think of sex games. We say yes to everything she suggests. She pulls a very expensive-looking metal sculpture out of a drawer next to the bed. She licks my vagina a little and then my asshole, preparing for the pricey toy. I can feel how she tries to move vaginal fluid from the front to the back with her tongue. Of course, vagina mucus is far better lubrication for anal than spit—the water in spit just grips everything. She twists the metal sculpture so the two acornlike knobs on it are facing in the same direction and then slides one into the front and one into the back. It's cold at first, but feels great. She pushes the two ends in farther and I sing silently in my head: *Everything has an end, except a sausage which has two.* Lumi continues to lick my clitoris the whole time.

I relax completely, spread out my arms, look up at the ceiling, and I no longer care where my husband is inserting himself in her. I can't help laughing inside about how cool we are, about how fearful I used to be, and about how I've managed to silence Mother and Alice Schwarzer. I now am nothing more than my clit and my lust. Nothing can embarrass me; I'm not trying to maintain control; go with the flow, Elizabeth. When can you really do that these days? I'm on vacation in the middle of town. We try out every position, fingers disappear into every hole. I take the stoppers out of me once in a while but quickly shove them back in. Everything is allowed—except one thing. Georg will not stick his cock into Lumi and will not come inside her. I've told him a thousand times: "Go ahead, stick it in, man. Why wait. You want to, so go ahead, goddamn it." He just won't. He refuses. He just doesn't want to put his cock inside a prostitute. I guess I don't have to understand. After he and I have extensively explored her beautiful dark-red vagina and stuck things in everywhere, after two or three hours of pure lust, after I've come who knows how many times, I sit on him and ride him and clench the muscles of my well-trained vagina with all I have—while Lumi sticks a finger in each of our asses—and he comes. Finished. Now we just lie around and goof. We have a drink on the bed, still naked. We know each other now, inside and out. We ask her to tell us a few stories about extreme customers, then we pay—we're allowed to pay afterward because we're regulars—get dressed, and head home.

On the way home we constantly smell our fingers. Because they smell like Lumi, we have to laugh. She got three hundred and fifty euros for that. I still have a rush—and I think I'm the coolest person ever. All that I am able to do, as a heterosexual woman. I impress even myself. For ages afterward we still smell of her perfume and everything else.

I accompany Georg home and have to hurry so I'm not late to therapy. I go as I am, reeking of an orgy. She wouldn't expect it any other way, as she always says. She can just air the place out well after I leave again, and everything will be fine.

I apologize to her for the way I smell, again. I certainly don't want her to think it's my own perfume that smells like that. And I definitely want her to know about our sexual adventure. I describe it in minute detail. Surprisingly there is still time left when I'm finished.

"In that case, I can talk to you about my best friend, Frau Drescher. Just so I'm clear about it in my head. She was in therapy for a brief time, but she doesn't like to talk about the past, so she stopped going. As a result, she just silently carries around all the shit her mother foisted on her. She doesn't understand what the past has to do with her current life. But I always think, *Go ahead and think that way, but without me.* I can see it all but can't say anything. You told me that people have to figure these things out themselves. You can't convince people. But you can leave when it gets to be too much to be around those who should go to therapy but won't. And that's the point it's gotten to—it's too much. I constantly feel as if I'm crazy, and yet she convinces herself she's healthy in the head because she doesn't need to go to therapy. Though she gets tips from me that I pick up from you. I think she's a ticking time bomb, just like my mother. And ticking time bombs scare me. Probably because I am one, too.

"My best friend and her craziness account for a large part of my own therapy with you. That's got to stop. I keep thinking that my life would be better off without her. But it all seems wrong somehow. I think the reason is that deep inside, I don't really believe it's all right to abandon someone even if you realize they are not good for you. I think I need to pick a fight first and then leave her. But you can just leave if you really want to—right? The problem is, she'll surely be irate as a result, and that makes me fear aggression from the best friend I will have abandoned. And what aggression she has! I've told you about it before. She is definitely the most aggressive person I know, and despite that fact I constantly try to pacify her with gifts, compliments, and ass kissing. But you can't pacify her. Nobody can help her to become a better person except herself. And she refuses. Funny how it takes so many years to realize that. It takes so long for a sense of self-preservation to prevail.

"I imagine it would be very liberating if I were able to do it. If I were able to get up the nerve. You have taught me that it's important to be able to fight within a friendship. Cathrin and I have never done that. We've always been a very harmonious unit. No criticism is allowed. We're like two psychopaths—everyone around us is mean to us, but we are nothing but nice to each other. But of course there's been aggression, from her side. Envy about my husband, child, relationship, success, money, orgasms, actually about fucking everything. You should run screaming from the words *best friend*! There's only room for one god. Just as with my mother. Help! Monotheism. Again. I keep stumbling over the same thing. Always the same with me, Frau Drescher. I can't take it anymore. I don't want any part of a relationship like that anymore. I've got to end it soon. I just don't know how. She scares me. A lot, actually. My best friend. And I'm afraid of her. How did it all go wrong?

"Since I've started entertaining the idea of breaking it off with her, I've had such terrible thoughts. Like, for instance, I've always acted around her as if I think I'm ugly. So she feels better. We've convinced ourselves we're ugly as a result of this awful relationship."

Suddenly a thought occurs to me.

"Cathrin has infected me with her anorexia. I almost sent her to a clinic at one stage so her daughter wouldn't have to see her body degenerate any further. And the whole fucking thing because she thought good clothes only looked good on a thin body. And now I want to look good, for my husband, too, and for my daughter. For everyone, but first and foremost for myself. I want to eat what I want! I'm short, I have a child, I have short legs, and I'm thirty-three. People should be able to tell how old I am. I want to be allowed to look my age. Because of my gray hair, my daughter says, 'Whoa, you're old!' She actually said that recently. And she's right.

"To Cathrin, the fact that I don't dye my hair is something horrible. Help! Aging, death. She once told me that an old American feminist said the greatest invention for women—greater than the pill—was hair dye, because women become invisible to men when they have gray hair. I can't accept that it's supposedly feminist to try to look young as long as possible—for men. The only good man is one who accepts me as I am, with gray hair and wrinkles. I have no desire to act like her and try to combat aging. Fuck that. Why is it taking so long for me to end this masochistic relationship with her? But I'm afraid of her now, afraid of her vengeance. Whatever form it would take. Could I have saved this relationship at some stage? Instead of now trying to save myself from it? We never learned to talk to each other about unpleasant topics. So many years and I never managed it. You have often asked me whether I believe I can change something by talking about it. But in this case I think it would have had the same result as my breaking it off with her, as I will soon do."

"I think so, too," says Frau Drescher, "after all I've heard you say about her."

"It's really nice to hear you say that. I'm taking note of that, Frau Drescher. Because normally you never let me run away from something. Whenever I have a problem with Georg and want to run off and think I can't take it anymore, when I want to run off and leave Liza with him, you forbid me. Every time. But with

Cathrin now, when after a thousand years I realize for myself that she is bad for me, you haven't contradicted me. Uh-huh. I noticed. You're not the only one here who observes, Frau Drescher. Ha!"

Agnetha laughs.

"Cathrin always said she wanted to get pregnant but wanted to stay thin when she was pregnant. To me that's horrible. She's waited all these years for a baby from her wife-beating husband, hoping the entire time it wouldn't be a son, because then she'd get hit from both sides, become a punching-bag sandwich. She smokes, drinks, does tons of exercise, especially swimming— not for her health, but for her figure. A typical gym and yoga abuser. And then she wonders why after all these years nothing has nested in her hostile womb. And she's always loading me up with questions she wants me to ask you. And I spend good time getting you to answer her questions instead of getting you to help me."

"Yes, I certainly remember all the questions you've asked on her behalf."

"If she ever managed to get pregnant, the gynecologist would tell her, 'A bit of swimming is fine, but not at your usual level of exertion.' But she wouldn't let herself be swayed, I'm sure of it. Her gynecologist couldn't tell her to do anything. She would drive me crazy if she were pregnant. I can't even stand thinking about it, despite the fact that she would be the one who would have to suffer from it all. And the way she always says, 'Good that you're going to therapy so regularly. You need it. But I can live my life without therapy. I don't need any help.'

"My husband always knew how negative our friendship was. Once in a while he would cautiously ask whether I had lost my mind when it came to Cathrin.

"I want to be able to look at myself in the mirror and say, 'Man, do I look sexy, and, man, will I be happy to be rid of her.' That's what I want. I don't want to be unnecessarily obsessed with beauty. And I don't want to starve myself anymore. I'm a little, sexy, healthy, well-built woman. Fuck, yeah!

"For someone like me, who has an African ass, it's also a good idea to get yourself a man who likes Tinto Brass movies. Then you can eat what you want. You don't have to have one of the boy butts that are the style these days—no hips and all the rest of that misogynist shit. You can have a real woman's ass. And a woman's tummy. Awesome."

I can't help smiling. I feel so much better—physically better—now that I know I can abandon Cathrin. I stop and take a few breaths. That way Frau Drescher can say something, too.

"Yes, Frau Kiehl, I've also noticed an improvement in your physical well-being. I consider that at least in part another indication of the success of your therapy."

"So do I, Frau Drescher, so do I. As you well know, I've had a bad breast complex for years. We've already determined that this complex started back in my school years. But I actually need to begin the story much earlier. My first contact with breasts was naturally with those of my mother. She would often stand in the bathtub and take sponge baths. We all learned to do that to save water. I come from an environmentally conscious family. You didn't bathe or shower every day—that was considered a waste of water. Not to mention bad for your skin. I was taught just to wash the smelly parts with a bit of soap and water every day. Feet, crotch, and armpits.

"I always paid close attention when my mother stood there and took her sponge baths. I was allowed. I looked at her breasts and asked myself whether I, too, would get such big breasts. She actually had small breasts. But from my perspective as a child, with zero breasts, they seemed huge. I used to often ask if I could feel them. She let me. I weighed them—I'd hold out my hands like a beggar and put them beneath her breasts with the palms up. Only instead of coins I got a handful of breast. I would poke my finger into her breasts, too, and my mother said that it hurt and that I shouldn't do that. But I wanted to feel those protrusions of hers. Now of course I know they are mammary glands, but back then I had no idea what breasts were. She had very dark areolas and nipples. Really dark reddish brown. I found them sometimes disgusting, sometimes beautiful. The most beautiful breasts I'd ever seen. Also the only ones at that point. I went back and forth between being afraid of getting breasts and feeling head-over-heels excited about getting them.

"Now I know both from you and because my daughter does the same thing that this is a strong point of competition between mothers and daughters. Often when Liza sees me naked in the bathroom, taking a sponge bath, she says, 'Yuck, I don't want to grow up, Mama. I don't want to get breasts like that.' And then she says, 'Can I touch them?' I think the worst part for me, when I think about it now, is the way people say 'She has *no* breasts' about a woman or girl who has small breasts. That sounds terrible. *No* breasts. Nothing, nada, completely flat. And I always thought to myself, *But that's not true! I do have breasts. Why doesn't anyone notice them? You just have to look more closely—there are breasts there, just small ones.* I felt robbed of my femininity. Back during my school days, no boys were confident enough to say, 'Hey, I like small breasts,' or 'Forget breasts, I'm an ass man.' These days, as an adult, I hear statements like that all the time, said with confidence. But when I was a kid I found myself living in a dictatorship of the breast. Everyone was fixated on big breasts. It's embarrassing to admit that it affected me so much, but even to this day it's still important to me that men find me attractive. It'd be tough for me to become a lesbian out of protest because I can't get past this problem. I think society and the media are more and more fixated on breasts, too. A few years ago, back when my complex was really bad, some friends of ours brought an old *Playboy* magazine to a party. It was the October 1978 issue. I was so happy to find out that not so long ago women with small breasts were considered beautiful. The woman on the cover had smaller breasts than I do. And she was on the cover of *Playboy*! Seeing those pictures really helped me.

"Obviously I know that having implants doesn't help with the complex in the long term. It's a problem in your head, of course, and can't be surgically altered. You've taught me that well, Frau Drescher. I know now that giant-breasted woman with toothpick arms still carry around their complexes along with the two uncomfortable hard breasts up front and the back pain they eventually cause. Ha! That will never happen to me. I'm not going to have people gawking at me like an alien, a freak, with a pair of balloons beneath my throat and arms that are far too thin. My husband and I have been to couples therapy for my breast complex, as you know."

I met Georg in a professional context. After we got together, I often visited him at his office. I looked around his office with a new set of eyes. A different perspective from the one I'd had during the relaxed getting-to-know-you phase. It was a cold, distrustful, controlling perspective. Among a bunch of otherwise harmless images he had a B-movie poster of a woman who reminded me of Jayne Mansfield. Busted. He said it was just something he'd thrown up on the wall. Yeah, right. Uncool and inhibited as I am, I immediately asked him about it. The trashy movie had been about a giant woman. All I could see were the breasts. I could tell what was going on. There was no other possible explanation for the poster being hung in his office. Then he took me to a concert to see his favorite musician, Iris DeMent. I practically fell over when she came onstage. I was overwhelmed by hate—for him, for her, for both of them. They were in cahoots, I was sure. She was wearing a dirndl and her breasts—at least D cups—were spilling out of it. And then he tried to tell me that she was just a good songwriter and that her breasts didn't come into it. Of *course* not! Naturally I did not believe him. I preferred to drive myself crazy with my breast envy, or, in more folksy terminology, tit envy. Of course, you don't bitch at your husband for fun or out of boredom; it's because of real fears. It's not fun for anyone to be so uptight. To be so petty and pathetic. My husband couldn't listen to his favorite music at home anymore. I just glowered at him every time until he finally gave up trying to listen to it. Before we entered couples therapy, it was simply not an option in our relationship to go against my will. There was no way he was going to get that music past me once I had concluded she was a breast peddler.

Once we were sitting with our two children at our favorite pizzeria. On a door inside was a poster of a naked woman lasciviously dangling a spaghetti noodle into her mouth. When I saw those breasts, I got furious. Because they were so beautiful. A big handful on each side. Beneath each nipple, the breast had that perfect hanging-pouch effect. The nipples and areolas were not too dark, not too pale, not too soft, and not too hard. Horrible for someone like me, who struggled daily with a breast complex. Whenever the family wanted to go eat there I thought to myself, *No, please, not the perfect-boobs pizzeria!* I would immediately lose my appetite because of anxiety and rage. Another time we went—of course there was a table available, right near the door with the poster—and my stepson said, "Look, Papa, that woman looks like my mother when she's naked, doesn't she?" Aaaaaaargh! Until that moment, I didn't know about the big breasts of my predecessor. My husband suffered for years because of that sentence uttered by his son. "Aha, I didn't know that your ex-wife had such large breasts." Completely insane of me. He left her for me. But when you are as riddled with complexes as I am, you actually attack your own husband for the fact that he was with someone—*anyone*—before you, and that he didn't show you photos of the breasts of all his previous women, and that he hadn't ripped out the hearts of all those women just to show that he loved me more than all the rest put together. How awful it must be to be together with me. Stress, stress, stress. And everything that was said during that breast-envy fight was said. Unfortunately. You can't go back and erase it, rewind, undo it. It kills a certain amount of love when someone—in this case me—lays landmines all over the place.

"Oh, excuse me, Frau Drescher. Another breast attack."

"Frau Kiehl, it's obviously a major desire of yours to continue to talk about it until you have made up your mind. You're not boring me, don't worry."

"Okay, but I've strayed completely from the topic of Cathrin. I want to get away from feeling bad about my body, and I want to get away from my friend—away from harsh, evil attitudes toward women's bodies and back to healthy attitudes. I want to be on good terms with the actual body I have. And that's not possible while I remain friends with Cathrin. But how can you address it without leaving scorched earth behind? I need absolution from you, Frau Drescher, the same way my husband does from me for his porn films and hookers. Because I feel so bad for wanting to abandon her. But I'm allowed. You're allowed to leave people. It's true, right?"

"Of course. I always tell you that. You are allowed to leave. But apparently you don't really believe it."

"Yes, you do say that: participation is voluntary, even when it often doesn't feel that way. But free will played only the smallest part in that friendship. I have been mentally liberating myself from her for the last few months. Oddly enough I don't think I will miss Cathrin for one second. No idea how I will make the break, but it will be great. As always, you are far ahead of me, just like my husband and even my ex-husband. Even the children think there's something funny about this skewed relationship."

"Frau Kiehl, I'm afraid I must interrupt your review of Cathrin. The time is up."

I swing upright on the couch and look bashfully at Frau Drescher. We haven't seen each other for the entire session. I have said everything to the painting of the devil.

She looks me straight in the eyes and assures me.

"I'll say it again: you are allowed to leave. Every relationship between adults should always be voluntary, always based on free will."

"Thank you."

"Of course. Have a nice weekend."

"Oh, yeah," I say, as I do before every weekend. "It's the weekend again."

For us the entire year is the weekend. I mean, as far as work goes, it seems to me and my husband as if it's always the weekend, because we have made our hobbies into careers. Which is also why I'm so messed up—I have too much time to deal with my trauma. I think for me personally, a war or becoming a refugee or at least an apprenticeship as a bricklayer would be better. Then I'd be diverted from thinking about my parents, my husband, my psyche, my sexuality.

I drive to the notary quickly—but not so fast as to risk killing anyone. I have only a few minutes. Otherwise my husband will notice that I stopped off somewhere else. That's the downside of being so symbiotic, of spending so much time together—you end up being a bit Stasi-like, whether or not you mean to be.

The clerks at the notary office know what to expect. I come in having already sent in all the desired changes to my will. We read it through together, I sign it, he signs it, and then he makes a copy of the new version. In the event of my death, he is the executor. Wow, that sounds ominous: *executor*. I take the original with me. I have to stash it secretly and quietly in the cabinet where all the important papers are—the wills, the long-term care insurance documents, copies of our organ donation cards, everything to do with our no doubt impending death. Somehow I have to get it in there without my husband noticing. Otherwise he'll look at me all worried, thinking I'm going downhill again psychologically.

Now, however, I want to get home and shower off Lumi's scent. When you are alone at the notary's office, smelling like sex is not as amusing as when you're walking down the street with your husband. I had the impression that the clerks at the notary's office were sniffing oddly at the air. Once everything's taken care of, I drive home with loud music on in the car.

I park the car in the spot we own right in front of the building and scurry into the apartment. My husband is expecting me. He's freshly showered. At least one of us is. He spreads his arms and I hug him. He's in his long underwear and an old-fashioned men's undershirt. I put my cheek on his muscular, hairy shoulder. We are a well-choreographed team. As we let go of each other, he turns around, and I am struck by the hair on his back. Once again. I'm convinced that my husband is so hairy because he's bursting with testosterone. He has hair growing out of his ears, like a werewolf. I like it. But despite that, when it gets out of hand he goes to a Turkish barbershop where a pretty woman—I'm very jealous of her because she has great breasts—removes his hair with this wonderful threading technique. She twists his ear hair in the threads she has wound between her finger and mouth and then does something so the thread pulls out all the hair. I always beg him not to have the hair on his back removed. When he's on top of me and inside me and I can stretch my neck just far enough to see over his shoulders, I feel tiny and flat and covered and have the impression I'm peering through a grassy landscape. I run my hands through his silverback-ape hair and know that we are all descended from them.

You also feel cold when you remove all your hair. I have a lot of hair under my arms, and once, under the bad influence of my best friend, I had it all removed. She tried to convince me women aren't supposed to have hair there. And my husband jumped all over me for the naked-mole-rat-looking armpits I had as a result. For the first time in my life, someone told me he loved the hair under my arms above all else. I also found it uncomfortably cold without hair there. I let it grow back and made my husband promise to leave his back hair alone for me.

I can see from the hall that he's put coffee cake on the table. He's in a great mood and hasn't noticed that I stopped off somewhere else after therapy. No questions and no questioning look on his face. Super. When I see he has something to do here upstairs, I'll creep downstairs to our death cabinet and stash the notarized additions removing my soon-to-be-former best friend from the will. You can't really hide it, since it needs to be found. Otherwise it will be like an Easter egg hunt for adults after your death. I just have to be observant and not miss the right opportunity. So I don't get caught.

I take off my shoes in the front hall and slip into the orthotics I got from my mother-in-law to stretch my toes. We both have ganglia on our feet that cause the big toe to go crooked and press against the other toes. It's genetic, but exacerbated by wearing shoes that are pointed and too narrow. My mother-in-law had to have operations on both big toes, but the surgeon who operated on her told her that if she had used orthotics her whole life she could have avoided the painful surgery. When she told me that, I figured I would buy myself a set of orthotics. I don't want to have surgery later in life, so I always wear the devices at home. They pull the big toe back where it's supposed to be.

"I picked up some cake at Café Heimweh. All organic. Eggs and everything."

My husband knows how to charm the pants off a woman.

"Super, thanks. I'm hungry. Do you have a couple of slices for me? Now that I'll soon be free of Cathrin, I can eat cake again."

"Yeah, two pieces for each of us."

I take the beautiful slices of cake off the pink tissue paper and put one each on small plates for us. Then I get two glasses of tap water. This is the first time since Liza's been at her father's place that we have sat down together at the table, just the two of us. We almost never do that when she's away. When Liza is home we all sit at the table for every single meal. When she's not here we usually eat on the couch.

I sit down and immediately start to eat. We used to always fight about the fact that he doesn't come to the table when I call him. But we figured out in couples therapy that I shouldn't get upset about it. I don't need to make him into a copy of myself, unfortunately.

As I sit down I notice a sensation in my asshole. It's a bit battered from this morning's sex with Lumi and Georg. It must have been Georg. Lumi was far too gentle and cautious to have hurt it. Anal sex was always a big deal for my boyfriends, but never as big of a deal as it is for Georg. They were all Catholics. I think that has something to do with it. I used to do it as an occasional show of love for a boyfriend. But these days I like to do it often and properly. I love him so much more than any of the previous boyfriends. At first he brought it up very cautiously. Then he begged to try it out with me. You have to beg a woman for that, because it can be quite taxing and painful.

But you have to get through it—for love. Fucking love. I would never offer it on my own. But he asks me to do it for his sake. I agree, though I'm scared and anxious. But I always say yes. I simply can't imagine saying no to him regardless of what he asks. Fortunately he doesn't ask me to do any bad things. Or nothing too bad, at least.

Georg finally comes to the table, sits down opposite me, and begins to stuff cake into his mouth. We don't talk. What do we need to talk about?

I can still remember exactly how he oiled the skin around my asshole the first time. Then he stuck first one finger in, then his thumb, then two fingers. We take our time—which is one reason we have anal sex less often than normal sex. You have to be so cautious and move so slowly so as not to hurt the woman (me!). It's a lot of work, usually too much for us to bother. Though once we've stretched out my asshole enough so his cock can go in without hurting me, it's a lot of fun.

When I have anal sex I think about the leader of the German women's movement, Alice Schwarzer, and listen to my body and feel an inner sensation that starts in my asshole and spreads through my entire body. It's completely different from the feeling I get during vaginal sex. Though even with vaginal sex the women's movement says there are no orgasms. Of course, I've learned from my trusty *Geo Kompakt* that there is definitive scientific evidence of vaginal orgasms. I'm certain there are anal orgasms as well. With my husband's cock in my ass, my women's movement head always tries to talk me out of the possibility that it can feel good, even as my rectum is telling me how good it feels. Who should I believe?

At some stage the women's movement came up with theories that are politically correct but scientifically indefensible. And they are never permitted to be altered. But I can feel in my own body, during sex, that the women's movement got a lot of things wrong.

Our first pieces of cake are almost gone. I smile about the thoughts running through my head.

"What are you laughing at?"

"Nothing."

He takes his second piece of cake and serves me mine as well. He always eats poppy-seed cake and I always go for apple. Always the same so I don't go crazy. That's how our life is.

When you've been stretched by a thick cock, it really feels as if your sphincter muscle is about to explode. My husband always compliments me on how relaxed I am and how coolly I endure it. He probably has other experiences to compare it to. But I don't ask him about it because I'd have a fit of jealousy. I keep saying to him, "Slowly, careful, wait a second." It really takes ages before the cock can satisfactorily slide in there. I used to compare myself to the women in porn films and wonder why they could handle it so easily—whoop, cock out of the vagina, whoop, into the ass, no problem. I thought, *Man, I'd love to be able to do that for my husband.* I saw it hundreds of times in movies and thought something was wrong with me. Why can't I just shove it up there, too?

Then one day came the wonderful explanation. In the documentary *9to5: Days in Porn* I saw a scene that was very enlightening for my sex life with my husband. Before shooting an anal sex scene, the women carefully and slowly and lovingly introduced increasingly large objects into their asses. I rewound that scene and watched it several times. It freed me forever from the thought that something was wrong with me. *I'm too tight. I'm the only one it hurts so damn badly if you go too fast.* They distend their assholes beforehand—stretching like athletes before a competition. And here I was always starting from scratch and wondering why when he put his cock in it was so painful that it felt as if I were going to throw up. They don't show the stretching of the asshole and the tedious preparation in real porn films. They want to maintain the illusion that the women are so horny they can just shove anything up their asses with no problem and no pain.

I can never ask my husband to check if anything is wrong with my asshole after anal sex, either, because he always says he wants to deal with disease and injuries only when they are emergencies. Frau Drescher also says I should leave him in peace and not force him into my idea of a relationship, which involves partners squeezing each other's pimples, checking each other's stool for worms, and checking on rectal wounds. Even if, as is the case with us, one partner has inflicted the wound on the other. *Pfff,* Drescher.

When we first got together, we had a really bad mishap having to do with my asshole. Because of the drugs and booze, I don't remember anymore why exactly we ended up in the bathroom. But the image in my mind—just before the pain—is of us both naked in the bathroom mirror. I was leaning forward against the sink, and he was behind me. I had on a blindfold, but it had slipped so I could see us in the mirror. I was sneaking peeks. He was so turned on that he just rammed his cock into my ass. I pulled it out immediately. But something got fucked up. You learn in school that you can catch all sorts of things very easily from anal sex. Because there's often blood. That's how it was with me that time. So there we were, two naked cokeheads in the bathroom with no idea what to do.

We both had a very unpleasant comedown. And an image in our heads that would never go away. I've thought about it every time we've tried it since. It's a major barrier, which makes it that much tougher to relax. My asshole. A vicious circle.

Since that injury, anal sex has become a major event for us. Like having the whole family over for cheese fondue. It's rare, but when we do it, it's a real party! He apologizes a hundred times a year for that one time. Says he doesn't know what came over him. I know—I did! And it drives him crazy that he hurt me so badly that time. Yeah, yeah, no problem. It's just difficult to put it out of your mind whenever the head of his cock knocks on the back door again. I have to talk to my asshole: *Take it easy. Everything's going to be fine. Relax. Stretch on out. It's better for both of us. Don't worry, that's never going to happen again. Open up. Don't cramp up. It'll hurt both of us less.* And within a few minutes, his fat cock fits right in.

He's finished both of his pieces of cake.

"May I leave the table?"

"Sure."

That's how it works at our place. We always ask—really just to set an example for the children. But it's become so routine that now we do it even when they're not around.

He stands behind his chair and something occurs to him: "I ordered something online. A surprise. It's a DVD called *Glory Hazel*. A compilation of scenes from cool 1970s sex films. Two women in Switzerland put it together. Some kind of art project. Want to watch it?"

"Sure."

Insatiable, my husband. Especially when the children aren't home. When they are, sex is pretty much out.

I sit alone with the rest of my second piece of cake and continue to think of our anal past. He's off to clean something, no doubt. Funny. How can someone possibly be so tidy? Of course I know what he would say: how can someone possibly be so messy?

After the mishap with my asshole, he suggested we measure the diameter of his cock and then find an object the same size and stick it inside his ass. That way he'd understand what it was like for me. But also, I'm sure, because he likes to have things shoved up there. He's Catholic, after all. I'm small, so naturally my asshole is correspondingly small. He's big, and his cock is actually large even for his size. Disproportionately large. So, since Georg is larger than I am and therefore has a larger asshole, whatever is going up there has to be bigger and thicker than his own cock for him to have an experience comparable to mine—to feel a comparable strain on his sphincter muscles. Woohoo!

We bought a giant rubber dildo in a sex shop. I was very uncomfortable at the register. I'm sure the cashier was smirking. I would love to have explained to him that it wasn't for little old me, but rather for an experiment. An experiment in equality. But I just played it cool and didn't let myself get dragged into worrying about whatever the sex shop cashier was thinking. What would be the point? He knows me well—we've bought almost everything in our forbidden bag of tricks at this shop. We keep it all hidden from the children. Most of the things have broken after one use. Made in China. The springs of the battery compartment in one vibrating dildo broke, for instance. With any other electronic device, you'd go back to the store and complain. But for some reason, you don't do that with sex toys. For one thing, the salesman has an idea where it's been.

As a result, our bag is full of useless things. Everything from tiny vibrators to the giant jackhammer we got for the experiment on my husband. We also have all kinds of things we got when we were playing around with bondage at the very beginning of our relationship. An all-in-one device with ankle and wrist manacles. Blindfolds (that was part of the reason the asshole mishap took place). We have strings of electric beads that would vibrate thrillingly inside me, if they weren't from China.

After a session that took forever, we managed to get his asshole stretched wide enough—using butt plugs, increasingly big dildos, and other objects—to get the huge dildo inside him. Ever since, he's had more respect for my inner anal dialogue. He's also a lot more careful since then.

For any heterosexual woman who wants to lead a more comfortable life, it's a good idea to make men put themselves through anything that they ask you to do. Just like us with the giant dildo in the ass. It made my life a lot easier. He totally admires me now whenever I let him in the back door, ride the Hershey Highway, access all areas. Because he knows exactly how much pain it caused him and how difficult it was for him to relax his mind and rectum enough so his asshole wouldn't tear. What an incredibly long time it took just to get the tip of the giant dildo in him. Such a long time! Ha!

After he'd finally managed to get the huge dildo into his ass—having taken way longer than it does for me, since he had no experience in letting someone in the back, the way we women do—I said to him, "Now the next thing you have to try is swallowing a mouthful of sperm. If you can do that, I'll happily start doing it for you again."

I stand up and walk over to the window facing the garden. I don't like it when my daughter's not around. I look at the quince tree in the garden. Up in the top branches, a magpie has built a nest. I'm obsessed with things like that. Since the death of my brothers, I find myself drifting more and more into magical thinking—the kind of stuff kids always come up with, or crazy Christians. I learned the phrase "magical thinking" from Frau Drescher. She uses it to describe things that fall under the category of superstition in the broadest sense of the word. Like my obsession with the number three, for instance. Three dead children. Then my traumatized, wounded wartime brain spins out from three dead children to completely different things. If I see three flies buzzing around the kitchen I think they represent my brothers. I still swat them and kill them. I don't want them to bother me. And anyway, my mind is too crazy even for myself sometimes. Besides, it's no problem: if the flies really are my brothers; they already managed to be reincarnated once, so they should be able to do it again. When I'm out in the world, I always look up into the trees to try to see clumps hanging in them. There are three types of clumps I look for: the first are magpie nests, like the one in our back garden. They're sloppily built and you can recognize them by the loosely thrown together roof that the clever magpies build as umbrellas over their nests. The second kind of clumps I keep an eye out for are parasitic mistletoe bushes hanging in trees. They feed themselves by penetrating the bark of a host tree and drawing all their nutrients from it. You see a lot of them when you drive along the autobahn. Sometimes you see huge colonies of mistletoe. Oddly enough, in England there's a Christmas custom based on mistletoe: if you kiss someone under a branch of mistletoe, it means you'll soon get married. It's an apt fit—parasitism and marriage. The third kind of clumps I look for are squirrel nests. They are very tidy, and nice and round, unlike magpie nests. They are the rarest of the three sorts of clumps that stand in for my three dead brothers. Whenever I see one, I tell myself I'm going to have a lucky day even as I chide myself, since, as an enlightened person, I shouldn't believe in that kind of crap.

The other magical thinking that dogs me has to do with the silver acorn. Although the acorn—the "something old" from my wedding—caused the accident as far as I'm concerned, I have kept it. It's hidden in the basement in a trunk where I keep all the things from our canceled wedding. I keep hoping it wasn't a mistake to keep it. I'm deathly afraid of that evil object. But I always thought that if I got rid of it, it would exact revenge. Like my best friend. I'm afraid of their aggression. So the acorn remains down there in the cellar. It's probably responsible for all the strange things that happen in our apartment.

For instance, we have all kinds of electrical problems. Something's wrong with the circuitry in the apartment. Either it's the acorn or it's my dead brothers themselves. Whatever it is causes constant outages that wreak havoc on our lamps and lightbulbs. We go through bulbs and lamps incredibly fast. Yep, entire lamps stop working, not just bulbs. Many different electricians have failed to figure out what the problem is. I feel as if my brothers are following me. I once read that when human flesh is burned, it smells like bacon.

I hate to be alone with thoughts like this. Horrible thoughts. Death and anal sex. Isn't there anything else in my head?

I firmly believe that they were burned alive. I don't try to make it easier for myself or fool myself by clinging to comforting beliefs. No. I assume the worst so I'm not as stupid as all the believers. Don't console yourself; be tough. Don't run away; look the facts in the eye. *God works in mysterious ways; he has his reasons*. Fuck off. Things happen that we simply have to live with, deal with, go crazy over, whatever. Just not turn religious over, that's for damn sure.

Turning religious is just too easy. Too easy on yourself. *Things happen for a reason, even if we aren't privy to God's plan.* Yeah, right. You wish! That's not how it is. I'll never see them again. At what stage of evolution from ape to Neanderthal was a soul suddenly breathed into us? At no stage. We are animals who will never see one another after death, just as all the force-fed Frankenchickens we breed will never see one another in chicken heaven.

I have an overwhelming desire to save someone, because I was unable to save my brothers. I would love to save someone's life. I might feel better then. I keep a note in my wallet listing locations in our neighborhood where there are defibrillators, and I know just how to use one. I wouldn't have to read the instruction manual. I don't care who I save—it could even be some old Nazi for all I care. Though of course I'd like it to be a child. Even if it were a bad child. I've learned how to do mouth-to-mouth and how to make an incision in the windpipe and insert a breathing tube.

All because she never turned around to look at the backseat.

* * *

Georg's cell phone rings. "Hi, Michael," I hear him say. A work colleague. Michael! The only other thing I ever wish for is to be with another man. Have I mentioned that? I won't be able to stand being with just one for much longer. I've tried to talk to him about it many times, to tell him he has to let me do it—sleep with other men—or I'm going to explode. What my husband doesn't know is that I constantly get infatuated with other men. It's been happening for about a year, though nobody has realized. We get to know new people, usually couples, and I instantly become infatuated with the man. It lasts only a few days. When my fantasies—which are so vivid they almost drive me crazy—don't take shape in reality, my infatuation wears off in a few days or weeks or months. And knowing myself, I'm pretty sure what I call an infatuation is what others experience as lust. Horniness. That would explain why earlier when the same supposed feelings of infatuation would pop up, I would quickly have that person as my new partner.

Up to now my infatuations have always worn off. But I can't guarantee that will always be the case. I feel as if I'm stuck in some fucked-up experiment about lust. I want to stay with him. We are good together. We have a patchwork family that doesn't need to be shaken up any further. But I need to be allowed to have sex with somebody else. In my head I'm constantly cheating. I fantasize about having sex with almost all of our friends. I want to have sex with someone—pretty much anyone at this point—without that person destroying my family.

* * *

Georg is still on the phone. This is my chance. I grab my bag, pull out the documents, and slip downstairs to hide them in the sacred death cabinet. I feel like my mother. She was constantly doing things behind her husband's back.

"Elizabeth?"

Fuck. He's off the phone and looking for me. I don't answer. Don't move, like a bunny caught in a car's headlights.

"What are you doing in the cabinet down there?"

There's no getting out of this.

"Yes, yes, just made a tiny change. Thanks for asking. Now leave me alone."

It's terrible the way nothing goes unnoticed when you live with someone. Especially when you get caught doing something. He's asked me a thousand times not to constantly deal with things related to death—with my own death or death in general.

I'll have to go upstairs now and tell him the truth.

I take the folder and the papers from the notary. I might as well rearrange the papers upstairs at this point. On the way to Georg and the couch, I grab the hole punch in the kitchen.

"Yes, okay, I stopped by the notary because of a small detail. I had to take Cathrin out of the will, you know? So you and Stefan and Liza and Max get more. If something happened to me and the will hadn't yet been changed, she'd get quite a lot. I couldn't let that happen."

I look at him. He looks back at me very upset. He doesn't say anything. Fuck. I know, I know, I always have some reason. Some reason to continue to screw around with it. I go to the notary about ten times a year to make the tiniest little changes. The will must always be perfect, in case . . . And this has been going on for eight years. My husband won't be able to stand it much longer. He learned through our couples therapy that he needs to try to keep me from doing it. And he's trying to do that now, insofar as he is giving me the evil eye. Yeah, man, I get on *my own* nerves. I know that I shouldn't do it, but I can't stop. I don't want someone I love to get less and someone I no longer love to benefit because of an error I didn't correct. I find the thought of that unbearable.

I'm his problem child. Will it ever stop? Anything he could do now is just absurd because we've been through this so many times before. Everything. All the possibilities have been exhausted and nothing has helped. Nothing can break my notary addiction. Because it is an addiction to death. I've promised him time and time again and never kept my word. Nothing works. Not even Agnetha in this case.

"Rip up your will—for me," says Georg calmly, quietly, in a steady voice.

What? He must be crazy! My beloved will? Never. I'd rather cut off all my limbs. No.

"No."

"Yes, and you're going to do it now. Trust that whoever is left behind will handle it in a way that reflects your wishes. Trust in that."

"No, I can't count on anyone else. I have to take care of it myself."

"That is your problem. Which makes it my problem, too. You don't think you can depend on me, on anyone, on anything. You want to control everything, even things that can't be controlled. Do you really think the worst part about you dying would be some shortcoming in the will? Do you really believe that? No. The worst part for me and Liza would be that you were gone. The will wouldn't matter. You can't control the fact that we would be sad. Inconsolably sad. For a long time. There is nothing you can do while you're alive that would make your death any easier for us. And you know what? The more you mess around with your will, the more I think you want to check out. To kill yourself. You always keep that option open, don't you?"

Why does he have to be so smart? The love of my life. Yes, I'm sorry. Often I can barely stand to be alive. I want to have the possibility to end it if I want to.

"I think it's terrible that I have you and Liza. You keep me here even though I often don't want to be here anymore. And if I didn't have you two, I would have killed myself a long time ago. Which is why I always have to alter my will. In case the time has come, you know—in case I manage to pry myself away from you. In my will it says you and Stefan have to move in together and raise Liza together. Would you do that? Since it's in there?"

"I know what's in there. I know it all. All the amendments. It makes me so sad, Elizabeth, that you spend so much time preparing for your departure. It means that you're not really here with me, with Liza. That you're not really here in life."

"Yeah, I'm sorry. That's possibly true. I can't rule out the possibility that I might go someday, you know. And I don't want to rule out the possibility. I've already gotten enough bad news in my life. I don't want to hear one bit more. Ever again. And there's no guarantee of that. Nobody can guarantee that. No more bad news. I'm done if I hear even one more breath of bad news, done. No more will fit in my head."

"There's not going to be any more bad news. It really is possible that that was it. Really. But of course I can't guarantee it. Of course not. Elizabeth, please tear up your will. For me."

"No, Georg, I can't do that. Don't ask me to. Stop it."

I would love to, but I can't. I should choose him, choose life, choose my child. But I can't. Not yet, anyway. I start to cry. It's exhausting after a while—keeping one foot in life and one in the grave, always straddling the divide, unable to decide for one or the other. I don't want to love so deeply that it rips my heart out when someone has to go. I don't want to invest so much that I'm shattered when someone or other is gone. Always a foot on the brake, always vigilant. I'm watching you, Death. Who will you take next? I must do everything in my power to protect my husband and child from you. I won't commit any stupid fatal errors.

Georg takes me in his arms.

Oh, man, how often have we had this talk?

"Stick with me, Elizabeth. Stick with life."

He hugs me so tightly that he squeezes the air out of my lungs. I make a noise as though I'm being deflated.

"Yeah, yeah, I'm not going right away. No time soon."

"Shall I tear it up for you, then?"

"Come on! Please. Don't. I know what you mean. I'm working on it. But don't rip it up, okay?"

"Then you do it. Rip it yourself."

"No, I'm not going to do that, either. I'll leave it alone, but I won't rip it up. Please. Please, please, please."

I snuggle up to him. I put my hand in the arm of his undershirt so I can feel the soft skin on the inside of his upper arm.

I feel totally spent. Life is so difficult. I can't do anything I want to do because it's bad—either for me or for others.

In desperation, I say, "Let's change the subject."

He knows this move. It means I need to be distracted because my head is buzzing and I'm afraid I'm going to lose my mind.

Georg holds me more tightly. We stay that way a long time.

I get myself together again and ask, "What's the story with the Swiss artists you mentioned? What is it they do better than other people?"

"They just spliced a bunch of movies together. It's one sex scene after another, with a sound track. No bullshit, no humiliating dialogue. And all from the era when porn stars looked like real men and women."

Good, distracted already.

My husband learned all the tricks he uses on my vagina—and there are a lot—from porn films. They are verifiably responsible for my sexual happiness, for every time I've come in the last seven years, every flushed splotch on my skin after an orgasm. The leaders of the German feminist movement would certainly approve of the movies in our collection. No rape, no debasement of women. Just loads of clitorises getting diddly-diddly-doed.

A little bit of my sexual satisfaction originates with me, from within. It's not 100 percent my husband and his porn film socialization. For instance, my old gym teacher taught us in high school how to tense the Kegel muscles and strengthen the muscles in the pelvic floor. I think I have her to thank for the fact that I come so preternaturally hard every time. And that I can decide when my husband comes once I've had enough of the rubbing. At some point everything is just rubbed raw.

* * *

Georg gets a plastic case out of the drawer beneath the TV and puts it in my hand. I look at the cover. It reads *Glory Hazel*. Cool name. I see a pixilated black-and-white image of a woman kneeling down in garters. A man's head is squeezed between her legs. Her arms are spread wide and she's clawing the velvet bed covers.

"Looks great," I say to my husband.

I open the plastic case and pull out a paper pamphlet inside. I unfold it and out jumps a beautiful vagina, with the hair only slightly trimmed, as was the style back then.

We both laugh. I look at it for a long time. Then I take out the disk and put it in the DVD player. I run to the refrigerator and grab two beers, open them with the bottle opener we have fastened to the wall—everything is set up well at our place—and sit back down with my husband on the couch. We wrap ourselves in an oversize wool blanket.

Even the intro trailer is good. Porn without all the embarrassing shit.

Under the blanket, I put my hand on his cock and balls and hold these two oddly shaped structures firmly. I'm finally free of myself. Watching other people having sex is a great substitute for drugs. It gives you a real rush.

We've been immersed in this art-house sex world for a few minutes when the doorbell rings. I yank my hand out of his pants and, feeling like a teenager busted while heavy petting in her room, jump up.

Georg laughs. He knows how I am. Always on the spot, immediately covering things up instead of just lying there and not opening the door. He looks at me amusedly. Then he looks at his crotch and says, "I can't get the door just now."

I wrap myself in the blanket. Not because I'm naked but to protect myself from whatever is about to hit me. I push the PAUSE button on the remote and walk to the door.

With my hand already on the doorknob, I breathe deeply and try to look relaxed as I open the door. Our friend Jochen is there with his baby daughter in his arms. I'm always happy to see him. He's not good-looking, but he's funny and very dirty. His sense of humor is dirty, I mean.

He doesn't want to bother us and apologizes for waking us up. Huh? Do I look so disheveled? Ah, who cares.

Georg calls from the living room with false indignation, "Who is it? What stranger are you talking to?"

"It's just me, Jochen. Don't worry."

Yeah, as if. No worries? If I could, then it would be him! Definitely.

He hands me a DVD case—something Georg lent him. I let my fantasy play in my head and try to catch his eye. He's got something else on his mind, though, and as he rocks his baby he says he has to get out to his car—he's double-parked. He says good-bye and squeezes the baby between us so we can kiss on each cheek, right, left. Nice. He calls out, "See you later, Georg," and is gone. My top candidate for an affair.

I breathe in and out once more in the foyer, gather myself after the rush of wild thoughts, and go back to the couch. I put the DVD down on the table.

"Want to watch some more?" asks Georg, pressing PLAY on the remote. We try to get back into it. A beautifully made-up actress from the late 1970s with particularly striking pubic hair is masturbating on a paisley bedspread accompanied by spacey synthesizer music.

Suddenly Georg says, "If I absolutely *had* to agree to someone, then it would be Jochen."

What's going on? I look at him out of the corner of my eye and suppress a grin. He is looking at the TV screen, seemingly unperturbed. The woman is now clawing at the bed and moaning as a man licks and fingers her.

Did he just give me the go-ahead? I think he did!

He did, right? Right? Right? Yes!

But for now, concentrate on *Glory Hazel*.

Woo hoo. Here we go!

Tim Mohr is the award-winning translator of works by Alina Bronsky, Wolfgang Herrndorf, and Dorothea Dieckmann, as well as Charlotte Roche's prior novel, *Wetlands*. He has also collaborated on memoirs by Doff McKagan, Gil Scott-Heron, and Paul Stanley. Mohr's own writing has appeared in the *New York Times,* the *Daily Beast, New York* magazine, and the *eXile,* among other publications. Prior to starting his writing career, he made his living as a club DJ in Berlin, Germany.